DATE DUE

FEB 24 2013 ½. ℓ.	
JUN 7 2013	
FEB 7 2014	
SEP 2 1 2017	

D1505523

GUNS ON THE CIMARRON

Center Point
Large Print

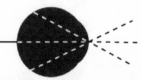

**This Large Print Book carries the
Seal of Approval of N.A.V.H.**

GUNS ON THE CIMARRON

Allan V. Elston

CENTER POINT PUBLISHING
THORNDIKE, MAINE

This Center Point Large Print edition
is published in the year 2011 by arrangement with
Golden West Literary Agency.

Copyright © 1943 by Allan Vaughan Elston.
Copyright © renewed 1971 by
the Estate of Allan Vaughan Elston.

First published in the U.S. by Macrae-Smith Company.
First published in the UK by Ward Lock.

The text of this Large Print edition is unabridged.
In other aspects, this book may vary
from the original edition.
Printed in the United States of America
on permanent paper.
Set in 16-point Times New Roman type.

ISBN: 978-1-61173-214-6

Library of Congress Cataloging-in-Publication Data

Elston, Allan Vaughan, 1887–1976.
  Guns on the Cimarron / Allan V. Elston.
    p. cm.
  ISBN 978-1-61173-214-6 (library binding : alk. paper)
  1. Large type books. I. Title.
  PS3509.L77G86 2011
  813′.52—dc22

2011023027

GUNS ON THE CIMARRON

CHAPTER 1

BOUND FOR SANTA Fe by way of Taos, Johnnie Cameron jogged his sorrel up Cimarron Canyon. A snow-cold stream ran here. After a three-day ride across prairies, it was good to hear the plash of riffles and to smell the freshness of these north New Mexico mountains.

The sorrel dropped its head to drink.

This struck Johnnie as a good idea and he swung to the ground. On hands and knees there he tilted back his sombrero to bury nose and chin in the stream.

He straightened with a smack of relish. "Beats an alkali water hole, yeh, Blazer?"

The sorrel blew through nostrils, then turned with reins dragging to begin cropping tall, tender bluestem.

"How we gonna make Santa Fe," Johnnie complained, "with you allatime picnickin'?" However, being kindly disposed toward all horseflesh, he got up and removed the saddle. He let the horse roll, heels up, in the grass there.

Johnnie himself propped his back against a pine, stretched out his long, buck-skinned legs and rolled a cigarette. Beside him lay the saddle with a rifle sheathed in its scabbard, and a slicker balanced across the cantle. The rider had avoided packing a bedroll by putting up at a settlement each night.

And because the rifle was dusty after the long ride from Granada, he now took the weapon from its scabbard to run a ramrod through it. The piece was a rimfire .44 carbine. Having polished its bore, Johnnie Cameron performed the same operation on his Colt's forty-five.

Then he heard hooves crunching gravel and approaching upcanyon. That, of course, would be the burro pack train he had passed only an hour ago.

The burros came straggling into sight. There seemed to be about two hundred of them, all with empty pack saddles. Four swarthy burreros, mounted on mules, were driving them. At the rear of the train came an elderly hacendado driving a buckboard.

The bed of the buckboard was empty except for blanket rolls and an assortment of commercial parcels.

"*Buenos dias, señor,*" smiled each of the four burreros as he came opposite Johnnie Cameron.

They could see that here was merely a young gringo cowboy with blue eyes and yellow, sweat-matted hair. They liked the friendliness of his range-bronzed face, and the softness of his drawl as he answered, "Same to you, *amigos.*"

The herd of unladen burros shuffled sleepily on upcanyon. But the elderly hacendado, obviously master of this outfit, stopped his buckboard beside Johnnie. "We meet again, señor," he greeted. He was puffing a corn-shuck cigarrita and offered Johnnie one. Not to offend, Johnnie accepted it although he would have much preferred to roll one of his own.

"Thanks," Johnnie said, and felt instantly that the response was inadequate. Always he had found himself at a loss when trying to match courtesies with one of these upper class Mexicans.

This one was clearly a ranchero of means, every inch a caballero from his wide-brimmed velour hat to polished boots. His face, spiked with a gray goatee, was both intelligent and sympathetic. The leathers which encased his slight figure were heavy with metal embroidery. A shotgun lay on the seat by him. Nevertheless the old gentleman presented a certain dapper dignity. The team he drove were matched roans, rangy, high-headed and of the best Spanish strain.

More than likely, Johnnie surmised, the man was on his way home after selling his season's wool at Granada, Colorado; Granada, in this year of 1873, being at the end of the Santa Fe railroad. Rumor had it that the railroad would some day be extended southwest into New Mexico; but until then the hacendados would have to freight their wool to it by cart or burro train.

"I'll be passin' you again before night," Johnnie smiled. The parcels in the buckboard, he guessed, were presents which this extremely agreeable country gentleman was taking home to family and servants.

"True, my friend," murmured the ranchero. "With these wretched burros I must travel like the snail."

Since the man had a spanking buckboard team, Johnnie wondered why he didn't drive on ahead and let the burros poke along home as they pleased.

From beneath the wagon seat the hacendado produced a demijohn of choke-cherry wine. "To drink your health, señor," he announced. "But serve yourself first."

Johnnie took the demijohn. "A pleasant journey for you, sir," he said, and took a long draught.

This clearly called for introductions. "My name's Johnnie Cameron," he announced.

"And I," returned the hacendado, bowing, "am Ygnacio Sandoval. For a week already I have been on the road home from Granada. My hacienda is one day beyond Santa Fe. It is yours, señor, whenever you will do me the honor to come there."

"Thanks," Johnnie said. "But I'm only going as far as Santa Fe."

"Ah! To the fiesta?"

Johnnie was about to ask "What fiesta?" but checked himself. Later he was glad he hadn't displayed ignorance of anything so sacred to New Mexican traditions. The Santa Fe Fiesta, he was soon to learn, had been celebrated each year for nearly two centuries to commemorate the reconquest by De Vargas.

"'Fraid I won't have any time to play," Johnnie evaded. "I'm headin' for Santa Fe on business."

"But during the fiesta there *is* no business!" Don Ygnacio protested.

He insisted on another round of the wine. Then, consulting an enormous gold watch, he heaved a sigh. "I must drive on, Señor Cameron, to catch up with my burros. *Hasta la vista.*" He touched the brim of his silver-trimmed sombrero, flicked his reins. His team of roans trotted on up the canyon.

Johnnie was in no hurry to follow. If he made Taos by sundown, he could still be in Santa Fe tomorrow night. So he continued to loll against the pine tree.

It was early September. Aspens on a high canyon bench were already turning yellow. From these same aspens a dozen or more steers emerged and began filing down a niche toward water. They were long-horned Mexico cattle, naturally, since the southwestern ranges knew no other kind. Johnnie Cameron had helped to drive great herds of them from Texas to the Kansas shipping towns.

The longhorns in sight now made him remember why he was riding to Santa Fe. Johnnie Cameron was taking an idea there. Could he put it over? It was an idea about cattle.

One of the steers arrived at the creek barely fifty yards downstream. The animal watered there, in profile, and on an impulse Johnnie Cameron took from his saddlebag a crayon and a pad of paper. He had a peculiar gift for sketching and now this posed bovine appealed to him as a subject.

Johnnie was always doing that. He had a habit of sketching almost any living thing that interested him; a horse, a cow, a deer, a buffalo, an old Indian, a beautiful woman.

So now he sketched a likeness of the steer on his pad. Artfully he portrayed the long, upturned horns, the bony legs, the slight flank, the narrow, curved back, the potbellied body, the shaggy neck.

Then, grinning, he deliberately caricatured the sketch a trifle; he made the horns even longer and the flank even more ribby. "That's our idea, Blazer," Johnnie murmured. "And I reckon we better be ridin' along with it."

He put the sketch with many others like it in his saddlebag. Then he saddled the sorrel and rode on at an easy jog up the canyon.

It was a twisting trail, the wall sheer on one side, sloping and pine-clad on the other. Frequently it forded the stream.

All at once Johnnie heard sharp, crackling sounds ahead up the canyon.

Rifle shots! The boom of a shotgun echoed them. Then came the dull, thumping blasts of a forty-five.

Johnnie jerked the .44 carbine from his saddle scabbard. He spurred to a gallop. Splashing across another ford he raced on to the next bend of the canyon.

Beyond this the canyon widened. After making the turn, Johnnie saw a drove of pack burros stampeding through the willows. The four burreros stood in a frightened huddle with their hands raised high. Don Ygnacio Sandoval, on the seat of his buckboard, also had his hands up. Three masked men were shooting from saddles.

One of the masked men had a rifle. The other two were thumping away with forty-fives. The rifleman was churning dust with his bullets around the feet of the burro drivers, while the pistol-shooters rode close to relieve Don Ygnacio of his wallet. The wallet was fat, presumably holding the proceeds of a large wool sale at the railhead. Johnnie, immediately sensing a planned ambush by outlaws with a foreknowledge of the wallet, reined to a halt and whipped up his rifle.

The rifle-armed outlaw was the first to notice the intrusion. This man sat his horse well apart from the others. Later, Johnnie vaguely remembered him as tall, slim, dressed in black leathers and riding a rangy bay. At the moment he couldn't take in details. His attention centered mainly on the two who brandished forty-fives at the wheel of the buckboard.

"Fork it over, mister," one of them yelled in clear gringo accent. He reached to snatch the wallet from Don Ygnacio just as Johnnie began shooting.

Johnnie saw the man buckle, then slither from his saddle. Then bullets from the aloof rifleman began zipping about Johnnie's ears. The sorrel reared, spoiling the aim of a second shot. But the animal's rearing saved Johnnie by screening him for a moment. A bullet meant for Johnnie's brain struck the upreared sorrel's breast.

Blazer fell, squealing. Johnnie landed on his feet and jumped for the shelter of a pine tree. From back of this he sent a hail of lead at the masked rifleman. Answering bullets splintered bark by his cheek. A shotgun boomed from the buckboard. Don Ygnacio, taking heart from Johnnie's intervention, had snatched his wagon gun to resume fighting.

His blast blew the second pistol-wielding bandit from his saddle.

Johnnie fired again at the masked rifleman. But

the man was in retreat now, upcanyon. He had never been closer than a hundred yards. Johnnie sent a final bullet after him. The man disappeared upcanyon. The fight was over.

The burreros cheered.

"A thousand thanks, señor," gasped Don Ygnacio. He jumped from the buckboard and came running to Johnnie. "You are not hurt, my friend?"

Johnnie shook his head. "And you?"

"Not even a scratch." Then the hacendado's face clouded. "But you have lost your horse, señor!"

Johnnie went to his horse and kneeled there a moment, stroking the mane. "I'll make him pay for this some day, Blazer old boy." The sorrel quivered. He had been shot through the heart and in a minute more was dead.

Johnnie turned away with the look of one who has lost his best friend.

"To save my purse you have lost a fine horse." Don Ygnacio said it with both sympathy and humility. "So the debt is mine, señor. You must permit me to pay. I have many horses at my hacienda. The best of them shall be yours."

Johnnie shrugged. "Forget it, Don Ygnacio."

The four burro drivers came rushing up, half exultant because two of three bandits had been shot down, and half fearful lest they should be scolded for their own sorry showing.

"Only one *ladron* got away!"

"The next time he will not be so fortunate, Don Ygnacio."

Johnnie went to the buckboard and removed masks from two men who lay dead there. Both of them appeared to be frontier ruffians of a stripe Johnnie had often seen swaggering about Dodge City and Abilene. The marshals of Kansas and the rangers of Texas had driven many such men west of the Pecos.

And now Johnnie realized why Ygnacio Sandoval, after selling his wool at the railhead, had chosen to journey back home in the slow company of his burreros. If he had driven on ahead and alone, he would have had no protection against such an assault as this one.

Retrieving his saddle, slicker roll, blanket and bridle, Johnnie lugged them to the buckboard. "I'm on foot," he said wryly. "So I reckon you'll have to gimme a lift to the next corral."

"But of course," agreed Don Ygnacio. "You must ride with me all the way to Santa Fe." He glanced down at two dead outlaws and then added with a shrug of distaste, "But first, it is our misfortune that we must deliver these *ladrones* to the nearest law."

"You mean we gotta turn clear back to Raton?"

"No, my friend. There is a new mining settlement just ahead called E-Town. Because of a boom in the mines, this county keeps a deputy there. It is only a trifle out of our way to Santa Fe."

The hacendado gave sharp orders. Two of his peons dashed away to round up the stampeded burros. The other two wound wagon sheets about the dead men, preparing to load them into the buckboard.

While they were so engaged, Johnnie walked about a hundred yards to an eminence which had been occupied by the masked rifleman. He was hoping to find some evidence of a hit.

Readily he found hoofmarks of the man's horse. Why had this fellow kept aloof, instead of advancing boldly, with his two companions?

On the ground there, Johnnie saw the stubs of half a dozen cigarritas. They were Mexican cigarritas, wrapped not in paper but in covering taken from an ear of Indian corn. At once Johnnie was fairly sure that this third outlaw was a Mexican. *Anglos* rarely used these cigarritas. That being the case, perhaps the man had kept at a distance for fear of being recognized by his victims.

At least this was a possibility. Johnnie looked the ground over carefully for some further clew. To have smoked half a dozen cigarritas, the rifleman must have been many minutes here.

Something half hidden in a clump of columbines caught Johnnie's eye. He picked it up and saw that it was a riding gauntlet. A glove for the right hand. By the warm sweaty feel of

17

it, it had been dropped here within the hour.

The rifleman quite naturally would remove his right glove for a more facile use of his trigger finger. While shooting, he must have dropped the glove without noticing.

Johnnie picked it up. It was doeskin and of a quality likely to be worn only by a fastidious caballero. But what struck Johnnie was the glove's size. It was much too small to fit an ordinary man's hand. This glove was extremely narrow. A woman might wear it. But certainly that tall, bullet-throwing *ladron* was no woman.

Johnnie put the glove in his pocket. He went back to the burro train resolving to say nothing about it to Don Ygnacio. From here on, though, he meant to keep his eyes open for a Spanish dandy with an effeminately slender right hand.

This narrow glove should fit that hand—just as a narrow slipper had fit the foot of Cinderella.

"*Listo, señor?*" inquired Don Ygnacio.

"Ready," Johnnie said.

The burros had been assembled and were already proceeding up the trail. Two canvas-shrouded outlaws occupied the wagon bed. Johnnie took a seat beside the hacendado.

But before whipping up his team, Don Ygnacio poured out two cups of wine from the demijohn. He gave one to his guest.

"Let us drink damnation," he proposed, "to all *ladrones.*"

CHAPTER 2

WITH JOHNNIE seated by him for protection, Don Ygnacio Sandoval had no reason now to lag along with his burro train. He instructed his burreros to follow him to E-Town, only a few miles ahead. Then the buckboard team moved on at a smart trot. Johnnie held his carbine ready in case of further encounter with the escaping outlaw.

"I think we shall not see him again," predicted the hacendado.

They came to a steep cascade of the stream. Here, at the canyon's head, the trail climbed to a gap which gave into a wide, mountain basin.

"It is the Moreno Valley," announced Don Ygnacio.

The valley appeared to be about ten miles wide and twenty long, its floor lush with tall grass, its walls graciously pine-clad and rising to snowy peaks. "What a range!" Johnnie murmured. He saw bands of wild horses and a few long-horned cattle grazing there.

"Is it not *magnifico*?" echoed Don Ygnacio. He was proud of his New Mexico.

"It's a cowman's paradise," Johnnie said.

On the near side of the basin, a feeder ravine led a short way to the new and booming camp of E-Town. A half hour of brisk driving brought them into its single pine-board street. Johnnie saw a row of cheap stores and restaurants and false front saloons. Booted miners were drifting to and from nearby shafts. Beyond, slag heaps and derricks and tipples made unsightly streaks against the mountain.

Don Ygnacio stopped his buckboard in front of an unpainted shack. He called out, "Señor Billy, are you at home?"

A thickset, bearded man came out. There was a forty-five swung low on his right thigh and a deputy's badge pinned to his checkered shirt.

"Howdy, Don Ygnacio," he greeted. "Get a good price for your wool? Didn't run into any grief, I hope."

"I have met three griefs, Señor Billy. One of them has escaped. The other two are in the wagon."

The deputy, all this while, was staring quizzically at Johnnie. "Haven't I seen you somewhere before, podner?" he inquired.

"Maybe. I'm Johnnie Cameron."

Recognition lighted the deputy's eyes. "Sure I recollect now. Three summers ago you rode into Abilene with steers from Texas."

Johnnie admitted it.

"And two winters ago you was huntin' buffalo outa Caldwell. Had a side-kick named Ogallala, didn't yuh? He can sure make a six-gun sing, Ogallala can. Whatever happened to that old buzzard?"

"He's hopin' to join me out here pretty soon," Johnnie said. "That is, if you don't slap me in jail for that roughhouse in Abilene when Ogallala—"

"Fergit it," the deputy cut in. He held out a hand. "In case you've forgot, my name's Billy Biglow. Truth is, I was glad to see you and Ogallala and Sweetwater Smith run them gamblers outa Abilene. Lots of gents right here need runnin' outa town too. Is your gun limber, Johnnie?"

"Take a look under the wagon sheet," Johnnie suggested.

Biglow rolled back the canvas and exposed two dead men. He gave a low whistle, then cocked an inquiring eye at Don Ygnacio.

"Three masked *ladrones*," the hacendado explained, "tried to rob me in the canyon. I returned their fire. Then Señor Cameron has come to my aid and we kill only two of them. *Que triste!*" He made a gesture of regret with his cigarrita. "To you, Señor Billy, I apologize that we did not kill all three."

"You didn't do a bad job at that," Biglow grunted. "Know who these jaspers are? They're Ripper Drake and Cherokee Conly. Both wanted for killings in Kansas. They had a date with a noose, these jiggers did. So you saved the law a peck o' trouble."

"If you need witnesses," the hacendado said,

"you may inquire of my burreros when they arrive here."

Biglow nodded. "Now you gents go right in my shack and make yerselves at home. I'll drive this evidence to the morgue and be back in a shake."

Disembarking, Johnnie and Don Ygnacio went into the shack. Odors of venison, coffee and frijoli beans greeted them. A Chinese cook was setting food on a table there. They heard the buckboard rumble away toward whatever passed for a morgue in E-Town.

The entire camp would be a morgue in a few years, Johnnie predicted. These gold towns usually didn't last long.

"It's Colfax County we're in?" Johnnie asked.

"*Si, señor,*" said Sandoval. "Just west over the pass is Taos County, where we shall be tonight. To the south of Taos is Santa Fe County. And to the west of Santa Fe is Sandoval County, where lies my own rancho."

Billy Biglow rejoined them. As a pure formality, he asked Don Ygnacio to make out a statement and sign it. Johnnie signed also and the incident was closed.

The three men then sat down to eat and Johnnie made the most of his opportunity to get information about the country.

"It's a sweet range fer both men and cows," Biglow explained. "Only trouble is a lot o' no-good *hombres* has got pushed into it from the prairie strips between Texas and Dakota. These Taos mountains makes a good hideout fer 'em. They figger they ain't no law west o' the Pecos, and so they plan to raid ranches and mines and stages and wool shippers along the Santa Fe trail."

"Of which last we had a sample this mornin'," Johnnie said. "By the way, Biglow, if you run onto a tall slim dude with a woman's size hand, save him for me."

"How come?" Biglow questioned.

Before Johnnie could answer, a rattle of gunfire came from a saloon across the street.

Biglow stood up, hitching at his gunbelt. "Wonder why them fellers can't behave. 'Scuse me a minute, gents." He went outside.

"Need any help?" Johnnie called after him.

"Nope. Stay right there, Johnnie. No sense lettin' yer victuals git cold."

They saw Billy Biglow cross the street and disappear into the saloon.

A moment of silence followed. Then a single shot came from the barroom.

Johnnie saw a man dash out and jump to the back of a horse tied at the hitchrack. The man wore a battered felt hat and corduroys white with mine dust. His chin was spade square and covered with a stubble. Before Johnnie could get more than a brief glimpse, the man had galloped out of view.

Customers were tumbling from the saloon. They were all excited and talking at once. A few of them had revolvers and began shooting after the runaway. Others ran to get mounts of their own.

Johnnie Cameron picked up his rifle and ran into the street. A posse was forming. Having no horse himself, Johnnie couldn't join it. He went on into the saloon to inquire.

Billy Biglow lay dead on the barroom floor.

"Who shot him?" Johnnie asked the bartender.

The bartender used his bar rag to mop beads from his own pale forehead. "Pete Adler got lit up," he explained. "He was shootin' bottles off the bar. Billy Biglow come in and told him to put up his gun, and Pete blazed away at him. Pete allers was quick-fingered. Too dern bad, I say. We allers liked Billy around here."

Johnnie helped him carry the victim across to Biglow's shack. The body was placed on a cot there and covered with a wagon sheet. Johnnie and Don Ygnacio stood by with heads bared.

"Perhaps," the hacendado suggested sadly, "this Pete Adler is the *ladron* who escaped from us in the canyon."

Johnnie shoot his head. "Don't think so. That masked fellah was tall and slim."

"But we only saw him on a horse, señor. So of his tallness we cannot be sure."

"I'll check on it," Johnnie said. He returned across to the saloon.

"Does Pete Adler," he asked the bartender, "have small, ladylike hands?"

"Him? No. Pete's got big mitts, red and raw. He's a miner. Staked a claim here but it didn't pan nothin'. Heard him say he aimed to pull out and head further west."

"Was he hangin' around this bar all mornin'?"

"He sure was, stranger. But don't worry none. That posse 'll ketch up with him all right. He'll be stretchin' hemp before sundown."

It was clear that Pete Adler couldn't have been at the canyon hold-up. Johnnie reported this certainty to Don Ygnacio. Sympathetic friends of Billy Biglow now crowded the shack. Of these, one was a cousin who had accompanied Biglow here from Kansas.

"Reckon there's nothin' we can do," Johnnie said.

"We are only in the way, señor," agreed Don Ygnacio.

He fed his team and left word that his burreros should camp here for a day before proceeding on, in case authorities should want to question them about the canyon hold-up.

Johnnie and the hacendado then drove on toward Taos.

For a few miles they followed the westerly rim of Moreno Valley. Then they turned up a canyon toward Taos Pass. Giant spruce and fir sentineled the trail here. The way steepened in air crisp with the tang of high altitude.

"Folks don't use this prong of the Santa Fe trail so much, do they?" Johnnie asked.

"You are right, señor," said Sandoval. "Most of the heavy wagons go by way of Las Vegas. They cross the upper Pecos and enter Santa Fe from the east. This fork goes over the pass and down into Taos; from there it follows the Rio Grande to Santa Fe."

The sun was low when they reached the pass. From there Johnnie looked out over a down-sloping bank of green and gold, with the brown of Taos Valley in the cup below; beyond all of it reared the red spikes and domes of the Rio Arriba.

On the summit the hacendado rested his team while he brought out the demijohn of wine.

"Know a banker in Santa Fe named Stephen Elkins?" Johnnie asked him.

"Do I know Don Stephano? But of course." A glow came to Sandoval's saddle-brown face. "He is a great man here in New Mexico and my very good friend. He is a friend of your too, señor?"

"No," Johnnie said. "But I've got a letter of introduction to him from a stockman in Missouri."

"Si. Often Don Stephano has told me that he came from Missouri."

"Does he know anything about cattle?"

"All bankers must know about cattle, señor."

"Sure," Johnnie admitted. "They couldn't make stock loans if they didn't. This Stephen Elkins is some popular out this way, is he?"

Don Ygnacio's assent was emphatic. "He is a great favorite with all our New Mexicans—both with the Spanish and the *Anglos.* Someday he may be a governor—or even a senator to the Congress."

Johnnie puffed his cigarette. "Well, anyway, right now he's president of the First National Bank o' Santa Fe—and I'm askin' him for a fifteen thousand dollar loan."

Don Ygnacio arched an eyebrow. But he was too polite to express surprise.

Johnnie laughed. "I reckon you think I got plenty nerve. A lone cowpoke ridin' into a strange range to borrow fifteen thousand."

"No doubt you offer good security, señor."

"The main security I've got," Johnnie said, "is an idea. It's an idea about cattle."

"Let us drink to your success," proposed Don Ygnacio.

They drank of the choke-cherry wine.

"Tell me about your own rancho," Johnnie said presently. "Is it a big place?"

The hacendado shrugged in deprecation. "It is not so big a ranch as the one we have just crossed."

27

"Didn't know we'd been on one," Johnnie said.

"For the last hundred miles, señor, you have been on one rancho. It is the Maxwell Grant, which ends at this pass. And it has more than two million acres."

Johnnie whistled. "And yours isn't quite that big?"

"No, señor. Mine is a little one of only a hundred and thirty thousand acres. It is a grant from the King of Spain to my ancestors. On it are many sheep and horses. The best of the horses is for you, Señor Cameron."

Don Ygnacio clucked to his roans and sent them trotting down the trail to Taos.

CHAPTER 3

NIGHT WAS TWO hours old when the buckboard pulled up under spreading alamos in front of the Taos tavern. A chubby Indian boy came out and Don Ygnacio tossed him the reins. "You will see that my team is fed, *niño*."

The tavern, a flat-roofed adobe of one story, covered an entire side of the plaza. The long sala which Johnnie entered had a hard-packed earth floor with rugs of homespun wool strewn about it. Flickering candles gave light. In one corner piñon logs crackled on a mud hearth. On one wall was a mounted elk head over a buffalo gun on brackets. On another hung a framed portrait of Kit Carson, until five years ago the most distinguished citizen of Taos.

Two guests were smoking cigarritas by the hearth. They happened to be unacquainted with Don Ygnacio. Nevertheless they stood up and each gave a slight bow as the hacendado came in with Johnnie.

"Caballeros," they murmured in salute.

"Caballeros," echoed Don Ygnacio.

He rang a bell which brought the tavern's host.

"You are well arrived, patron," the hotel man greeted cordially.

"We desire comida and your best rooms,

Alfredo. This is my friend, Señor Cameron."

"The friends of Don Ygnacio are mine, Señor Cameron." Alfredo bowed low, then tossed an end of his serape over his shoulder and picked up candles. They followed him down a hallway so wide that a cart could have been driven through to the patio beyond.

Crossing the patio, they came to an outbuilding which contained the more select rooms. Evidently the best was none too good for Ygnacio Sandoval.

"Comida will be at your pleasure," announced Alfredo. He ushered Don Ygnacio into a room with a high, four poster bed of laces and many pillows, taking Johnnie to another quite like it. Then Alfredo clapped his hands and half a dozen Indian boys came running. Some brought tin tubs for bathing. Others brought kettles of warm water.

An hour later Johnnie had bathed and shaved. He joined Don Ygnacio in a dining sala, where comida was served for two. Alfredo in person brought in soup, which to Johnnie seemed to be a mixture of chile pods, meat balls, minced onion and garlic. Then came blue cornmeal pancakes swamped with chile sauce and green peppers stuffed with chicken and cheese.

At last Alfredo served sherry wine and withdrew.

With a contented sigh, Don Ygnacio lighted a

cigarrita. "By another sunset, my friend, we shall be in Santa Fe."

"But you still won't be home," Johnnie reminded him. "You said your grant is a county west of Santa Fe."

"Ah, but also I have a house in Santa Fe. My family is there now, for the fiesta. They will welcome you too, Señor Cameron."

After a single glass of wine, the hacendado was ready to retire. "I am not so young as you, señor. We must drive seventy miles tomorrow. So with your permission—*buenos noches.*"

"Good night," Johnnie said.

He went out on the plaza. Shops and saloons on three sides of it were lighted and still enjoying patronage. It was ten o'clock, too early for anyone as young and full of life as Johnnie Cameron to go to bed.

So he made a circuit of the plaza, stopping here at a cantina where guitars made rhythm with clinking glasses, and there to watch a hatchet-faced Mexican deal monte to a pair of trappers. All doors were wide open. Soft lights and hard voices came from them. Gunslung men moved in and out. An owl hooted from the plaza cottonwoods. Horses champed and stamped at the hitchracks. From dark lanes came the smells of hollyhocks and dust and chile peppers.

In the main gambling place, Johnnie saw gun-armed *Anglos* at poker. He felt sure that some of

31

them were border fugitives of a kind with Ripper Drake and Cherokee Conly. Johnnie stood back of them for a while, watching hands. He failed to see any hand slender enough to fit the glove dropped by a masked rifleman in Cimarron Canyon.

Yet that escaping *ladron* might quite well be in Taos. Pete Adler might be here too, in his flight from E-Town. Johnnie moved from game to game, carefully observing all faces and hands.

Roulette was in full whirl; chuckaluck dice were dancing in a five gallon bottle; a swarthy halfbreed dealt blackjack to vaqueros, sheepherders and miners.

But Pete Adler wasn't there. Nor was any slim Spanish dandy with markedly effeminate hands.

Johnnie took the glove from his pocket and looked at it again. On the lining of the cuff he saw a trademark. Or rather the name of a retailer was stamped there. It read:

LA TIENDA GRANDE
TAOS

Which meant that the glove had been sold on this very plaza. Johnnie went outside and crossed to a general store with the name "La Tienda Grande" over its door. This being Saturday night, the place was open even at the late hour.

A genteel Mexican proprietor bowed to Johnnie as he entered. "May I serve you, señor?"

"I'm on my way to the Santa Fe fiesta," Johnnie said. "So maybe I better doll up some. What about a red silk bandana with horseshoes on it?"

The proprietor clapped his hands, summoning his staff of clerks. They brought down from the shelves not only the establishment's entire stock of silk handkerchiefs, scarfs and serapes, but also everything else in the way of gentleman's wear suitable for the fiesta.

Johnnie purchased a blue silk bandana and a serape of gay stripes. By then the store's staff had been won to his confidence. "By the way," Johnnie said casually, "did you sell this glove?"

The merchant looked at the trademark. "*Si, señor.*"

"Who bought it?"

"*Quien sabe*? Of the cash sales we keep no record, señor."

"But this is an odd size. See? It's too tight for an ordinary man's hand. Might fit a boy or a woman."

"Verdad. It has the width of a boy's glove and the length of a man's. Once such a pair of gloves were in stock here, but we do not know to whom they were sold."

The merchant was quite sincere and so were all four of his clerks.

"Perhaps it was Pancho who sold the glove," a clerk suggested.

"Fetch Pancho here," the proprietor said. He explained that Pancho Archuleta was the store's bookkeeper and cashier, and that sometimes he waited on a customer.

Pancho was found in an adjoining barroom and brought in. He examined the glove and then denied having ever seen it before.

His eyes were sly and shifty. They evaded Johnnie's. The man's entire manner seemed overly cautious and his response did not convince Johnnie at all. "I know nothing, señor," he kept saying too promptly, as though he had been accused of something. A faint nervousness tainted his voice as he inquired, "Why do you ask, señor?"

"Because the man you sold the glove to," Johnnie said, "is a *ladron*. He stuck up a pack train in Cimarron Canyon."

"I know nothing, señor." Pancho slipped away, not back to the adjacent barroom but out into the gloom of the plaza. Johnnie saw him fade between the adobe walls of an alley.

It occurred to Johnnie that he might have scurried away to warn someone. Chances were he knew quite well to whom the gloves had been sold. Johnnie followed to the alley's entrance. Ahead in the darkness he could hear the man running. Why would he run, unless to warn a friend who could be incriminated by the glove? No use chasing him in the dark. Johnnie waited there at the alley's end, on a chance that the man might return this way. Waiting, he leaned his back against a hitching post and rolled a cigarette.

Ten minutes passed. No one came. Lights at the plaza shops began winking out. Then came the whirr of a rope. A noose dropped neatly over Johnnie's shoulders. Before he could move, the noose tightened. It pinioned his arms against his body. The noose had settled also over the post. The pull of a taut rope now made Johnnie helpless against that post. His right hand could touch the holster of his forty-five, but he could not crook an elbow for the draw.

The rope stretched out tightly to the horn of a saddle. Under the saddle stood a stiff-legged cow pony, trained to keep a roped steer helpless. The horse was braced and pulling; the pull made the rope cut like a knife across Johnnie's chest and arms.

Seated in the saddle was a tall, slim man wearing black leathers. A mask obscured his face. A cigarrita glowed at his lips. On his left hand was a glove. In his right was a cocked forty-five.

The gun was aiming at Johnnie's heart. He was at the mercy of this ladron, beyond question the same tall, masked rifleman who had escaped in Cimarron Canyon.

The man said nothing. In the darkness, with plaza cottonwoods hiding the moon, he was barely more than a silhouette. It was clear to Johnnie that a furtive-eyed clerk had recalled a sale of gloves, and for reasons of his own had dashed away to warn this masked horseman. The masked horseman must have ridden directly here from the hold-up, taking refuge in some hideout known to both himself and the clerk.

Suddenly the rope slackened. But only for an instant. During that instant the mounted man threw a hitch which again looped Johnnie, pinioning him all the more securely. In the same instant the horse advanced a step nearer, taking up the slack and then again bracing forefeet to keep the rope taut.

"Shall I shoot your ears off, señor?" The masked man spoke softly, and yet in a tone dagger sharp with malice.

Johnnie's impulse was to shout. Pride kept him from it. He wasn't used to calling for help, even in a straight-jacket like this. Perhaps the man would realize that his victim could make an outcry and so bring customers tumbling from the saloons.

Again an instant of slack. Again a deftly thrown hitch which dropped another loop about both the post and the prisoner. The horseman advanced with each hitch, his gun at aim all the while.

Johnnie strained to get at his own gun. Its butt was six inches too high for him, with his arms pinioned this way. He should be wearing it low on his thigh, like Ogallala and Sweetwater Smith. Throwing hitch after hitch, the rider kept closing in. He was an artist with a rope. Impotent and humiliated, Johnnie could only stand seething while the horse came step by step nearer. Arriving at arm's length, the man could smash his gun barrel down on Johnnie's head. No noise that way. Shooting would bring witnesses, but a blow on the head wouldn't. It was too late for Johnnie to shout now. The last hitch had looped his neck, and the tautness of the rope all but choked him.

The horseman was so close now that his stirrup touched Johnnie. But instead of clubbing with his gun, the man drew off his single glove. With it he slapped Johnnie full across the lips and drew blood.

"After this you will mind your own business, señor."

The man disengaged the rope from his saddle horn and dropped it at Johnnie's feet. Also he dropped the glove. Then he pulled his horse to haunches, made a rearing whirl and was off at a hard gallop. The night swallowed him.

Even with the rope slack, it took Johnnie more than a minute to disentangle himself from the loops. His arms and chest burned from the rope's bite. He staggered free from the post, at last, and again pride kept him from advertising his defeat.

He'd tell no one, not even Don Ygnacio Sandoval.

At his feet lay a glove. Johnnie picked it up. It was more than a glove. A conviction fired through Johnnie that he was picking up a challenge flung to him by an invisible outlaw empire. This particular ladron was only one of a breed. There were many others like him, west of the Pecos.

Johnnie put the glove in his pocket. He had both gloves now. He also picked up the rope and coiled it over his forearm. With it he crossed the plaza to the tavern.

The main sala was deserted. But Johnnie saw a desk with ink, paper and a quill pen. Late as it was, he decided to write a letter.

He wrote:

Dear Ogallala:

I lost Blazer in a gunfight. An all right hombre picked me up. His name is Ygnacio Sandoval. Except for too many ladrones, this is a good range.

Keep feeding those heifers, Ogallala. Haven't located that Pozo Hondo country yet. Soon as I get to Santa Fe, I'll try to sell our idea to Banker Elkins.

Regards to Slim and Rosy and Sweetwater.
Yours,
JOHNNIE CAMERON.

CHAPTER 4

A KNOCK ON HIS door at daybreak aroused Johnnie. Alfredo called in to him, "Don Ygnacio is already at breakfast, Señor Cameron."

The tolling of a mission bell reminded that this was Sunday morning. Johnnie found Don Ygnacio dressed for the trail and eager to be off. "I have ordered a fresh team," the hacendado announced, "so that we will not be late for the fiesta."

When they went out to the street the team was waiting. An Indian boy appeared with Johnnie's slicker roll and put it in the buckboard. The gloves and rope of the outlaw were inside the roll.

Three riders came up on jaded horses and dismounted in front of the tavern. Johnnie recognized one of them as a miner seen yesterday at E-Town, and so concluded that this was part of the posse that had ridden after Pete Adler.

"Did you catch him," Johnnie inquired.

"Catch Pete Adler? Nope, he got clean away." The three possemen shuffled wearily into the tavern for breakfast.

Johnnie climbed to the seat beside Don Ygnacio and the buckboard, behind a span of skittish broncos, rolled south out of the plaza toward Santa Fe.

They splashed across Pot Creek and rattled by the adobes at Ranches of Taos. The grade being down from here, the hacendado made record time. Soon they had traversed a sagey plateau and were winding down a ledge trail into the canyon of the Rio Grande.

The Grand River of the North riffled a hundred yards wide here, almost from wall to wall of the gorge. The buckboard rumbled along its brink, bumping over rocks.

"I must not be late," Don Ygnacio murmured. "For this year at the fiesta my household shall receive a great honor."

He did not explain about this.

Soon the canyon widened, giving room for patches of alfalfa here and there. They began to pass bullock carts and burros and scrawny nags, all bearing peon families toward Santa Fe. Mexicans afoot and Mexicans on mule-back. Children piled high on the carts. Black-shawled women and gay young caballeros. Many of them knew Don Ygnacio and greeted him as a citizen of distinction.

A passing ranchero called out, "It will be a great day for your little Josefita."

"And for all New Mexico," beamed Don Ygnacio.

At many roadside settlements he was invited in

for wine. Always he presented Johnnie Cameron. "This is my good friend who saved me from *ladrones*."

The hearers heaped praises on Johnnie and maledictions upon all outlaws. Giving details made them late, and so the sun was low when they left the river and turned up a range of piñon hills toward the capital.

"Who," Johnnie inquired, "is Josefita?"

"She is my granddaughter." Pride brightened the hacendado's leathery old face. "Tonight she will be much excited, my Josefita. For tomorrow she will be first lady of the fiesta."

The sun slipped behind red hills across the Rio Grande. The trail was crowded now. Ahead of him in the twilight, Johnnie saw a tiny bonfire beside the road. Then another. And another. The dusk became spotted with flickering beacons.

They came then to a crest and looked down upon Santa Fe. Johnnie saw a tangle of narrow streets with adobe boxes lining them, low and flat-roofed. Then he heard bells. He saw moving people, each holding a candle. A thousand candles in as many hands, in single file, all moving in solemn procession up a hill. A church stood on that hill, reaching its Cross above the dusk-dim piñons.

"Always the fiesta begins this way," Don Ygnacio whispered. "With vespers at the Cross of the Martyrs."

They let the team rest while the dark deepened. Johnnie Cameron looked down on Santa Fe, heard no sound except bells, saw no light except candles. In this, his first sight of it, the Royal City of the Holy Faith was living up to its name.

Then Don Ygnacio drove on down into quiet, winding streets. He turned into the Agua Frio Road where an irrigation ditch murmured, and where willows dropped lazily over the roadway. A high adobe wall ran here and Don Ygnacio drove through a gate in it. "We are home, señor," he announced.

The house was one-story but seemed to cover an acre. Here again was quiet, because all of the family and most of the servants were attending vespers. One old man came out and Don Ygnacio greeted him affectionately as Miguel. "Put away the team, Miguel, and then bring everything inside. There is a small gift with your name on it."

"*Mille gracias, patron,*" Miguel murmured.

They went inside and again Johnnie found himself on a hard-packed earth floor covered only with an occasional Indian rug. The lamplight showed carved wooden saints recessed into the walls. The walls were adobe, tinted blue. An organ was at one end of the sala. At the other end was a fireplace with two formal, high-backed chairs in front of it. The other chairs were merely cushioned benches. An ancient sheep dog came up to sniff as Johnnie entered.

"I'll just stop long enough to meet your folks," Johnnie said. "Then I'll go bed down at the hotel."

The hacendado wouldn't hear of it. "You must not disappoint me, Señor Cameron. No, you are my guest here for all of the fiesta. Then you must come to my hacienda where I will select for you a horse."

His insistence couldn't be denied. Johnnie permitted himself to be led back through a long adobe tunnel which emerged into a patio. A great cottonwood grew here with lanterns hung from the lower branches. Wings of the house enclosed the patio on four sides. Two more sheep dogs came up to leap joyfully upon Don Ygnacio.

Miguel brought Johnnie's slicker roll in, then ushered Johnnie to a cool room in the rear wing. Johnnie groomed himself to meet the Sandoval family. In a little while he heard them arriving from vespers.

When he emerged into the patio he found his host surrounded by a chattering crowd of his kinfolk and many servants. Don Ygnacio was passing out presents he had brought from the railhead.

He saw Johnnie and cried out, "Ah, and I have brought you also a guest. He is a brave gentleman. But for him I would have been killed by ladrones."

They crowded up to Johnnie with excited

welcomes. He had never before found such friendly people. Or people so embarrassingly grateful. "Did you shoot the ladrones, señor?" a grandson of Don Ygnacio's demanded. A matronly niece exclaimed, "Ah! señor, a million thanks for your courage."

All of them seemed to be cousins, nephews, nieces or grandchildren except a widower son whom the hacendado presented as "Don Santiago." Santiago carried his right arm in a sling. "Caramba!" he exclaimed. "Except that a runaway horse threw me, Señor Cameron, I would have gone with the pack train myself."

Most all of them, it seemed, lived with Ygnacio on the old family grant in Sandoval County, coming only to Santa Fe upon occasions of fiesta.

"But where," Don Ygnacio demanded, "is Josefita?"

"Here I am, Papacito." His favorite grandchild came running into his arms.

Spanish girls weren't new to Johnnie. He had met them in San Antone and San Angelo. But this one was different. She was different even from the cousins who surrounded her in the patio here. She was taller, more slender. Her hair, no longer than her shoulder, was dark but full of sunshine glints. It curled loosely and, flung back, revealed a skin so clear that Johnnie could trace the beginnings of a blush as she saw him staring.

She caught up her vespers mantilla and covered her head.

Don Ygnacio presented her with pride, "This is my Josefita, Señor Cameron."

"I thank you, señor," the girl said with a little shudder, "for saving Papacito from the ladrones."

"No such thing," Johnnie murmured. "He had 'em licked before I got there."

He was suddenly conscious of his dustiness. He had changed to his other shirt, but his jacket and trousers were the same travel-worn garments of the trail. If only he hadn't shown so much sales resistance, last night, to those clerks in Taos!

"I am sure," Josefita insisted, "that you were very brave."

"And how is thy handsome novio, child?" inquired Don Ygnacio.

Johnnie didn't miss that. He saw the hacendado look at him as though there might have been a hint in the mention of a novio. And so the girl had a handsome fiancé!

"Don Ramon is out at his mine," she said. "He arrives only in time for the pageant."

So the novio's name was Ramon and he owned a mine. No doubt he was due for some important part in the parade tomorrow. All of which made Johnnie feel dustier and dustier.

Johnnie and Don Ygnacio sat down to supper.

The others had already dined, not having expected Don Ygnacio until tomorrow.

After the wine Johnnie retired to his room. There would be family confidences in this first hour of home-coming upon which he preferred not to intrude.

He tried brushing off his trail buckskins and then decided they were hopeless. If he could find a store open tomorrow, he'd outfit himself to match the best of these caballeros.

Now he threw himself on the bed. The clean bare room, with its cool, whitewashed walls, lulled him and he fell asleep.

He awoke to hear a guitar in the patio. No voices. Just a single guitar strumming chords. Johnnie looked out and saw Josefita in a swing under the cottonwood. She began to sing softly an old Spanish love song. Near her sat an elderly duenna, half asleep. A sheep dog lay at her feet.

Moonlight filtering through the cottonwood leaves made dappled shadows there. Johnnie watched them shimmer on the girl's face. A good thing she had a novio! Otherwise he wouldn't be keeping his mind on that cattle deal with Elkins.

She sang another verse of her song. Johnnie stood in his open door, watching. "Lordy, lordy!" he told himself. "She sure is pretty."

She looked up and saw him there. "Is there anything you need of service, Señor Cameron?"

46

"Not a thing," Johnnie said. He advanced into the patio. "Please don't stop singing."

"I sing because I am so excited," she said. "It is the first time I am allowed to be in the fiesta pageant."

"You'll have to tell me about this fiesta," Johnnie said. He sat down with his back to the alamo. "I'm a stranger out this way, you know."

"But of course. First I will sing a song of old Mexico to put you in the humor."

Her song of the conquistadores charmed Johnnie. All the while he kept wondering why she should seem so unlike all the other daughters of Spain he had ever known. Johnnie felt a subtle mystery about her. As he saw her profile in the moonlight now, she didn't look Spanish at all.

Presently her song was finished. The guitar hung loose from her fingers.

"It is like this, señor," she said. "In the year so long ago, 1610 if you know the history book, the conquistadores built the palace of the governors that we still have on our plaza here. But seventy years later the Indians rebelled and drove all our people back into Mexico. That was very bad. Señor Cameron, for our people, and for the Indians too."

"But the Spaniards came back," Johnnie said.

"Yes," said Josefita, sitting up very straight. Her eyes were alive with fire and pride. "Yes, they were brave people and so they came back. In 1692 Don Diego de Vargas marched up the Rio Grande and recaptured Santa Fe. Was he not a fine caballero, this De Vargas?"

"I reckon he was," Johnnie admitted.

"So each year now, señor, we choose the finest caballero in all New Mexico to be De Vargas. In our fiesta we have him march into Santa Fe, with all his plumes and armor and fine horses. It is a very grand parade, señor."

"And this parade comes off tomorrow?"

"Si, mañana." A little choke of excitement all but stifled Josefita. "And what do you think, señor? Don Ramon Montoya, the man I will marry when I am eighteen—he is the one chosen to be this so splendid De Vargas!"

Johnnie rolled a cigarette. So she wasn't quite eighteen yet. Just a kid, and about to become Señora Montoya. The idea ruffled Johnnie a bit. Also it made him feel a little lonely.

"I savvy," he said. "You'll be sort of queen of this fandango, won't you? High combs and lace mantillas and all that?"

"Verdad, señor. Do you wonder that I am excited? At the Palace of the Governors tomorrow night, with Don Diego de Vargas y Lujan Ponce de Leon, I shall lead the grand ball."

Johnnie grinned. "I'll be on the sidelines," he promised.

• • •

Early in the morning Johnnie went out to join a crowd lining the Camino Real. Over the hill came a cavalcade of plumed horsemen. The people cheered. Guns were fired into the air. Johnnie Cameron couldn't fail to catch the spirit of it as he saw Don Diego de Vargas on a prancing white stallion, and seated on a silver saddle, come riding into Santa Fe at the head of an armored troop.

Spears flashed in the sun. Plumes waved in the wind. Blooded horses champed at bits and spurs jingled. De Vargas, man of the hour, made a gallant figure. A tall man with a handsome, proud face—Johnnie could hardly deny that he might well be the finest caballero in New Mexico.

Then Johnnie remembered that he wasn't really De Vargas, but only a fellow named Montoya who was playing a part. But he played the part well. "Viva De Vargas!" the people shouted as he rode by. "Viva el Conquistador!"

More guns were fired skyward. Johnnie felt a bit like firing his own. He fell in with the crowd and trooped along in the wake of the parade.

He missed nothing of the vivid spectacle of the *entrada*, with the cross and banner of Spain planted once more before the Palace of the Governors exactly as it had been planted there by the real De Vargas. And Johnnie saw the alcalde of Santa Fe in his brocade satin coat read again the ancient edict of conquest. Soldiers and padres and war-painted Indians then followed De Vargas back to his camp beyond the river.

The household of Don Ygnacio Sandoval went home to make ready for tonight's ball at the palace. But Johnnie lingered on the plaza. Time he was looking up the banker, Stephen Elkins, and getting down to brass tacks on a cattle deal.

But when he went to the bank he found it locked. Every business in town, he was told, was closed and would stay closed until after the fiesta.

However, Johnnie did manage to find one open shop. In it he purchased a jacket of creamy doeskin, corduroy riding breeches to match and a checkered silk shirt. He had a boy polish his boots. After putting on his new outfit, Johnnie wandered to a plaza bench and watched the populace at play. All of New Mexico seemed to be milling about, some in seventeenth century costumes, some masquerading as eighteenth century frontiersmen. A thousand Pueblo Indians crowded into the plaza and opened sidewalk stalls to show blankets and pottery. Vaqueros circled at full gallop, shooting and shouting.

Not to intrude too much upon the Sandovals, Johnnie sent word by messenger that he would take comida downtown. All the while he kept wondering how he could sidestep Don Ygnacio's persistent invitation to go on with the family to the Sandoval hacienda. He must be careful not to offend. At the same time it was quite out of the question to let the old hacendado take him out to the ranch and present him with a fine horse.

Thinking of horses reminded Johnnie that he didn't feel quite dressed up without one now. Especially with every other caballero in town riding a horse. So Johnnie hunted up a livery barn and rented himself a mount for the evening. "I'll be needin' it off and on for the next few days," he said.

After eating supper at a cantina off Burro Alley, Johnnie found a barber and got a shave. The barber chattered at length about the current fiesta hero, Don Ramon Montoya.

"He is a fine caballero, señor. An old family, the Montoyas, that one time was very rich."

"And isn't now?" Johnny suggested.

"Not now, señor. Of late years Don Ramon has lost everything. His silver mine on the west mesa does not pay any more. Still, he is a *muy grande* caballero. Soon he will make marriage with a daughter of *los ricos*, la Señorita Josefa Sandoval."

"This Montoya fellah can't be quite broke," Johnnie argued, "else he wouldn't have a top braunk like that white stallion I saw him forkin'."

"But he only borrowed the stallion, señor. It belongs to Don Pablo Lucero, a wealthy ranchero who lends it to Don Ramon only for the fiesta."

Evening came and Johnnie hitched his own rented nag on the plaza. Costumed ladies and plumed gentlemen were already riding toward the palace. Lesser folk swept in from a dozen radial streets to dance on the plaza.

Johnnie himself crowded into the palace. He was there when the grand march began. He saw a lovely bejeweled lady of old Spain lead the march on the arm of Diego de Vargas. She was Josefita Sandoval. Her cheeks were flaming. Her hair was coiled high on her head with two big turquoise combs there.

If Johnnie was aware of Josefita, other señoritas were aware of Johnnie Cameron. More than one raised dark lashed eyes as she passed him. "Que rubio!" one of them murmured, and seemed frankly fascinated by his blondness. Johnnie didn't realize that blond men were at premium out here. He only knew that his feet itched to be dancing.

The grand marchers circled the room, formed in figures, weaving a tapestry of color. Twice Josefita and her cavalier passed Johnnie, Josefita with a gay smile, Don Ramon quite ignoring the yellow-haired, gringo cowboy waving from the sidelines.

Then the march was done and the couples began dancing.

"You like the *baile*?" a voice asked. Johnnie turned to find Don Ygnacio by him. "Will you come and sit with my household, señor?"

Johnnie followed him to the Sandoval box. It was empty, because young and old were on the dance floor.

The dance was a minuet now.

Later the music changed to the soft, dreamy, heartbreaking tempo of old Mexico.

"Looks sort o' like a waltz," Johnnie said to Don Ygnacio.

"It is called the cradle, señor."

Johnnie watched Josefita and Ramon. They were dancing toe to toe, each with hands looped back of the other's waist, and leaning far back so that their bodies formed a cradle as they whirled. Josefita's full and ruffled skirt boiled about her ankles. The ends of her *reboza*, crimson like her cheeks, streamed back of her and her high-coiled hair caught light from a thousand candles.

The dance came to an end. "Looks easy," Johnnie murmured. "Wouldn't mind takin' a fling at it myself."

"You like it, no?" smiled the hacendado.

A flurry of skirts and a breath of perfume brought Josefita to them. With her came he who wore the velvet and lace of De Vargas.

"Don Ramon, you must meet our guest," she said. "I have told you how he saved Papacito

53

from the ladrones. Señor Cameron, may I present Don Ramon Montoya?"

Don Ramon bowed from the hips. An odd smile flashed on his face. "My lady has spoken so well of you, señor," he murmured, "that I am already jealous."

The man's handsome face was clean-shaven, a rarity in Santa Fe, except that deep, narrow sideburns dropped from either temple. He was extremely tall and slim and sure of himself. "A friend of the Sandovals is mine," he said, and extended his right hand.

Johnnie took it. The touch sent an icy shock through him. This hand was narrow—like the hand of a woman. It was too slim for a man's.

A voice, too, echoed from last night. It seemed to Johnnie that he could again feel the sting of a glove on his lips.

He remembered well the timbre of that voice—"After this you will mind your own business, señor." And now, he was sure, he heard it again.

Johnnie looked Don Ramon in the eyes but his answer was spoken to Josefita. "Yes, miss, your granddad and I *did* get held up on the trail. A fellah never knows where he'll meet ladrones."

The dark eyes of Ramon flickered. He said smoothly: "That is true, señor. One never knows. So if one is wise, he will always beware."

"I'll keep my eyes open," Johnnie said.

All of it was lost on the Sandovals. They could hardly guess that Johnnie Cameron had just accused Don Ramon of being a ladron; and that Don Ramon, he who wore the golden braid of De Vargas, had just promised a bullet for Johnnie's heart.

CHAPTER 5

"LET US NOT speak more of the wicked bandits," insisted Josefita. Her slipper tapped impatiently. "Will you dance with me, Señor Cameron?" She curtsied prettily to her grandfather and Don Ramon. "You will excuse, please?"

Johnnie looped his strong brown hands back of her waist. Toe to toe and leaning far back, they whirled away. Other couples jostled them as the floor filled. Music and laughter and gay badinage rang through the old palace.

Johnnie saw Don Ramon staring at him. He could read a challenge in the man's eyes; and partly to defy it, Johnnie asked Josefita: "How many dances do I get tonight, Josefita? Is four too many? Naturally I want 'em all."

She looked up at him. Then her eyes sought Don Ramon across the room. "Two times we may dance," she said. "Once because you are my guest, and once because you have saved Papacito."

"What about once just for the thrill of it?" Johnnie begged.

She laughed. "You are very bold, señor."

He delivered her back to Don Ramon. But the ball did not break up until nearly dawn and most of that while Johnnie Cameron stood by. His reward was four dances with Josefita.

After the last one, Johnnie went out into the plaza with worry furrowed between his eyes. He must decide how to deal with Montoya.

That Montoya was the masked rifleman of Cimarron Canyon Johnnie could not doubt. Nor could he doubt the reception such an idea would get from the Sandovals. Don Ramon a bandit! Incredible. Certainly the Sandovals would believe no such charge against the chosen husband of Josefita.

"They'd think I'm loco!" Johnnie worried.

Outside he found rows of carriages. At the hitchracks were tethered mounts of the cavaliers. Johnnie saw a big white stallion with a silver-trimmed saddle. On this one, he remembered, Don Diego de Vargas had made the *entrada* into Santa Fe.

Which meant that Ramon Montoya would ride home on it, when the dancing was over. No doubt he'd ride at the carriage wheel of his novia, Josefita Sandoval.

It gave Johnnie an idea. Pressing through a throng of revelers on the plaza, he found his own droop-necked livery nag. Johnnie mounted and loped up Agua Frio Road to the Sandoval house. Again he found the house deserted except for the old servant Miguel. All others were at play at the plaza.

In his room at the rear of the patio, Johnnie

retrieved from his slicker roll a coiled rope and two gloves. With these he went out and rode back to the Palace of the Governors.

Johnnie dismounted at a hitchrack where a white stallion was tethered. He looped the coil of rope over the stallion's saddle horn and tied the gloves to a latigo.

When Ramon Montoya came out to mount that saddle, he would now find on it the equipment of a ladron. Let Montoya make the most of it. The man would know that Johnnie knew. It would frighten him, Johnnie hoped. It might make him overplay his hand.

Riding back up Agua Frio Road, Johnnie considered Montoya from every angle. He remembered gossip from the barber. Montoya was bankrupt and had had to borrow a horse for the fiesta. The man had a silver mine which no longer paid a profit. An aristocrat with a flat purse. Was it logical for a man like that to hold up a pack train of burros?

"It fits him like a glove," Johnnie muttered, meaning no pun.

For Ramon Montoya, being close to the Sandovals, would surely know that Don Ygnacio was returning from market with cash received from a wool crop. And Montoya, with the prospect of playing number one cavalier at the fiesta, would desperately need cash. How easier could he get it than by donning a mask to hold up his prospective father-in-law in the canyon? It was clear that Montoya had friends among outlaws of the Cherokee Conly ilk. He might even be the brains of many outlaws who had been driven by Kansas marshals into the Taos Mountains.

True, his prospective father-in-law might have been killed. But would Montoya care about that? What other effect would it have than to hasten the inheritance of Josefita?

Johnnie dismounted in the Sandoval patio and told Miguel to send his horse to the livery barn. He himself retired promptly to bed. Before falling asleep he made a decision. He would see this thing through. He'd accept, after all, the continued hospitality of Don Ygnacio and even go along to the ranch and receive the gift of a horse. Montoya, as Josefita's fiancé, would be sure to appear frequently there. When the showdown came, Johnnie wanted to be there himself.

He awoke in midmorning to hear the knock of a mozo. The mozo came in, serving at Johnnie's bedside a cup of rich chocolate and sugary sopapillas.

At noon breakfast in the patio, Johnnie found only Don Ygnacio. "The others have fatigue, after the baile," the hacendado explained. "But you and I have the habit of rancheros. Our day begins with the sun."

"I'd sure like to see that banker," Johnnie said as Miguel served him with chicken broth.

"Ah yes. You wish to see Don Stephano Elkins. He was at the baile last night, señor. When I told him my guest has a letter to him, he said he will arrange an appointment soon."

"How soon?"

Don Ygnacio shrugged. "Mañana perhaps. One cannot hurry business in the week of fiesta."

Nevertheless, Johnnie sent for his livery horse and then rode downtown on a chance that Elkins might appear at his bank. The bank was locked and deserted. Nothing was open except barrooms and cafés. Gay crowds in costume were still on parade. Vaqueros raced around the plaza, tossing riatas over laughing señoritas and occasionally shooting off guns.

Johnnie still wore his own holstered forty-five. This morning he had considered leaving it in his room. Then, recalling a thinly veiled threat last night from Montoya, he had decided to keep himself armed.

He spent most of the day sitting on the bank steps, watching the fiesta crowd and hoping that the banker might appear.

At sundown he gave up and rode back to the Sandovals'. As he was entering the gate there, a Mexican mozo stepped forward to inquire, "You are the Señor Cameron, yes?"

"Yes."

The mozo handed him a note. Johnnie saw that it was on stationery of the First National Bank of Santa Fe. It read:

Dear Mr. Cameron:
 My good friend Don Ygnacio tells me you have a letter to present. Unfortunately I will not be at my office today, and am leaving for Albuquerque in the morning. However, if convenient to you, I can receive you at my home at six this evening.
 The bearer will be glad to show you the way.

Sincerely,
STEPHEN ELKINS.

Johnnie looked at his watch. It was exactly six now.

"Bueno," he said to the mozo. "Take me to the house of Mr. Elkins."

"It is only a little way, señor. Come."

Walking the horse, Johnnie followed the messenger up the Agua Frio Road. Less than ten minutes brought them to an adobe-walled residential courtyard much like the Sandovals'. "This is the house, señor." Johnnie dismounted, dropped his bridle reins and followed the mozo in through the gate. He found himself facing an imposing, pueblo-style residence with out-hanging girders and blue-trimmed windows.

They crossed the courtyard to its door. The mozo opened the door and said, "Enter, señor."

Johnnie Cameron took off his sombrero and stepped inside. The gloominess of the sala surprised him. Light came only from one oil lamp on the center table. The musty smell, as well as a cobweb spanning between girders, did not seem to fit the home of a distinguished Anglo like Stephen Elkins.

Johnnie sensed a trap a half second before three men stepped from behind a drapery and aimed forty-fives at his head. Ramon Montoya was not one of them. These three were all Anglos, bar-blistered toughs of a kind one might encounter in a Dodge City honkatonk.

Assassins, Johnnie guessed instantly, planted here by Montoya! The Elkins note was a forgery. A fine fathead he'd been not to expect just such a trick!

One of the gunmen took a step toward him. The other two kept their guns level and Johnnie heard hammers click to cock. "Shut the door, Pedro," the nearest gunman directed the mozo. The door back of Johnnie swung shut and the gloom deepened.

They had the drop on him, all three. No use grabbing for his own gun, Johnnie reasoned. He stood for a moment, sombrero in hand, wits groping desperately. On the table an oil lamp flickered. That lamp was his only chance.

Johnnie forced a grin. "Well, here I am, gents," he said. "Might as well hang up my hat and stay a while."

He gave the hat a sail toward the lamp. The toss was aimed to ring the lamp as a horseshoe might ring a peg. The aim was true and the deep-crowned range hat settled exactly over the glass chimney. It smothered the light there. At the same instant Johnnie dropped flat to the floor and rolled.

Flame split the dark as three guns roared. Bullets raked the space just vacated by Johnnie. "Blast him!" a voice yelled. And another: "Don't let him get away, Zeke."

They were charging across the sala, still firing. Johnnie was on his hands and knees now, crawling. He drew his gun and kept moving, not toward the door but away from it.

"Light a match, Zeke, and crack down on him."

Johnnie could have shot at the voice, but didn't. He knew they'd expect him to try fighting his way out by the way he had entered. So he crossed them by groping toward draperies at the far end of the sala.

His fingers touched velvet just as a match flickered in the hand of a gunman. Johnnie fired at the light, heard a man drop cursing to the floor. Two guns blazed at him. The bullets chipped adobe from the wall by Johnnie's head. He dived back of the drapery and groped through an arch there. He was in a rear hallway with faint twilight coming from an open window at the deep end.

Johnnie raced toward it. He got a leg over the window sill. Then two of three ambushers came plunging into the hall. Johnnie let fly four quick shots. He saw one of them fall. The other tripped over the first, firing as he fell. The bullet smashed glass at Johnnie's window. He slid on out over the sill and found himself in a garden.

Across forty yards of September twilight he saw a high mud wall. Johnnie made a run for it. He holstered his forty-five and jumped, catching the top of the wall. As he pulled himself up a gun blazed from the house window. At forty yards in dim light, the man missed. Johnnie clambered to the top and dropped to the other side.

He stood panting there, gun out. But he heard no pursuit. At least two of those thugs were accounted for. The third appeared to have lost stomach for shooting it out, in the open, with Johnnie Cameron.

Johnnie slipped down an alley and circled back to the street. He reclaimed his horse, swung to the saddle and started down the Agua Frio Road. Then he saw an old leñador driving two burros. Each burro carried piñon firewood cut to stove length and packed in an arc over a wooden saddle. When the leñador came opposite, Johnnie accosted him to inquire, "Who lives in that house, compadre?"

"No one, señor," the old wood peddler said. "Once it is the house of Don Ramon Montoya. But the bank has foreclosed it for many debts."

"Thanks." Johnnie tossed down a coin and rode on homeward toward the Sandovals'.

He knew that Montoya had plotted the ambush. Apparently the man had innumerable bushwhackers at his beck and call. Yet it couldn't be proved. Johnnie could summon no witnesses. He'd put himself in no convincing light if he carried this story to the law.

If it came to Johnnie's unsupported word against Montoya's, Don Ygnacio would be impelled to credit the word of Josefita's novio. What about confiding in the banker, Elkins?

Again Johnnie foresaw an impasse. He was here to solicit a cattle loan from Elkins. If the banker were to disbelieve Johnnie's charges against Montoya, Johnnie would find himself discredited at the outset. As the purveyor of unbelievable scandals, he would be ineligible to receive a loan.

On the other hand if the banker did believe Johnnie's story, the loan would still be denied. For a bank wouldn't consider it sound policy to loan money to a man likely to be shot at any moment by vindictive outlaws. A dead man, they would say, can never pay a note.

Nothing was left except to keep everything to himself until he could get positive proof implicating Montoya.

Arriving at Don Ygnacio's, Johnnie turned through the gate and was admitted to the house by Miguel.

"They are waiting for you in the patio, señor," Miguel said.

The family and many guests were in the patio. A long table was set with at least thirty plates. The elite of Santa Fe were there. Among them Johnnie saw Ramon Montoya.

"A perfect alibi," he thought, "if those fellahs had drygulched me!"

Montoya would have been quite unimplicated. He could disclaim all knowledge of a fight in a vacant house up the road.

Just now the man was exchanging pleasantries with Josefita. Johnnie approached them, smiling, and Montoya looked up with a start. His black eyes met Johnnie's and fear flickered there.

"You have enjoyed the fiesta, Señor Cameron?" asked Josefita.

"Yes, ma'am," Johnnie said. "I had a right excitin' time."

"I will tell Papacito you are here." The girl left them.

All at once Johnnie remembered he was hatless. His sombrero was draped over a lamp chimney up the road. The hat could be identified. When two dead men were discovered there, how would he explain?

A bold idea came. Johnnie said crisply to Montoya: "I left my hat in a house you used to own, up the road a bit. Take a run up there and bring it here."

To Don Ramon Montoya, any such blunt command could be nothing less than insulting. Blood rushed to his face. "You are insolent, señor," he said.

Johnnie produced a forged note. It was the message signed "Stephen Elkins" which had lured him to the trap. He displayed the note to Montoya.

"Get this straight, Montoya. If my hat is hanging on the sala rack by the time we finish comida, I'll tear this note up. If it isn't, I'll show it to Don Ygnacio Sandoval."

Murder stared from Montoya's eyes. But he kept his voice low and restrained. "I am not concerned, Señor Gringo." He turned with perfect composure to rejoin Josefita.

His own bluff, Johnnie admitted, was none too strong. Montoya could deny all connection with the note. He could probably brazen out any charge preferred by Cameron.

Still, it was worth a try. Montoya might take the course of least confusion. He might much prefer to avoid being even accused.

"Señoras y caballeros," announced Don Ygnacio, "comida is served."

The entire company sat down, Don Ygnacio at the head of the table. To his right sat Montoya, to his left Josefita. Johnnie watched Montoya's face through three courses.

It was during the wine pudding that Montoya excused himself. He left the patio and was gone about twenty minutes. Then he reappeared with a box of imported cigars, explaining them as a gift to his host which he had left in his saddlebag.

Johnnie grinned. He arose at the conclusion of comida and looked into the sala. His sombrero was on a rack there. Since a promise was a promise, Johnnie tore up the forged note.

CHAPTER 6

NEXT MORNING THE fiesta began tapering off. The principal bank of Santa Fe resumed business and Johnnie was escorted there by Don Ygnacio Sandoval.

Stephen Elkins was a much younger man than Johnnie had expected to meet; he seemed barely more than thirty. His beard was fine and silky, his eyes keenly discerning and there was a confidence-compelling strength in his face.

Elkins gave a cordial hand to the hacendado. "You came in to deposit the wool money, I suppose?"

"Si, Don Stephano. But had it not been for my young friend here, I would have lost it to ladrones. He is the Señor Cameron from Missouri."

Johnnie presented his letter of introduction. Elkins read it through, then looked up with a smile. "You come well recommended, Cameron." To Don Ygnacio he added, "The letter is from Abe Marshall, who runs a stock farm near Kansas City. Abe and I were together at Missouri University, class of '60."

The banker paused to reread the last paragraph of Marshall's letter. Then he looked Johnnie over with shrewd appraisal. "You seem rather young, Cameron, for the experience Marshall mentions.

He says you trailed steers north from Texas in the summers of '70, '71 and '72; and that in each of the succeeding winters you hunted buffalo on the plains."

"I'm twenty-four," Johnnie said.

"What's more, Marshall says you've saved your money. Something strange about that. Never heard of a cowboy saving his money. He always blows it in. As for buffalo hunters, they're even worse."

Johnnie laughed. "Most of 'em are. I know 'em all pretty well, you see."

Elkins made his callers sit down and offered a box of cigars. "How did you happen to meet Abe Marshall?" he asked Johnnie.

"Well, it was like this," Johnnie said. "There's always been about a month between the end of the cattle drivin' season and the beginnin' of the buffalo season. We don't usually go out after hides until late September."

Elkins nodded. "Naturally. Hides are a better quality in the winter time. How did you spend your time in this month between cattle and buffalo?"

"A bunch of us would loaf at the market square in Kaycee," Johnnie said. "In late August you can find lots of the old-timers there, gettin' outfitted for winter. Jack Gallagher, Billy Dixon, Tom O'Keefe, Billy Ogg, Jim Hanrahan, Wild Bill Hickok and Wyatt Earp. Mostly they just sit around the market square, swappin' lies, drawin' lots for the best patches of buffalo range for the comin' season, and makin' bets on who'll bring in the most hides. Far as I know, the best tally ever scored was made by Bill Hickok, two winters ago. Bill brought in five thousand dollars' worth of skins that season."

"But where," Elkins asked, "does a stockman like Abe Marshall fit in?"

"One day," Johnnie explained, "we Market Square loafers began arguin' about how long it would last. How long would the Chisholm Trail last, to give us summer work? And how long could we keep raidin' buffalo herds in the winter? Some of the boys said it would last indefinitely. I said, no, we'd be all washed up in one or two or three more years. We had a hot argument. I stuck to my guns. I looked up and saw a local stockman standin' there. He said, 'You're right, son.' This fellah was Abe Marshall.

"Marshall took me out to his stock farm for dinner, and we got to be right good friends. And I saw some cowstuff there the likes of which I'd never seen in Texas. It gave me an idea."

Johnnie picked up a pencil and began sketching on the envelope which had enclosed Marshall's letter, and which now lay on the desk at Johnnie's elbow.

Elkins leaned forward with sharp interest.

"If it's an idea about cattle, Cameron, let's hear it," he said.

"Did you ever see any Hereford stock, Mr. Elkins? Or Shorthorns? Or Galloways? Or Muley Blacks?"

"Not this side of Missouri," Elkins said. "I'm familiar with the facts, though, about the introduction of Scotch-English breeds into America. I believe a few Herefords were imported thirty-three years ago, in 1840; and I understand a few Durhams were brought to Maryland in 1833."

"They've been crossin' those breeds in the East," Johnnie said, "these last twenty years. Abe Marshall's got a herd of grade Herefords. Not purebreds, you understand; just grade whiteface with a little Durham blood in 'em. And look, Mr. Elkins; there's as much difference between 'em and Mexico longhorns as there is between Belgian hares and cottontails."

By now Johnnie had completed his sketch on the envelope. He had drawn there from memory a profile of one of Marshall's blocky, beefy Herefords. Beside it Johnnie now put the slightly caricatured sketch of a Mexico longhorn he had drawn in Cimarron Canyon. "As much difference as that, Mr. Elkins."

Elkins puffed thoughtfully on his cigar, his eyes more interested in Johnnie than the sketches. He saw that conviction had flushed

Johnnie's face. "No doubt you're right, young man," the banker said finally. "Our southwestern cattle run mostly to horns and legs." He glanced again at the letter from Marshall. "But Abe mentions four friends of yours named Ogallala, Rosy, Slim and Sweetwater Smith. Where do they fit in?"

"I took 'em out to see Marshall's cowstuff," Johnnie explained. "We sat on the corral fence and watched those heifers all day. Curly-maned ballies they are, prettiest stuff you ever saw. Backs so broad you could play seven-up on 'em. Deep dewlaps. Short legs. Meaty rumps. Stubby horns curved down." Johnnie spoke with fervor, holding up his own envelope sketch as an illustration. "And hides as smooth and soft as a red and white bed quilt. By sundown that day, we decided we didn't want to eat any more dust kicked up by dogies an' buffalo. We figured we ought to start us a real cowranch and raise real beefstuff like Marshall's."

"A rancho!" Don Ygnacio Sandoval broke in with a beam of approval. "You have come here to look for a rancho, señor?"

Johnnie turned toward him and said: "Ogallala's already got one spotted. He's been all over, Ogallala has. He's trapped beaver with Kit Carson. He's ridden shotgun messenger on the Deadwood stage. He's fought Apaches in Arizona. One time he ran across a range in

73

northern New Mex, and camped there a week, and he swore if he ever settled down, that was the spot for him. He says it's not far from Santa Fe. He says there's a basin cupped by high hills. It's mostly dry land, he says, but there's five good springs that flow the year around. He claims that if five men would file homesteads at those springs, they'd control sixty thousand acres of good grass. They call this basin, he told me, the *pozo hondo*."

"Ah! *El pozo hondo*!" Don Ygnacio exclaimed. "It is not far from my own hacienda."

"*Pozo hondo*," Elkins said, "means deep hole. I hunted there once. Yes, it's a good range. But I understand it's already occupied."

Johnnie's face fell. "That's bad news, Mr. Elkins. I was hopin' we wouldn't be too late to file."

"You're not too late to file. The land is still open to filing. What I meant is that a rather notorious and extremely slippery crew of border thugs use the pozo, off and on, for a hideout. Am I right, Don Ygnacio?"

"Si, Don Stephano." The hacendado shrugged. "No one is there but ladrones. And when a posse goes to find them, even the ladrones are gone."

"Outlaws, huh?" Johnnie's face brightened. He realized that wanted men never file on land, because if they were to appear at a land office they'd be promptly arrested. "In that case, we're all right. We'll run those fellahs out, pronto."

"They are *muy mal hombres*," murmured Don Ygnacio.

"If you ran them out, young man," Elkins admitted grimly, "you'd be rendering a fine service to the territory. But let's not worry about land just now. The country's still pretty well open, except for the old Spanish grants like Don Ygnacio's. What interests me is your idea about cattle."

"In short," Johnnie said, "my idea is this: instead of shippin' Mexico cattle out, I figure to ship Scotch cattle in."

The eyes of Elkins gleamed. He caught the genius of it at once. "You've got something, Cameron. It's big. I'll go further and call it epic. While your neighbors are driving longhorns *out,* to market, you'll be driving shorthorns *in,* to breed."

"But when you're ready to sell," objected Don Ygnacio, "you'll have to drive them out."

"No, I won't have to drive a hoof out," Johnnie insisted. "I can sell calves to my neighbors, for stockers and breeders. I figure that everybody that sees my stock 'll want to improve their own."

Elkins smacked a fist in his palm. "I said it's a big idea, Cameron. That's too conservative. As far as the evolution of the cattle industry is concerned, it's the biggest idea that ever came west. Why didn't we think of it before? All these years we've been shipping bones and horns east, when we ought to have been shipping beef."

"Which is exactly why I'm here, Mr. Elkins," Johnnie said. "I've got to finance this deal. So I want to borrow fifteen thousand."

"Just what are your assets, Cameron?"

"Ogallala and Slim and Rosy Ryan and Sweetwater Smith and I," Johnnie said, "have pooled our savings. We've all had three good winters skinnin' buffalo, and so among us we can put up ten thousand dollars. We need twenty-five thousand in all. Because Abe Marshall has offered to sell us five hundred two-year-old heifers at fifty a throw. Grade Herefords. And he'll toss in ten yearlin' bulls."

Elkins picked up Johnnie's envelope sketch and studied it thoughtfully. "I see. You want to borrow fifteen thousand dollars, giving back a mortgage on twenty-five thousand dollars' worth of Hereford cattle."

"I'd sure like to get those heifers started west," Johnnie urged. "Is there telegraph service out here?"

Elkins nodded. "Yes, we've had the telegraph into Santa Fe for four years now."

"You'll make the loan?"

This frontier banker had known Johnnie less

76

than an hour. Don Ygnacio had known Johnnie less than a week. Abe Marshall had known him less than a month. Could any such impudent stranger from the range be worth a loan of fifteen thousand?

Weighing the decision, Stephen Elkins had to employ all his keen foresight and judgment of men which in later years was to place him not only in the United States Senate but in a presidential cabinet.

He looked at the tension on Johnnie's young face and his own relaxed. "I'll make the loan," he announced, "on three counts. Tell you what they are soon as I get off a wire." He rang for his secretary and a slim, somber Mexican came in with a quill pen behind his ear.

"Take a telegram, Refugio, to Abe Marshall. Marshall has a stock farm near Kansas City. You'll find his exact address in the files."

"Bien, Don Stephano."

Elkins dictated:

"Am extending credit of fifteen thousand dollars to John Cameron and four partners. Start those heifers rolling west.
S. ELKINS."

Don Ygnacio was hardly less elated than Johnnie. "I am happy that you will soon be my neighbor, Señor Cameron."

Johnnie dictated a wire of his own, addressed to Ogallala in care of Abe Marshall.

"Ship to Granada and then drive to Las Vegas. At Vegas, turn west to the Pecos ford. I'll meet you at the Pecos."

Don Ygnacio said warmly: "And you'll be riding the fine horse I have for you, Señor Cameron. Until your friends come, you will be a guest at my hacienda."

"A good place to scout the pozo from, too," Elkins inserted. "Well, everything seems to be settled, gentlemen."

He walked to the exit with them, his arm hooked affectionately in Sandoval's. "Adios, Don Ygnacio," he said at the door.

"Adios."

Johnnie said, "But you forgot to tell me the three reasons you're making the loan."

The banker smiled. "First, because this territory needs new ideas. Second, because it needs new cattle—the right kind of cattle. And third, because it needs new men—the right kind of men. Welcome to New Mexico, Johnnie Cameron."

CHAPTER 7

AT COMIDA THAT evening Don Ygnacio related with much gusto the outcome of Johnnie's conference at the bank. "Soon he will be our neighbor and have a great rancho of his own. He has compadres who will bring out many fine cattle from Missouri."

All of the Sandovals were cordial to the idea, but a few were dubious at mention of the pozo hondo.

"The pozo is a good range," Don Santiago admitted. "The vega there grows to the stirrup of a horse."

"*Verdad, primo,*" agreed a country cousin. "But also it has many ladrones."

"Which imports nothing, *primo*," echoed a town cousin. "The Señor Cameron knows well how to deal with ladrones."

Josefita turned to Johnnie with a question. "You come from Missouri, señor? Then perhaps you have seen a place called St. Joseph."

"It's a river landing about six miles above Kaycee," Johnnie said. "But I've never been there."

Before he could ask why she should be interested in St. Joseph, one of Don Ygnacio's many nephews came in with sensational news. "*Oiga!*" exclaimed the newcomer as he sat down at the table. "Have you heard? They have found two ladrones right here in the Agua Frio Road. There has been a fight, and these ladrones are both dead with bullets!"

"Where?"

"In the empty house where once lived our good friend Don Ramon. Is it not strange?"

Johnnie became absorbed with his plate of frijolis. Nothing could be gained by explaining. He must wait until he could present positive proof that Don Ramon was himself an outlaw.

Talk veered back to Johnnie's venture as a ranchero. The fact that he had won the confidence of Don Stephano Elkins made a deep impression. Johnnie quickly felt a change in their manner toward him. From the outset they had been both courteous and cordial, as well as grateful for the rescue of Don Ygnacio in the canyon. He now sensed a solid respect, a recognition that he was more than just an amiable cowboy with a straight-shooting gun.

When Miguel brought bedside chocolate early the next morning, the old servant addressed Johnnie as "Don Juan." It acknowledged that the guest was now to be considered as a gentleman of estate.

He went out into the patio and one of the younger Sandovals announced jubilantly, "We are going to the rancho this morning, Don Juan."

To the more formal adults of the family he was still Señor Cameron.

Johnnie found that Don Ygnacio's team and buckboard, as well as three spring wagons and various saddled burros, had been assembled in the courtyard. Ramon Montoya appeared at the gate. He was mounted on a calico ranch pony. Johnnie remembered that the prancing white stallion had been borrowed only for the fiesta.

Montoya announced to Don Ygnacio, "I will ride with you as far as la Plata Blanca."

" 'La Plata Blanca,' " Josefita explained to Johnnie, "is Don Ramon's silver mine on the mesa above our rancho."

A saddled mare was waiting for her by the gate. Don Ramon helped her to mount, and the two of them led the procession which shortly proceeded west out of Santa Fe.

Don Ygnacio, with Johnnie beside him on the buckboard seat, followed next. Then came spring wagons and burros bearing all the rest of the Sandoval clan and the servants.

A twisting down-trail through piñons brought them to the Rio Grande. As they forded hub deep through the river's riffles the hacendado said, "We are now in Sandoval County, señor."

"Is the pozo hondo in Sandoval County, too?"

Don Ygnacio motioned northerly. "Only a little of it," he explained. "The most is in Rio Arriba.

The land is very rough up there. It makes good hiding for ladrones."

Johnnie looked back. They had outdistanced the burros, but Don Santiago was just behind in a spring wagon. Ahead rode Don Ramon and Josefita. The girl gathered up the full sweeping skirt of her riding-habit, looping it over a horn of her sidesaddle to keep it out of the riffles.

A mile of upgrade beyond the ford put them again in piñon hills. A long, pine-sloped mesa loomed ahead. The hacendado puffed at his cigarrita and kept his team trotting directly behind Josefita and Ramon.

"Do they not make a fine couple, señor?"

Johnnie admitted it. "Been engaged a long time, have they?"

"Si, señor. It has been arranged since Josefita was ten years old."

The statement startled Johnnie. Then he realized that in Don Ygnacio's world it was quite usual for parents to arrange marriages.

"Don Ramon's father," Sandoval said, "was my best friend. He died eight years ago and it was his last wish that Ramon should marry my Josefita."

A sense of relief came to Johnnie that it might not be, after all, a love match. Since it had been arranged, it could be disarranged the minute Johnnie succeeded in pinning an outlaw's label on Montoya.

The buckboard was bumping over stones. Don Ygnacio slowed to a walk as they climbed the mesa trail.

"Why," Johnnie inquired, "is your granddaughter interested in St. Joseph, Missouri? She asked if I'd ever been there."

"It is because she was born there, señor."

Again Johnnie was startled.

"But she herself does not know this, señor, until only a few years ago. Now, when anyone comes here from Missouri, she always asks if they have been in St. Joseph."

Don Ygnacio drove on another steep mile, wheels creaking in the gravel. Johnnie was too polite to inquire further. His attentive silence, however, at last drew the hacendado out.

"It is nearly seventeen years ago, Señor Cameron, that I go with wool in bullock carts all the long Santa Fe trail to Missouri. My son Santiago is with me. There are no railroads then, even in Kansas. At Independence we sell our wool and return homeward toward Santa Fe."

"That," Johnnie put in, "would be about in '56, before the war."

"Si, señor. We trail back across Kansas and are on the Purgatoire River, in what is now Colorado. There on the trail we find a covered wagon. It is burning. Arrows are sticking in it. Its mules have been driven away. Its people have been killed. We know that the Indians have raided it, and are still not far away.

"So we are afraid for ourselves and are about to drive on fast to be safe, when we hear a cry in the sagebrush. We look and there we see a buffalo robe. It is in a sagebrush by the trail, where the wagon is still burning. Por Dios, señor! In the buffalo robe we find a one-year-old niña."

"A baby girl!" exclaimed Johnnie. "Gosh!"

"While Santiago takes the niña on his saddle, I look for identification on the wagon. The Indians have robbed it before setting it afire; but they have dropped one sack of seed corn because it is too heavy to carry away on their little horses."

Don Ygnacio looked fondly ahead toward the figure of Josefita.

"We are afraid of the Indians," he resumed, "so we do not have time to look for more. But on the sack of seed corn we see a writing which shows it came from San José, Missouri. So we think that these people have come from there. It is all we ever learn about them. That is why," Don Ygnacio concluded, "that we have called the niña Josefita."

"You wrote to St. Joseph?" Johnnie asked.

"Si Señor Cameron. But the mail is very slow then. It must go by stage or pony express. In a long time we hear from the man who sells seed corn at St. Joseph. He says he has outfitted many

84

wagons. He does not know which this is. He cannot inform us any more.

"So we have taken the little niña to our hacienda, and we love her very much. As you can see for yourself, señor, she has become *muy linda*. If she has people in St. Joseph, we are very sad if they claim her. But we must be just. So when she is fifteen we tell her that she is not born a Sandoval."

They were heading a small canyon whose creeklet riffled east toward the Rio Grande. From here the trail climbed in zigzags to the mesa. On the second switchback above, Johnnie could see Don Ramon Montoya riding attentively beside Josefita.

Wild cherry and scrub oak grew thickly here. Suddenly a band of wild mustangs dashed out of the brush and raced by them, disappearing with a clatter of sliding rock into the next ravine.

"That big white stallion Montoya rode in the fiesta," Johnnie remarked, "would make two of those mustangs."

"Si," the hacendado agreed, "and yet they are all of the same stock. Do you know how they came here, señor, these wild horses?"

"Came from Old Mexico, didn't they?"

"That is true. When Don Hernan Cortez came to Vera Cruz in 1519, and burned his ships there, he brought ashore sixteen fine horses. The best horses of Spain. From these have been bred

85

many thousands that range in both the Mexicos. Some have run wild, like the antelope, and so their colts have become small and wiry like the antelope. A few have been held in service through all the generations. They had been fed at the haciendas and kept in good flesh, and so their colts have grown big."

"Like that white stallion in the parade," supplied Johnnie.

Don Ygnacio smiled. "Si, and like a chestnut gelding that is waiting at the boundary of my rancho, señor. I have sent word ahead to my mayor-domo. He is to fetch your horse to the mesa for you, my friend, so that you may enter my land as a caballero."

Johnnie's desire to feel good horseflesh between his knees stifled any protest he might have made.

They drove on up the switchbacks and came to the mesa. This high tableland was long and narrow, its westerly rimrock forming the east boundary of the Sandoval Grant.

After crossing the mesa, Johnnie looked west down a timbered slope to a wide, flat plain reaching to the Rio Puerco. The adobes of a rancho made tiny dots down there. White, slow-moving patches were flocks of sheep. He saw a fast-moving tan patch and knew it was a band of antelope.

"What a range!" Johnnie exclaimed.

Don Ygnacio explained to him that the distant Puerco marked the grant's west boundary for twenty-five miles. To the south loomed two volcanic cones, an imaginary line joining them being the south boundary of the grant. While to the north, a fence of majestic mountains again made a side of the Sandoval estate, as defined by decree from a Spanish king.

Don Ramon and Josefita were waiting there at the rimrock.

"I must leave you here, Don Ygnacio," Montoya said. He motioned up a mesa trail which led northerly toward his mine.

"*Vaya con Dios*, Don Ramon."

The spring wagons rolled up and Montoya exchanged good-byes with the other Sandovals.

"And to you, Señor Cameron, *hasta la vista*."

No phrase could have been more conventionally polite, Johnnie knew. Yet Montoya's tone gave it a subtle shade of meaning. The man's black eyes gleamed and Johnnie saw his slim, gloved hand brush the butt of his gun.

Only Johnnie noticed the challenge. "Until the sight," he repeated literally.

"Ah!" cried Don Ygnacio. "But here is my mayor-domo with your horse."

A black-mustached ranch foreman had appeared through a niche in the rimrock. He rode a mustang and led by a rope an animal of such beauty and splendid lines that Johnnie caught his breath at the sight of it.

The horse was chestnut with dapples of deeper brown at the flanks. About five years old, Johnnie thought. He knew horseflesh. Here he saw endurance, speed, dependability. A fine proud horse fit for the best of caballeros.

"Montese, señor," smiled Don Ygnacio. "Your saddle is in the wagon bed."

Johnnie didn't need urging. He jumped out and took the lead rope from the mayor-domo's hand, while his own reached forth to stroke the chestnut's soft muzzle.

"His name," the mayor-domo said, "is Muchacho."

"We're pals already," Johnnie grinned. "What about it, Muchacho?"

He bridled the gelding, tossed on blanket and saddle. Then Johnnie swung up with the easy grace of a rangeman; and Josefita said, banteringly for her novio's benefit: "Bueno. Just as I lose one cavalier, I find another."

The procession moved on, this time with Johnnie and Josefita riding at its head.

Looking back, Johnnie caught a malignant stare from Montoya. It was as though the man sensed a prophecy in this exchange at the very gateway of the Sandoval domain.

"Hasta la vista," he called after Johnnie.

"Until I see you!" Johnnie echoed.

CHAPTER 8

THE MEANING WAS clear to both men. Whenever the two should meet, at any lonely part of the range, each man must go for his gun. Montoya would shoot on sight, and so must Johnnie Cameron.

But although the entire Sandoval clan heard the challenge, it seemed only a casual word of parting. Hasta la vista!

Dipping below the rimrock, and riding stirrup to stirrup with Josefita, Johnnie soon found himself in dense aspens. Lower down, the aspens gave way to pine and then pine to scrubby oak. They could hear the wheels of wagons, with brakes rasping, sliding along behind.

A spring bubbled by the trail and Johnnie saw steam arising from it.

"We have many warm springs on the rancho," the girl said. "That is why it is called the 'Ojos del Espirito Santo' grant."

Springs of the saint's soul! A good name, Johnnie thought, for the ranch of the Sandovals. For where could one find warmer hearts than these?

The brushy slope gave way to grass and cactus and boulders. Again Johnnie saw skimming antelope. And miles ahead, on a flat vega, he saw a great castle of mud walls. About it lay

89

barns and sheds and bodegas and corrals. The sun was dipping now beyond the Puerco, balanced like a red ball on the line of willows there. A distant bleating came to Johnnie. A flock of many thousand sheep, ewes calling to the lambs, came creeping across the vega like a soft white cloud.

Johnnie saw only a few cattle. And no fences at all. A small bunch of mares grazed at the flow from a warm spring. A covey of blue quail whirred by. From hills to the north came the sunset song of coyotes.

The big mud castle loomed close, now. Servants and the children of servants ran from it. A dozen sheep dogs barked welcome to the homecoming Sandovals.

The house, two-story with rafters spiking from its walls, was built like a fortress. A quadrangle of outbuildings made a solid stockade for it. Strings of red pepper hung here and there on all outer walls. Johnnie saw a row of courtyard ovens, each shaped like a beehive. A huge cottonwood grew by the main entrance, and Johnnie dismounted under it. He helped Josefita to the ground.

"Entrez, señor," she said. "Our house is yours."

The wagons rolled up and all the Sandovals alighted amidst a chattering crowd of herders and mozos. Boys with fat and shining faces sprang forward to take the horses. There was a scramble for presents and souvenirs brought home from the fiesta.

Don Ygnacio ushered Johnnie in through what passed for a door, but which was more like a tunnel six feet long. For the outer walls of the house were six adobes thick, made that way to be proof against Apache raids. It gave a cave-like coolness to the sala which Johnnie entered. And here again he found an earthen floor, hard and clean. The sala was at least sixty feet long, with supper already spread on the table.

The smooth walls of adobe plaster were whitewashed, and covered with a calico screen head-high so that anyone leaning against a wall wouldn't be stained by lime dust. Solid spruce walls made the rafters and girders.

"I will show you your room, Don Juan." Johnnie found Miguel at his elbow, the old servant having ridden one of the spring wagons from Santa Fe. Johnnie followed him down a cool corridor to a small, almost bare bedroom. A narrow couch, a chair and a washstand made its only furnishings.

Later, at comida with the family, Johnnie heard Don Ygnacio receive a report from the mayor-domo. Everything had gone well during the master's absence. The sheep were in good flesh. Neither Indians from the west nor ladrones from the pozo hondo had disturbed the peace of this rancho.

"And we have had no visitors," the mayor-domo said, "except *el viejo.*"

"El viejo is always welcome," said Don Ygnacio.

Turning to Johnnie he explained. "It is a very old prospector named Jason Holt. We call him 'the old one.' Often he digs on the mesas yonder for gold which he never finds. He is very poor and so ragged that he scares even the crows. But he is a friend to all the just and an enemy to all ladrones."

"I might use him for a guide," Johnnie suggested, "when I scout the pozo hondo."

"No one knows it so well, señor, as el viejo."

The mayor-domo continued his report. "I have employed a new bodegero, patron, for the one who left us recently."

"You are sure he is honest, Arturo?"

The mayor-domo was quite sure of it. "He has much experience in keeping a bodega, patron. And I know he is honest, because he came only yesterday with a recommendation from Don Ramon Montoya."

"It is well, then." The hacendado dismissed his foreman who retired from the sala.

Josefita sat by Johnnie. "We are curious," she said, "to see the fine cattle you will bring from Missouri. When will they arrive, señor?"

"In about three weeks," Johnnie said. "About three days on a train and eighteen on the trail. It must be about four hundred miles from Granada to this range. And Ogallala doesn't believe in drivin' the tallow off o' cattle."

"You must let them rest on the rancho here," insisted Don Ygnacio. "My own vaqueros will help you brand these heifers before you take them on to the pozo hondo."

"They will not be safe in the pozo," Don Santiago put in, "unless they have your brand, señor."

"We'll register a brand at Santa Fe," Johnnie agreed, "as we bring 'em through. I telegraphed Ogallala I'd meet him at the Pecos."

When supper was over he said, "Guess I'll take a pasear out to the barn and say good night to Muchacho."

"My segundo will show you the way, señor." Don Ygnacio sent for his segundo, or assistant foreman, who conducted Johnnie out to the main barn.

Muchacho was munching vega in a stall there. He was well curried and a fresh bedding of oat straw had been provided. As Johnnie stroked the gelding's mane, he noticed his saddle on a rack in the barn vestibule. The butt of a Winchester .44 protruded from the saddle scabbard.

Usually Johnnie would have taken the rifle to his room overnight; but in this case it might seem discourteous to enter the host's house with rifle in hand, as though fearful lest it be stolen at the barn.

Dismissing the segundo, Johnnie took a stroll about the starlit grounds. On this side of the quadrangle were stock shed and corrals, with a shaded acequia flowing by. On another side were the blacksmith shop and tool sheds. On the third side Johnnie came to an adobe church whose gilt Cross reached toward the sky in perennial plea for all life here, like the upstretched hand of a priest.

Behind and flanking the church lay the peon quarters—flat, adobe huts rank with the odor of chile beans and peppers. A complete country village was this rancho of the Sandovals.

On the fourth side were still more flat sheds, each roofed with a stack of hay. And Johnnie could see two good reasons for stacking hay on roofs: it kept the roof from leaking; it kept the hay out of reach from roaming stock.

Completing the circuit, Johnnie came to the largest outbuilding of all. This, he could see, was the bodega, or commissary of the hacienda. Vaguely he was familiar with the system of labor on these Mexican ranchos. The hacendado kept many peons as herders, shearers, hay hands and house servants. Yet he rarely paid any of them in cash. When work was to be done, they were simply ordered to the fields. In return for this, a peon could draw anything within reason from the bodega, whether it be a sack of beans, a blanket, a reboza for his wife or tobacco for his pipe. If his record of work was good, he was given all that he needed. If not, he was encouraged to pack his burro and move on to the next ranch.

A mild form of slavery, and yet the slaves seldom complained. They were given much time to themselves. They could go to the mountains at will for chokecherries to make their own red wine. There was a siesta in the heat of each noon, whole weeks of fiesta and a *baile* each Saturday night. Plenty of antelope on the range to make carne for their chile beans. On Sundays, the church bells made them equal to the master. The hacienda priest was father to them all.

The bodega, tonight, was lighted. Johnnie saw sleek, contented Mexicans filing in and out of it. Here came one with a sack of frijolis; here came one with medicine for his ailing niño.

There was a new bodegero, Johnnie remembered. According to the mayor-domo, the man had arrived only yesterday with a recommendation from Ramon Montoya. A storekeeper of experience, the mayor-domo said.

Curious, Johnnie strolled to the bodega stoop and looked in. Back of a counter stood the new bodegero. And Johnnie recognized him at once.

He was the sly, bookkeeping clerk Johnnie had encountered in la Tienda Grande at Taos! The man who had sold gloves to Ramon Montoya. Pancho somebody, his name was. The man's rat-sharp face seemed craftier than ever, now. Here was the fellow who had skipped out to inform Montoya about a strange gringo who made inquiry about gloves.

It was clear that he had been planted here by Montoya. Why? A reasonable guess was that he had been sent to spy on the moves and plans of Johnnie Cameron. At any rate he was here to serve Montoya.

Nor could Johnnie with good grace report the situation to Don Ygnacio. He could prove only that this new bodegero had recently clerked at a store in Taos. That would merely confirm the man's experience and his qualifications for this present billet.

Johnnie promised himself to keep an eye on the bodegero. He returned to the main house and went to bed.

At daylight he was up. The household still slept, but Miguel served Johnnie a substantial breakfast. "The master has told me to inquire your pleasure for the day, señor."

"I'd like a snack o' lunch rolled in my slicker, Miguel. I'm ridin' for a look at the pozo."

"It is done, señor." While Johnnie ate, Miguel explained just how he could best reach the pozo. "You take the right fork at the headwater of the Rio Puerco, señor. At the top of it is a bald summit, with a gap between red shoulders. From this you look down into the pozo."

Soon Johnnie was astride Muchacho and riding toward the upper Puerco. As he rode, he drew his forty-five and twirled the cylinder. He might meet outlaws in the pozo; he might even meet Ramon Montoya.

"Hasta la vista!" The man's challenge echoed back to him. Johnnie hoped it wouldn't be today, though. Not that he minded shooting it out with Montoya. But if the showdown came before the man's crookedness was exposed, then Johnnie would lose by either outcome. Certainly he would lose if the other man fired first and straightest. And if Johnnie were to kill Montoya, how could he explain to the Sandovals?

Far to the right of Johnnie, as he road north, stretched the long high rimrock which marked the eastern Sandoval line. To his left ran the Puerco. The rimrock curved to meet the river far ahead on a high skyline.

Johnnie kept Muchacho at an easy jog and made the top of the grant by midmorning. From here he followed the Puerco's right fork to a bald summit.

Red shoulders made a gate there from which he looked down into the pozo. "There she is, Muchacho! Home sweet home for both of us!" A glow came to Johnnie's eyes as he looked out over a basin of lush grass. Its walls were higher than the Sandoval grant's, its floor rougher. Interlocking box mesas seemed to enclose on all sides. Their slopes offered excellent shelter for cattle. Scrub oak, wild cherry and piñon. Rimming the higher walls grew pine and aspen.

Johnnie's practised range eye soon noted five bright green patches, where grass grew ranker than elsewhere. They should mark the five never-failing springs which controlled the pozo. Sixty thousand acres! That would make a pasture about ten miles in any dimension.

However many outlaws might be skulking in brakes or canyons of this mountain cup, the prospect ahead filled Johnnie with a mighty elation. With Ogallala and Slim and Rosy and Sweetwater Smith, he could build a great ranch here.

"Wait till we turn those bally heifers loose on this grass, Muchacho! We oughta get big-boned calves here—maybe four hundred pounds at weanin'. Wonder if there's any loco."

Johnnie rode on down into the pozo basin, keeping a sharp lookout for loco weed. He saw only one or two patches. Well, a fellow couldn't have everything. What about those waterholes?

Johnnie spurred on at a lope, eager to find the first of five permanent springs.

No use filing on it, though, until the others came. The law, Johnnie knew, did not permit him to file land claims for his friends. Each man must file his own homestead. As for filing for himself now, it seemed to Johnnie that he would only be advertising his plans to outlaws and to anyone who might be hostile toward settlers here. Seeing Johnnie's claim stake, such persons might file the other four waterholes themselves.

Definitely it was best to wait for Ogallala and the boys, when all five of them could file together.

Johnnie was well out of the brush now. He rode on across a basin of boulders and high grass.

Then he saw a horseman emerge from a barranca and gallop toward him. Johnnie reined Muchacho to a halt. The oncoming horse was a calico. Montoya had a horse like that. Johnnie's jaw squared. He wasn't looking for a fight; neither would he run from one.

The other man was a mile away and still coming. Johnnie pulled the carbine from his scabbard and held it across his pommel. He waited. The loping calico came nearer. A tall, slim man rode him. At half a mile Johnnie knew he was Montoya.

Montoya might open up at long range. Or he might ride close and then go for his forty-five. Either way Johnnie was ready. To be entirely in the clear, he knew he must let Montoya start the play.

At two hundred yards Montoya stopped. For a minute he sat silently in his saddle, eyeing

Johnnie. Then he shouted, "We meet again, señor."

Johnnie called back, "Kinda looks like you been hangin' around here waitin'."

"Perhaps I have, señor."

Ramon Montoya snatched a rifle from his scabbard, whipped it to his cheek and fired. The bullet whistled over Johnnie's head.

With ice cold and steady hands, Johnnie brought his own rifle to aim. It was kill or be killed, he knew. With a bead on Montoya's chest, his thumb crooked to cock the hammer.

Then Johnnie lowered the rifle, staring in dismay. His thumb had failed to cock the hammer for the simple reason that the hammer was gone. The hammer screw was missing, too.

During last night, someone had used a screw driver to remove the hammer screw. With the screw gone, the hammer would simply fall out. The screw was a spindle on which the hammer heel pivoted.

The rifle was utterly useless, now. Johnnie dropped it bitterly to the ground. Then another bullet sang by him from the rifle of Montoya.

The range was too far for a six-gun. Montoya was aiming his third shot, calmly deliberate and clearly aware of his advantage. That slippery bodegero, Pancho, had no doubt been responsible for sabotage on Johnnie's rifle.

"Until the sight!" Montoya had promised. And the man was sighting now.

CHAPTER 9

TWO CONVICTIONS flashed to Johnnie. First, that he wouldn't turn and run. Montoya had smothered him with humiliation at Taos, with the rope coup there. To run from him now would be a little more than pride could bear.

And second, that Montoya would quickly shoot the horse out from under Johnnie. Just as he had killed Blazer, so would Muchacho be served now. With Johnnie unsaddled, he would be more than ever at the mercy of a mounted rifleman.

Determined neither to run nor to lose his horse, Johnnie took the only possible alternative. Just as Montoya's third slug sang by him, he jumped to the ground. Turning his horse to face south, he gave it a slap on the flank. "Off you go, Muchacho."

Then Johnnie flung himself face down in grass a foot high. He began rolling to the left.

Bullets cut through the grass. But Montoya was still two hundred yards away. At that range a man prone in high grass doesn't make a good target. The grass almost obscured Johnnie. All the while he kept rolling toward a clump of boulders.

Halfway there he arose to his elbows. He saw Montoya to the north, Muchacho to the south. Muchacho was trotting toward the Sandoval grant. Had the reins been left hanging, the horse would not have deserted a master. But the reins were looped over the saddle horn. Moreover, the horse had been acquainted with Johnnie less than twenty-four hours.

Whatever else happened, Muchacho was now safe. The animal would trot a while, graze a while, and then move on toward home corrals.

Another bullet from Montoya made Johnnie flatten. He kept rolling on through grass toward the boulders. They were still fifty yards away. Johnnie's idea was to tempt Montoya into six-gun range. Short arm range would make them both equal.

Again Johnnie rose to his elbows. This time a bullet zipped through the peak of his sombrero. The hat brushed off as Johnnie resumed rolling toward the rocks.

As the ground became rockier, the grass grew shorter. So short, at last, that Johnnie got up and made a dash for shelter.

The biggest boulder was about four feet high. Johnnie ducked back of it. Kneeling there, he peered over the top. Montoya still sat his saddle a furlong away. He had stopped shooting and was lighting a cigarrita.

Johnnie drew his forty-five. "Come on up and fight," he yelled.

"There is plenty of time, señor," Montoya called back. "You are like a coyote in a hole, now."

The voice was more than derisive. It expressed complete confidence in the final outcome. Johnnie was afoot, trapped, unequipped to shoot except at close range. Keeping at a distance, a rifleman could besiege him indefinitely.

Johnnie looked up at the sun. Not quite noon yet. He calculated his own chances. If Muchacho arrived riderless at the hacienda, Don Ygnacio would assume an accident. He would send vaqueros to search in the pozo hondo.

But Muchacho, unspurred, would make a slow journey home. Stopping constantly to graze, the horse probably wouldn't get there before tomorrow. That would be too late. Or would it? Why couldn't he stand Montoya off until nightfall and then force the fight himself? He could advance in darkness with his forty-five and shoot it out at close range.

Evidently the prospect of a long siege worried Montoya. The man began circling for a vantage of fire to which Johnnie would be exposed. But there were a dozen or more boulders. Johnnie shifted from one to another, keeping himself screened from all angles.

When the rider edged a bit closer, Johnnie blazed at him with his forty-five.

He saw Montoya draw back to about three hundred yards. There the man dismounted and built a fire. He made the fire of sticks and cured grass. Johnnie wondered why, until he saw the besieger toss green grass on the blaze.

The result was a column of dense white smoke.

A signal! It was fairly clear that Montoya was calling to allies encamped somewhere in hills rimming the pozo.

With his smoke rising conspicuously, Montoya again mounted his horse. He rode in to a range barely safe from Johnnie's six-gun.

"It is unfortunate, señor," he called out, "that you have come to the pozo hondo." His glance toward a timbered slope to the west indicated his expectancy of an intrusion from that quarter.

In a little while Johnnie saw four horsemen trailing down the nose of a hogback into the pozo.

"Roundin' up some ladrones, are you?" Johnnie challenged.

"They do not like, señor, to have visitors in the pozo."

"They're due for some more," Johnnie retorted. "I got four fast-shootin' compadres on the way out here."

"It is sad, señor. Because when they come, they will not find you."

The four horsemen were approaching at a lope. The man in the lead rode a piebald bay. He was thickset and wore a battered black hat with the brim hanging low over a stubbly face. All four men carried rifles.

Montoya drew back and joined them for a conference. Johnnie saw Montoya thumb toward the boulders and explain. No doubt he was telling that the trapped intruder had killed two of their crowd at the Cimarron Canyon hold-up. And that he planned to make a nuisance of himself by filing in the pozo.

The man on the piebald bay yelled, "Smoke him outa, there, boys." He himself sent a bullet crashing against Johnnie's rock.

Johnnie crouched low. He was safe until they closed in. More bullets came and chipped limestone within inches of his ears.

Then he saw three of the newcomers circling at a two-hundred-yard range. A quarter of the way around, one stopped and two others continued the circle. In a few minutes the four had placed themselves in perfect besieging formation, one east, one west, one north and one south of Johnnie's shelter.

But they did not close in. And Johnnie saw Montoya ride away. Perhaps to establish an alibi in case he should ever need one. "Adios, señor," Montoya yelled. He waved a slim, gloved hand, then galloped toward the east rim of the pozo.

The man on the piebald bay shouted, "Hist yer hands and amble outa there, kid."

"Come in and get me," Johnnie invited.

"We'll getcha," the man promised.

He fired a shot at the boulders. Shots came also

from three other directions. But Johnnie kept his head well down.

He gave a sigh and wished for Ogallala. And Rosy Ryan and Slim and Sweetwater Smith. Those fellows were pulling out of Kaycee about now, with twelve cars of white-faced heifers.

If they could only come riding over the hill!

Thinking of them reminded Johnnie of a discourse he'd heard from Rosy Ryan, recently, on the subject of ballistics. A fancy shot, Rosy was. And a crank on the way bullets behave when they shoot out of guns.

Rosy had been admiring Johnnie's brand new Colt's .45 Frontier Model six-gun. It was the first centerfire gun either of them had ever seen. In fact, centerfire forty-fives had only been introduced the fall before.

"As between a centerfire six-gun and a rimfire rifle," Rosy had proclaimed, "gimme the centerfire six-gun every time. Big advantage in ballistics. What you lose by havin' a short barrel, you more'n make up by shootin' a centerfire ca'tridge. When the firin' pin hits the center of a cap it explodes the powder evenly. Savvy? And so it makes the bullet shoot true."

Recalling that speech from Rosy Ryan, Johnnie considered his present opportunity for testing it. His own sabotaged rifle was a Winchester .44 rimfire, 1866 model. As far as he knew, all repeating rifles were rimfire. All revolvers had been rimfire until only a year ago. Which meant that his adversaries would presume his own revolver to be the usual rimfire .44 Colt's, instead of a brand new 1872 Colt's .45.

All of which gave Johnnie an idea of campaign. He stood up, so that his head and shoulders showed above the rock, and took a shot with his forty-five at the man on the piebald bay. "Better not come any closer," he warned.

But in shooting, he aimed twenty feet to the man's left purposely. He saw the bullet cut grass to the left and short of the mark.

Then Johnnie ducked as bullets whipped at him from four rifles.

When next he peered over the rock, the man on the piebald had advanced a score of yards closer. He was taking the bait. From the sample of shooting Johnnie had offered, there didn't seem to be much risk.

Johnnie continued to give exhibits of poor shooting. He fired, plowing grass ten yards to the left and fifteen yards short of the piebald. The man jeered: "He can't hit the side of a barn, Chick. Close in on him, you fellahs, and burn him down."

All four men advanced a little. Johnnie fired in turn at them, careful to make his shots go wide and short. If he could only lure them to ninety yards.

"Gimme a rock to steady one of them centerfire

six-guns on," Rosy had declaimed last winter, "and if I can't shoot daylight through a man at ninety yards, then hang me fer a horsethief."

Johnnie had never trusted a short arm at much more than fifty yards, but he was willing to take Rosy's word for it. Rosy knew.

So the exhibition of poor shooting went on. Bit by bit it lured the besiegers nearer. Johnnie's shot flew so wide that the man named Chick laughed at him. "Don't skeer me like that, kid." To the man east of Johnnie he yelled, "Ever time he pots at you, Pike, he dawggone near hits me."

"What are we waitin' fer, then?" Pike yelled. He dismounted at a hundred and fifty yards, dropped to his knees and crawled on toward the boulders.

The other three did the same. Johnnie picked Chick for his first victim. With the barrel of his forty-five steadied on a rock, he took careful aim.

A hundred yards. Ninety yards. Johnnie squeezed the trigger. Chick screamed and pitched forward. Johnnie whirled his aim for a shot at Pike. Rifles barked from two other directions, spattering the rocks around Johnnie. But his finger was steady as it squeezed again on the trigger.

Pike crumpled in the grass out there.

Johnnie turned to the next man, saw him running for the piebald horse. Johnnie's shot seemed to trip him. He got up and went limping on to the piebald. The fourth man was backing away, crabwise, in the grass.

Johnnie reloaded and kept firing. He made no more hits. They were out of his range now, and likely to stay there. Two were down and another was limping.

Before the survivors could regain their wits, Johnnie dashed out of his shelter and made a run toward the man called Chick. Chick was to the north and the only unhit man was retreating southerly. Before he could turn and open up on Johnnie, Johnnie had his hands on Chick's rifle. It was a Winchester .44 rimfire, like his own. Johnnie put the stock of it to his cheek and walked straight toward the man on the piebald bay, pumping a bullet with every step.

The boldness of it routed them. The two survivors struck for the nearest cedar brake at a gallop.

Johnnie himself quickly retrieved Chick's horse. It was a scrawny mustang, underfed and unshod.

Next, Johnnie recovered his hammerless rifle. Then he mounted and spurred toward the Sandoval grant. The outlaws were certain to return with reinforcements. Let them bury their own dead.

CHAPTER 10

JOHNNIE FOUND THE trail of Muchacho. He followed it, hoping to overtake the horse before the sight of an empty saddle could alarm the Sandovals.

The trail took him through an open swale where Muchacho had stopped to graze. Beyond the swale, in oak brush, Johnnie lost the hoofprints. But he felt sure he could find them on the bald divide which separated the pozo from headwaters of the Puerco.

Looking back into the basin, he saw white smoke still arising from the signal fire. Definitely it proved a long arranged understanding with the pozo outlaws. Montoya's silver mine was somewhere on the mesa to the east. Was Montoya the leader of this pozo gang? Or had he merely established an alliance with them while playing a lone hand of his own?

Certainly Montoya had borrowed two of them for the raid on Don Ygnacio's pack train. The rest of them seemed to be at his beck and call. Why?

Puzzling over this, Johnnie rode out of the brush onto a high, open bench. There the sight of a man on a mule brought him to a halt. The man was leading Muchacho and riding directly toward the pozo basin. He might be a horsethief who had been lucky enough to find a fine saddled gelding.

Then, as the man on muleback came closer, Johnnie saw that he was very old. He rode without saddle, and seemed to be clothed in a patchwork of canvas and sacking. His appearance quite fulfilled the description of an old vagabond prospector known to the Sandovals as "El Viejo." His full name, Johnnie remembered, was Jason Holt.

"Hi, Jason," Johnnie yelled, and advanced with a grin.

El Viejo eyed him with suspicion. He reined in his mule and inquired cagily, "Who might you be, young feller?"

"My name's Cameron and that's my braunk you're leadin'."

"'Tain't no such thing!" Jason retorted. "I know this here crittur. He belongs to the Sandovals."

"Then why," Johnnie demanded, "are you leadin' him toward the pozo?"

Jason produced a plug of tobacco and buried the yellow snags of his teeth into it. His rheumy old eyes bored into Johnnie's without flinching. Johnnie saw that he carried a shotgun crosswise in front of him, and that he was wiry and tough in spite of his age. The beard which covered him from cheekbones to chest was snow white wherever tobacco juice hadn't stained it.

" 'Tain't none of your business where I lead this braunk, young feller, less'n yuh can prove it's yourn."

Johnnie dismounted. He put reins over saddle horn and turned his nag toward the pozo. Then he slapped the animal and started it running that way.

Which left Johnnie afoot with two rifles and a six-gun. He advanced and extended all the weapons butt first to Jason.

"If I was a horsethief," Johnnie asked, "would I hand over my shootin' guns? Take 'em till you're satisfied I'm on the level. One of the rifles won't do you any good, though, 'cause it hasn't any hammer. Ramon Montoya had it jimmied last night, while I was asleep at the Sandoval house, so he could drygulch me in the pozo."

Jason stared. "Montoya, you say? You mean you had a shootin' fracas with that skunk?"

"With him and a crew of his playmates."

The prospector's face relaxed. "I'd 'a' sure liked to've been in on it, young feller."

Johnnie grinned. "Let's ride to your camp and I'll tell you all about it."

"You wouldn't fool me, wouldja?"

"Sure I wouldn't, Jason. And if you need any references, I've got two. Don Ygnacio Sandoval and Stephen Elkins."

"You mean Elkins the banker?" El Viejo was really impressed now.

"No one else. He just loaned me fifteen thousand dollars."

"That's a lot o' money. What fer did he loan it?"

"To stock the pozo with white-faced cattle."

The idea shocked Jason. "You figger to file land here?"

"Why not?"

"Because you'd git shot plumb full o' lead. They's a passel o' right handy lead throwers around here, an' you wouldn't stand no chance with 'em."

"I've stood three chances with 'em already," Johnnie argued. "Each time they lost two men. I'll give you the straight of it at your camp, Jason."

El Viejo tossed Muchacho's reins to Johnnie. "I reckon this is your braunk, all right. All I kin say is you got more nerve 'n a henhouse full o' polecats to file land in this here pozo."

Johnnie swung to his saddle. He put his own rifle in the scabbard there. The outlaw rifle he retained so that he could use its hammer to replace his own. Both weapons being Winchester .44s, the hammer of one should fit the other.

"Lead the way, Jason."

Jason rode his mule up a steep trail into aspens. Johnnie followed on what was little more than a deer path. An hour's riding brought them to the sheer wall of a rimrock on the east side of the pozo hondo.

The old prospector continued along this wall to an overhanging cliff, with a cave under it. A fly of soiled canvas hung across the cave. Outside were picks, shovels, pans, a tin stove, ore sample sacks and miscellaneous camp equipment. Most of it was as shabby as Jason himself.

"I only figger to use the cave when it rains," he said. "Make yerself at home, young feller, while I warm up this kettle o' beans."

Johnnie removed the saddle and staked Muchacho to an aspen.

"I seen a smoke signal in the pozo this mornin'," Jason said as he made a fire to warm the beans. "I've seen them signals before an' it allers means they's devilment afoot. So I hopped my mule an' started down fer a look."

"I getcha." Johnnie nodded. "And on the way you ran onto my horse."

"And I hearn shootin'."

"The shootin' really started last week in Cimarron Canyon." Johnnie began with the burro-train hold-up and gave Jason a complete account to date. By the time he finished, the old man had set out tin plates of beans on a flat rock.

"That Montoya's a two-timer, all right," Jason said. "I allers knowed it. What he needs is a shaft o' daylight drilled through him."

"What's his hook-up with the pozo gang?" Johnnie wondered.

"Never could figger that out," Jason said. "Him bein' a high society 'ristocrat, and them outlaws bein' only third-rate gun bums what got swept outa Kansas barrooms, it don't seem hardly like they'd throw in together. Maybe Montoya needs 'em for his dirty work, and maybe they need him for his brains."

"Do they ever give you any trouble?"

"I got trouble for *them,* if they want any. Two barrels full." Jason thumbed toward his shotgun. "No, they ain't bothered me none. I reckon they figger I ain't worth shootin'." The old man grinned, then, adding with a wink, "Besides, they think I'm scoutin' fer a shipment o' gold what got buried in the pozo one time. They figger to let me find it, and then grab it away."

"A gold shipment?" Johnnie prompted.

"Some believe it and some don't. Seems a shipment o' gold coin got stuck up on the Chihuahua trail one time. Them that took it loaded it on stolen horses and packed it into this pozo. They buried it somewhere. Then a posse from Las Vegas come ridin' in to git back the stolen horses. There was a fight. Some of the crooks got shot; some of 'em got strung up; the rest of 'em scattered. Maybe them that scattered came back later and dug up the gold. Nobody knows."

Johnnie scooped up his last spoonful of beans. "What's your guess on it, Jason?"

"Personally, I ain't much interested," Jason said. "I'd a heap rather rap my gold off a ledge or pan it in a crik."

"How long you been at it, Jason? I mean prospecting?"

Jason took a reminiscent chew from his plug. "I made the run to Californy in forty-nine," he said. "Didn't make no strike there. So I drifted back to Colorado and follered the backbone o' mountains down here to New Mex. Been tappin' ledges around this pozo eight year now. Figger I'm too old to move on any further."

Johnnie eyed his host shrewdly. Back of that unkempt beard he saw the stamp of untold hardships—and mystery. Evidently the old man had made no strike here. And yet for eight years he had braved the hazards of the pozo. Johnnie had a feeling that a motive was still unexposed.

"Don't you freeze up in the winter time, Jason?"

"I'm kinda tough, young feller. I've dug my way outa plenty snowdrifts. But when a real mean blizzard comes along, I ramble down to the Sandoval hacienda. They allers let me have an adobe shack to bed down in. Real folks, them Sandovals."

"Then you'd like to do 'em a good turn," Johnnie suggested.

"I sure would."

"And so would I, Jason. The way to do it is to show up Ramon Montoya. He's due to marry Josefita on her eighteenth birthday."

"Which is less 'n three months off," Jason put in vigorously. "It's bothered me plenty, too."

"The devil of it's this, Jason: we know Montoya's a ladron but we can't prove it. We've got to throw our ropes around some proof—before wedding bells ring for Josefita."

El Viejo held out a gnarled hand. "I'm with yuh to the last puff o' smoke, young feller."

CHAPTER 11

IT WAS DARK WHEN Johnnie arrived back at the Sandoval hacienda. He unsaddled his horse and saw that it was fed.

In the barn he found a screw driver. With this it took only a minute to remove the hammer screw from a Winchester rifle. The hammer then fell out. Johnnie put it, and also the screw, in his pocket.

The bodega was lighted and Johnnie went to it. His sudden appearance there startled the bodegero. The man stood back of his counter, petrified by panic as Johnnie advanced with a Winchester rifle.

But instead of shooting Pancho with it, Johnnie merely tossed it on the counter. "It's not mine," he said. "Belongs to a friend of yours named Chick. Chick's dead. I'm keepin' the hammer outa his rifle to replace the one you jimmied outa mine."

The bodegero's knees sagged. His face was bloodless.

"Take it to Montoya," Johnnie said. "Start now. I'm goin' in to supper. Then I'm comin' back here to see 'f you're gone."

Johnnie walked out. He went to the house and found the Sandovals just arising from comida.

"Sorry I'm late," Johnnie smiled. "I been lookin' over the pozo hondo."

"A thousand pardons that we did not wait for you," exclaimed Don Ygnacio. "Miguel, bring comida for Señor Cameron."

Josefita herself filled Johnnie's wine glass. "Don Ramon Montoya was here this afternoon," she said. "He inquired for your health."

"Thoughtful of him," Johnnie murmured.

"You found good grass in the pozo, señor?" asked Don Santiago.

"The best. I can hardly wait to get those heifers in there."

"You found the five springs," Don Ygnacio asked, "where you and your friends will file claims?"

"Only got as far as the first one," Johnnie said.

"Did you meet any ladrones?" Josefita asked anxiously.

"A few. They didn't seem to like me."

Worry puckered the girl's brow. "I am afraid they will give you much trouble, señor."

"On the other hand," Johnnie amended brightly, "I found a *good* neighbor over there too. Your friend El Viejo."

"Ah!" exclaimed Don Ygnacio. "He is well, I hope?"

"Couldn't be better. He and I hit it off fine. Before I left him, he told me all about the stock water situation over there. Says there's a hundred seeps and springs, but only five of 'em can be depended on not to go dry after July fifteenth. That's why five quarter section homesteads can control all the grass in the pozo."

"That is true," said Don Santiago. "Other people would have done it long ago, only they are afraid of ladrones."

Johnnie grinned. "Jason told me I'd better be afraid of 'em too. Gave me plenty of advice, Jason did. First, he said I'd better accept your kind offer to let the heifers graze here in the grant till we get a shack and corrals built in the pozo. Then he said all five of us better hole up in one shack, till we get the outlaws licked."

"It would be very wise, señor," agreed Don Ygnacio.

"The risk is too big," Josefita protested. "I think you should take sheriffs there with you."

"Josefita is right," Don Santiago put in. "And you may take vaqueros from here to help you."

"Thanks. But it won't be necessary," Johnnie said. "Ogallala and Slim and Rosy and Sweetwater and I can handle those fellahs. First place, they can't shoot worth a cent. I saw five of 'em practise shootin' at a rock this morning." He omitted to mention that he had been back of the rock.

Before they could question further, the mayor-domo came in with an apologetic look. "I have an unfortunate matter to report, patron," he said.

"What is wrong, Arturo?"

"It is about the new bodegero, Pancho Archuleta. He says he does not like it here. So he quits and goes away."

"But why," demanded Don Ygnacio, "does he not like it here? Have you not treated him well?"

"I have used him well, patron. But now he is gone. *Que lastima*! Now we must find another bodegero."

"See that it is done," said Don Ygnacio.

Johnnie smiled into his wine.

Pancho Archuleta rode away on the same pony which had brought him to the hacienda. A certain steely blue light in the eyes of Johnnie Cameron had sent a chill through his heart. Not for any bodegero's pay was he willing to risk meeting Johnnie after comida.

And so Pancho rode hard away from there. By midnight he was on the mesa. By dawn he was at the silver mine of Ramon Montoya. He waited forlornly on the steps of the house there. Montoya emerged, at last, to find him holding a hammerless Winchester rifle.

"Carramba! What are you doing here, Pancho?"

"It is this gringo, Cameron," Pancho mumbled. "He is about to kill me, so I have run away."

"Cameron! Don't be stupid, Pancho. Cameron was shot in a fight, yesterday, in the pozo hondo."

"We have expected that, patron," wailed Pancho. "But it does not happen. He has come home to comida and he says he will kill me if I am there when he is through."

Montoya flushed. "Shut up, you fool." He shot a wary glance toward the shaft house where mine workers were assembling for the day's work. The crew here at La Plata Blanca all knew Don Ramon as a caballero without guilt or guile. "Come inside, you stupid."

Inside he said: "You should not have run away, Pancho. The gringo was only bluffing. He would not dare to harm you at the hacienda. And if he should accuse, he has no proof. Return to your job at once, Pancho. I need someone to keep an eye on Cameron."

"But it is too late, señor. I have resigned my billet there. So now I can come only to you."

Montoya puffed fiercely on a cigarrita. "I do not want you here, you bungler."

"But where can I go, señor?" Pancho whimpered.

He could not go back to his old job at the Taos store, because of a certain shortage in petty cash which no doubt was discovered by now. Montoya thought it over fretfully and came to the only possible conclusion. "You must go to Fadeaway Fallon's, Pancho. And at once. I do not want you found here."

Mention of Fadeaway Fallon both impressed and frightened Pancho. "But he is a great banditto, señor! He cannot make use of me, who am only a clerk."

"He can use you for a mozo. That's all you're good for, anyway."

All this while Montoya had been eyeing the rifle held by Pancho. Now he noticed that its hammer was missing. "What," he demanded, "are you doing with Cameron's rifle?"

"But it is not the Señor Cameron's. He says he has taken it from Chick. He says Chick is dead."

"Diablo!" Chick, Montoya remembered, had been one of four men summoned by his signal smoke. Armed only with a six-gun, how had Cameron been able to shoot his way out of that trap?

"He has used the hammer of this rifle to fix his own, patron. Then he tells me to bring it here to you."

The information stung Montoya. Fury smouldered in his eyes. He must destroy Cameron. Cameron would expose him to the Sandovals, otherwise.

"Get some sleep, Pancho." Montoya nodded toward a couch. "Soon as the mail comes in, I'll ride over to Fallon's with you myself."

Pancho went to sleep. An hour later a mozo returned from Santa Fe with supplies and a packet of letters.

A glance told Montoya that most of the letters were duns. Others were polite denials to requests for loans. Ramon Montoya had been exploiting every possible source for funds. His social obligations had been heavy during the fiesta. They'd continue to be heavy these next three months, with marriage to Josefita Sandoval due in December. Much would be expected of him. He'd promised Josefita to redeem the old Montoya mansion in Santa Fe. In the meantime he must entertain as became a caballero of distinction, and be prepared to provide a handsome gift for the bride.

But fiesta expenses had claimed his last dollar. His credit was gone. And here were a score of duns.

Of the last two letters, one was from the bank and the other was from la Doña Marta Calaveras. Doña Marta was a wealthy widow who operated the leading gambling saloon of Santa Fe.

She wrote:

Querido:
You ask for ten thousand pesos. *Sin verguenza*! Do you not have shame to treat me so?

When the grand Don Diego de Vargas rode by in the fiesta, he did not even see me. At the ball, he did not ask me to dance. And one time he has said that he loved me. I am still waiting. When will you come again to Santa Fe?

MARTA.

Montoya crushed the letter savagely. The fat fool still loved him. She was jealous of Josefita Sandoval. She'd be willing to give him ten thousand, all right. Or ten times ten thousand. But only on the condition that he give up Josefita.

Montoya read the letter from the bank. It was crisp. No, his credit could not be extended. Existing notes were already long overdue. The bank had refrained from pressure only to avoid embarrassing their client during the fiesta, in respect to his leading rôle therein. Would Don Ramon please appear at once and make a settlement?

Montoya spat out his cigarrita. He must raise money at once, and plenty of it. It was this same desperate situation which had impelled him to hold up Don Ygnacio's burro train. And that assignment had seemed so easy. Masked and keeping his distance, he had run no risk of recognition. But for the intrusion of that gringo Cameron, a fat purse in cash would have fallen to Montoya.

But it had gone awry, like everything else lately. His allies in the pozo were complaining. Why, they were asking, couldn't Montoya put them on to something good?

For many years Ramon Montoya had been fronting for them. From his secure social position among the hacendados of New Mexico, he had been coach and tipster to the banditry of the pozo. When a hacendado shipped wool, Montoya always knew the day and route of his return from market. He knew when and where the ricos gambled. For instance there was a one-eyed bartender named Enrico Robles at Doña Marta's place in Santa Fe, who served as an informer for Montoya. Pancho Archuleta had performed much the same service at Taos.

And Montoya knew when the big mines sent in to Santa Fe for their payrolls. He knew where the best horses were kept to graze. Well acquainted in political circles at Taos and Santa Fe, he always knew when posses were to be sent out; and from his mesa rimrock Montoya could always signal with a column of smoke to outlaws in the pozo. Black smoke meant run; white smoke meant come. More than once posses had combed the pozo in vain, black smoke having sent the outlaws in temporary retreat toward Arizona.

So in times past Montoya had served them well. In return, they had upon occasion furnished guns for Montoya.

Which reminded him that Fadeaway Fallon was sure to be growling about yesterday's fiasco. By riding over there with Pancho Archuleta, Montoya could mend his fences.

He aroused Pancho directly after lunch.

With Pancho he rode down a niche in the

rimrock, then down an aspen slope to a piñon hogback and from this down into the pozo basin. Crossing the basin Montoya asked, "What did you find out about the cattle Cameron sent for?"

"They are very fine cattle, señor. I have spoken with all the servants and they say the cattle cost twenty-five thousand dollars."

"I knew that already," Montoya snapped. "But how many men are coming with them? When do they arrive?"

"They come with four gringo vaqueros and they should be here in two more weeks, señor."

For the rest of the way, Montoya rode thoughtfully. As they ascended into timber on the far slope of the pozo, he asked, "Which way are they coming, Taos or Las Vegas?"

"They come by Las Vegas, señor. This Cameron will meet them at the Pecos River."

A good place for Fadeaway to raid them, thought Montoya.

High in an aspen park under the west rimrock they came to an old sheep camp. Here were three adobe shacks and a rock corral by a seep of water. Montoya counted eight horses in the corral and as many saddles draped over its gate. A rifle-armed sentinel sat in front of the main shack.

Montoya greeted him, *"Buenos,* Frenchie. Is Señor Fallon here?"

"Yeh," Frenchie said. "And he's on the prod about losin' a coupla hands yesterday."

The man who came out was slim, slight and shifty. In slippers, with suspenders holding up beltless pants, and with no gun in sight, he didn't look dangerous. Montoya, though, knew that he had killed a sheriff at Wichita, Kansas, and that since then had been raiding in New Mexico.

They called him "Fadeaway" because he had so often disappeared from posses. Even Montoya didn't know exactly where the man faded to, when necessary; but he had a suspicion that it was on the lower San Juan and close to the common corner of four territories, Utah, Colorado, New Mexico and Arizona. From it, with one step he could escape into any of three states. Some day Fallon hoped to start a hideout ranch there, stocking it with stolen cattle.

In the meantime, that more westerly retreat was too far from the Santa Fe trail to make a good raiding base. The pozo was three days' ride closer to loot.

Fallon cocked a cold eye at Montoya. "Blast you, Ramon. Seems like you been gormin' everything up lately. Chick and Pike took their last tumble. And Bitter Creek took a slug in the leg."

Montoya smiled and offered a cigarrita. "Which is all the more reason," he murmured, "for you to destroy this man Cameron."

"Who's that with you?" Fallon growled.

"His name is Pancho. You can use him to wash pots and bring wood."

Other men came slouching from the shack. Bearded, gun-slung border toughs, all of them. One was a stranger to Montoya.

"A new recruit," Frenchie explained. "Just blew in from E-Town. Name's Pete Adler. Seems like he had to salivate a depitty over there."

The gang here, Montoya knew, was in a constant state of flux. Men came and went. Some came because of a well-grounded rumor about a shipment of gold coin being buried in the pozo.

Montoya now drew Fallon aside. "How did Cameron get away yesterday?" he asked.

"Don't ask me," Fallon answered petulantly. "I wasn't there. I saw your smoke and sent four men. Chick and Pike and Bitter Creek and Nevada. We buried two of 'em."

"It was unfortunate, señor."

Fallon squatted on his spurs, picked up a straw, chewed viciously on it. His right eye had a slight cast and he cocked it up toward Montoya. "That makes six hombres we got to charge up against this Cameron. Looks like I'll have to handle him myself."

Montoya assented gravely. "Otherwise none of us will be safe, señor. Also there are four more like him on the way here."

"Yeh?"

Montoya's eyes made dark slits. "And they bring twenty-five thousand dollars' worth of cattle." He explained in detail about the plans of Johnnie Cameron.

Fadeaway chewed the straw and thought it over. "Prime heifers, did you say? They orta make a nice start fer that ranch layout I'm figgerin' on, over Arizona way."

"They will arrive by way of Las Vegas and the Pecos."

"The main Santa Fe trail, huh? When do they get here?"

"They will never get here, señor, if you do as I say."

"Yeh?" Fallon's cocked eye suggested that he didn't fully trust Montoya's judgment any more.

"There are many cottonwoods at the Pecos crossing," Montoya said. "Your men can hide there and attack while they sleep in camp. When Cameron and his four compadres are finished, the cattle will be yours."

Fallon screwed his thin face studiously. "An ambush on the Pecos, huh? Don't know as I like it, Ramon."

"Why not, señor?"

"Well, fer one thing because you figgered it out. You been figgerin' things out wrong lately. Anyway you sure messed up that Cimarron Canyon job. I lost two o' my best hands there.

And two more in Santa Fe. And two more right here in the pozo."

"But this time it is so simple, señor."

"I know somethin' a lot simpler," Fadeaway argued.

"Yes?"

"Simple as shootin' fish. Listen. Usually we gotta go out and get it. This time they're bringin' it right to us. Twenty-five thousand dollars in cowflesh right to our doorstep. Sweet, I call it. We don't move a leg until they push them heifers right into the pozo. Then we smack down on 'em."

The idea disturbed Montoya. He much preferred to have Cameron erased as soon as possible. As he debated this with Fallon, Montoya kept thinking about Josefita Sandoval.

The girl was young and so was Johnnie Cameron. Already Montoya had sensed an attraction between them. Risky to let Josefita see too much of that good-looking, yellow-haired gringo. Moreover, Cameron had knowledge which could hang Montoya—and lacked nothing but proof.

"They will not bring the cattle into the pozo right away," Montoya pointed out. "Until their claims are filed here, and while they build a house in the pozo, they will leave the cows on the Sandoval rancho."

"Where they'll get all the fatter," Fallon said.

"Suits me fine. We'll wait till them heifers hit the pozo, then we'll bounce this Cameron gent back out of it on a slug. Same goes for his compadres."

Montoya couldn't talk him out of this decision.

The shadows grew long and the men assembled around a rude table for supper. One whom Montoya had expected to see was not there.

"Where's Clegg?" he asked.

"He's on that Martinez job," Fallon said. "Ain't forgot the tip you handed us, have you?"

"Ah, Eduardo Martinez! Yes, it is tonight that he returns from Santa Fe. He has made a nice winning at roulette there." This was a routine tip passed along by the one-eyed bartender at the gambling saloon of la Marta Calaveras. Of this duplicity la Marta herself had no knowledge.

Fallon winked. "Easy pickings, this Martinez. As he rides home across the mesas tonight, Billy Clegg'll take it away from him."

Montoya grew thoughtful.

As the moon rose an hour later, he saddled his calico pony and rode away into the aspens. For the first mile he moved in the direction of his own mine. Then he veered.

A few hours' ride took him to a box canyon leading up out of the pozo. Spruce timber grew here. Montoya hid his pony among them and walked a little way up the trail.

By this route Billy Clegg was sure to return

after holding up Eduardo Martinez, Eduardo's winnings at roulette, according to Marta's bartender, amounted to three thousand dollars. A very nice purse. Ramon Montoya was due a small cut out of it—but why not have it all?

A single bullet should be sufficient for Billy Clegg.

Just after midnight, the single bullet was fired. Billy Clegg's body tumbled into the trail. Billy Clegg's horse raced on with an empty saddle. And Ramon Montoya rode home with the purse of Martinez.

After all, what did it matter if one double-crossed a ladron? Many more ladrones would be drifting west across the Pecos, to replace casualties in the pozo hondo.

CHAPTER 12

ALL THE SANDOVAL women were busy sewing. Night and day they made ready for Josefita's wedding.

The event was scheduled for her eighteenth birthday.

"But how do you know when that is?" Johnnie Cameron asked one evening. He was sipping wine in the sala with Don Ygnacio. "If you found her 'longside the trail, wrapped in a buffalo robe, I can't savvy how you figure when she was born."

"Does it matter, señor?" The hacendado waved a disparaging hand. "We bring her home and we christen her Josefita. The women are all there and they think the niña is about one year old. She is entitled to a birthday. So we decide that the day of christening shall be her first birthday. It was the twelfth day of December."

"Fair enough," Johnnie said. "So she'll be married December twelfth?"

"Si, señor. And you must be at her wedding."

Johnnie twisted a cigarette deftly. "Yeh," he said, "I'd like to be at her wedding." Under his breath he added, "But I don't mean Montoya's."

He still couldn't see any decent excuse for accusing Montoya. Any slight whisper against the man would immediately outrage the

Sandovals and convict the guest of poor taste.

"You ride for the Pecos *mañana*?" inquired Don Ygnacio.

"Bright and early," Johnnie said. "My outfit ought to be pretty well down the trail by now—and I promised to meet 'em at the Pecos." The name gave him a thought and he smiled. "Know what they say back east, Don Ygnacio? They say there's no law west of the Pecos."

The idea seemed to shock Don Ygnacio. "But it is not true, señor. Santa Fe is west of the Pecos. And my hacienda is west of Santa Fe. Is it not peaceful here?"

Strains of a fandango came from the peon quarters. "It's peaceful enough right here," Johnnie agreed. "I reckon they mean places like the pozo hondo."

"Even in the pozo there will be law, some day," sighed Don Ygnacio.

"Yeh, and it won't be long," Johnnie said. "The law says we can file land in the pozo, and we'll do it. The law says we can hold that land, with or without six-guns, and we'll do that. You just wait till Ogallala and Slim and Rosy and Sweetwater Smith start obeyin' law in the pozo."

The idea amused Don Ygnacio. He refilled the wine glasses. "To law in the pozo!" he chuckled.

It was late. Johnnie intercepted Josefita just before she retired. "I'll be off before you're up. So adios. You've sure treated me fine here."

"But you will be gone only a few days, señor. Then you will bring your friends here—"

"No use makin' a bunkshack out o' this hacienda," Johnnie interrupted. "Nope, the outfit 'll camp up the Puerco a ways, and we'll just drop in now and then of evenings."

She looked at him and her eyes were disturbed. "I'm afraid for you, señor. I mean when you go into the pozo."

"Don't fret about it," Johnnie said. "And by the way, mind passin' on a message to Don Ramon? I won't be seein' him again soon."

"But of course. What shall I say to Don Ramon?"

"Just say I'm sorry I missed him."

"Oh! You had an appointment with him?"

"That's it. But we missed each other. Adios, Josephine."

At daybreak Johnnie was away on Muchacho, riding east toward Santa Fe. His Winchester was in the scabbard, with hammer and hammer screw in place. After a few miles Johnnie tried it out on a coyote. The bullet kicked dust and proved there'd been no further sabotage.

Riding up through timber to the mesa was a risk. Any thicket might hide a sniper. Johnnie advanced with caution. He knew now that Montoya would stop at no trick of treachery. "He's out to burn us down, Muchacho. 'Cause he's scared we'll prove what we know."

136

The whirring of grouse startled Johnnie. Then it reassured him. If a sniper were lurking there, the grouse would already have been flushed.

Chances were that Montoya didn't know the schedule. Johnnie had been careful to say nothing about it until comida last night. And perhaps Montoya had as yet been unable to replace his spy at the hacienda.

It was a relief, though, to reach the open mesa. Johnnie loped across this and dipped down into a tributary canyon of the Rio Grande. Soon he was splashing across the big river. From here Johnnie kept an easy up-grade jog to Santa Fe.

It was past noon when he rode into the city. Santa Fe was slumbering. Along San Francisco Street Johnnie saw no life except an occasional tamale man dozing over his tray, with here and there a burro switching at flies.

Even the plaza was in siesta. But the bank was open. Johnnie went in there to see Stephen Elkins.

"Been expecting you, Cameron," the banker said. "Here's a telegram for you. And you'd better sign this note."

Johnnie signed a note for fifteen thousand dollars. The telegram had been sent from El Moro, a trail town in Colorado.

"Heifers in good shape. Ought to make the Pecos in six more days."

The message was signed "Ogallala" and had been filed five days ago.

"I'll meet 'em at the Pecos tomorrow night," Johnnie said.

Elkins sent out for coffee. "Did you have a look at the pozo hondo?"

"I did," Johnnie said. "It's just the range I'm hunting for."

The banker gave him a searching look. He smiled when Johnnie said no more. "Then you're not disturbed about outlaws over there?"

"No, sir."

Stephen Elkins liked the way he said it. "That's right, Cameron. The star of empire moves west and can't be stopped by the riffraff it pushes ahead of it. Our job's to bring along better tools. Steel plows for wooden plows. Wagons for ox carts. And now you're bringin' in Herefords to replace Mexico dogies."

"Some of the old-timers," Johnnie suggested, "claim it won't work. They claim nothin' but longhorns 'll do well in this greasewood country. They say it takes tough stock to live on a tough range."

"That doesn't worry me a bit," Elkins contested. "I've been reading up on these Hereford and Durham and Galloway breeds. They're tough. Their sires were toughened by the rigors of Scotland moors. So they should take to these New Mexico valleys like ducks to water."

The coffee came and he pushed a cup toward his client.

"That's my idea exactly," Johnnie said. "But these old-timers claim something else. They claim eastern cattle 'll starve to death in winter time if you turn 'em loose out west. Mexico dogies, they say, have been used to it for two hundred years. They're like mountain goats, and can paw their feed outa snow."

Elkins raised a shrewd eyebrow. "And what's your answer to that, Cameron?"

"I say good stock 'll get fatter 'n cheap stock. Good stock moves slower, so it doesn't run off its fat like dogies do. Dogies are nervous. They're built for speed, not for feedin'. A good cow'll keep her fat longer 'n a dogie, and so she has a better chance gettin' through a winter."

The banker pushed a box of cigars toward Johnnie. "I can see you know cattle, Cameron. I agree with you, on account of an incident that happened seven years ago in western Nebraska."

"What was that?"

"In the fall of '66 an ox team was heading toward Oregon," Elkins said. "A heavy snow made the drivers abandon it in western Nebraska. They turned the oxen loose, cached the wagon and returned to Missouri on horseback. Next spring they went back to get the cached wagon. They expected to find only the bleached skeletons of the oxen—but found instead the animals themselves, sleek, fat and ready for the block. Why? Because those oxen were good feeders. They weren't Herefords, of course, but they were stall-fed eastern cattle that had learned how to eat."

Johnnie went out and put up his horse for the night. Then he took a room at la Fonda tavern.

After supper he was getting ready for bed when a mozo brought him a note. It was on stationery of a gambling resort called El Silverado, and was signed by its proprietress, Doña Marta Calaveras.

"We have an interest in common, señor. Will you please come to see me?"

It might be a trap. Johnnie felt like giving it a wide berth. Montoya could easily be back of it.

He strolled out to the lobby desk. "Is Don Ramon Montoya in town?" he asked.

"No, señor. When in Santa Fe Don Ramon always stops here. But since the fiesta we have not seen him."

"What about this gambling joint, El Silverado?"

"One is safe to go there, señor. Our best people may be found at Doña Marta's."

Johnnie took a stroll down the street. He was curious. Maybe he was being lured to a gambling house where Montoya had posted an assassin to pick him off. Or maybe Montoya didn't figure in it at all. A rumor might be abroad that Johnnie was a cowman who had just been loaned fifteen thousand dollars. In that case any gambling house would want him as a customer.

He found the Silverado on lower San Francisco. Johnnie saw a carriage drive up to discharge an elderly caballero. This gentleman entered the Silverado, and others who turned in there seemed eminently respectable. Johnnie looked in, saw a long bar and rows of gaming tables. A Spanish girl was dancing on a stage at one end. Other girls were serving drinks at the games. Johnnie saw only two gringos. All other patrons seemed to be native New Mexicans of the ruling class.

Confident now that Doña Marta wanted only his money, and quite sure she wouldn't get it, Johnnie stepped inside. At the bar he inquired for the proprietress.

A swarthy, one-eyed bartender answered him, "She is in her office at the rear, señor."

Johnnie went back to a door marked "oficina" and entered. He found himself in a room furnished with an imported rug, cushioned chairs, a mahogany desk and a steel safe. Seated at the desk was a bejeweled woman with plump cheeks and flashing eyes. She might have been a charmer ten years ago. Even now only a double chin kept her from being more than commonly attractive.

141

"I'm Cameron," Johnnie said.

Her smile flashed. "You are welcome, señor. You will sit down, please?" She pushed a jar of cigarritas toward him, lighting one herself. "And now, if you will excuse me only a minute, señor?"

La Marta finished counting a stack of money on the desk before her. Then she carried it to the safe and locked the safe.

"I got your note," Johnnie said. "What's the idea?"

She sat down and her brilliantly mascaraed eyes appraised him boldly. "You have been a guest of the Sandovals, have you not?" she asked.

"That's right."

"Don Ygnacio is a so charming caballero, no? Do you like him?"

"Who wouldn't?"

Marta arched a teasing eyebrow. "And you like the Señorita Josefita?"

"I'd be blind and dumb if I didn't," Johnnie admitted.

"And she likes you too, señor."

Johnnie reddened. He was more annoyed than embarrassed, though.

Before he could protest, la Marta leaned forward to continue: "I know, because I saw her with you at the fiesta. There is a sigh in her eyes, señor, and it is not for Ramon Montoya."

Johnnie stood up stiffly. "You've got no call to talk like that, ma'am."

"Please do not be offended, señor. We speak disrespect to no one. And because we both wish the same thing, we should be friends."

"What same thing?"

"You wish that Ramon Montoya does not marry the little Sandoval. Is it not so, señor?"

"I reckon it is," Johnnie conceded.

"And so do I, señor."

Johnnie sat down again. The woman's intensity gave him the answer. She was in love with Montoya. For no other reason could she oppose with such bold directness his marriage to Josefita.

"There's nothing we can do about it," Johnnie said.

"I can do nothing, señor. But *you* can do much."

"What, for instance?"

"You can make love to Josefita."

Johnnie flushed and again stood up. "I can mind my own business. And so can you, lady. I get your drift, though. You want me to cut Montoya out so you can rope him yourself. You're welcome to him. But leave me out of it. Don Ygnacio treated me white. He took me right in his house. He gave me an A-one braunk. I'll put the skids under Montoya, if I can, but not by—"

Marta broke in with a sigh. "It is the only way, señor."

"There's a better way," Johnnie said. "All I need 's to get the deadwood on Montoya. I can show him up as a double-cinched ladron. A back alley killer, that's what he is. The number one, horse-stealin' drygulcher of the pozo hondo."

La Marta Calaveras gasped. Then she stood up with her eyes blazing. She was like an outraged Juno. "What? You insult my *querido* Ramon?" Her indignation took the pitch of hysteria.

Suddenly she snatched a pistol from the desk. "He is not a ladron," she asserted. "He is a fine caballero. The best caballero in all New Mexico. You will please get out of here, señor, before I shoot bullets through your head."

CHAPTER 13

RIDING TOWARD THE Pecos next day, Johnnie considered ruefully his none too graceful retreat from the doña's office. "She's sure gone on that buzzard," he confided to Muchacho. "I'd ought to 've known better 'n to talk him down that way. It just shows what I'd get myself into if I talked the same way before the Sandovals."

It was a clear morning with a touch of frost in the air. After topping the piñon pass at Glorietta, Johnnie headed down into the Pecos watershed and soon found himself in open country. No good ambush for a sniper here, and so he had plenty of time to think. It was clear that la Marta was an old flame of Montoya's and that she was far from ready to give him up.

Still, Montoya had fooled her as completely as he had fooled the others. And la Marta, as the operator of a gambling palace, could be classed as a woman of the world. Certainly she was in a position to know all the undercover intrigues of Santa Fe.

If Montoya could deceive Marta, how much easier could he deceive the Sandovals! "It's our job to show him up, Muchacho," Johnnie muttered. "And we'll have to work fast."

An hour before sundown he sighted

cottonwoods. He knew they marked that headwater fork of the Pecos which crosses the Santa Fe trail some thirty-five miles west of Las Vegas.

The ford was deserted, which disappointed Johnnie a little. He had hoped to find his friends already here.

Dismounting on the east bank, he staked Muchacho out to graze. Then Johnnie made a fire for supper. Coffee, beans and bacon were in his saddle roll.

And just as the coffee boiled he saw dust eastward along the trail. Cattle. Whiteface cattle! They came nearer and Johnnie gave a cheer.

"Hi-o, cowboys!" he yelled. Tossing the saddle on Muchacho, he went tearing down the road. "Hi, Ogallala! Hey there, Sweetwater! Who let you old buffalo skinners outa jail?"

"Look 'em over, Johnnie," grinned Ogallala.

"Whata yuh tryin' to do? Stampede 'em?" demanded Rosy Ryan. "Slap on the brakes, kid."

Johnnie was still shouting and waving his hat. Greeting his old cronies, and appraising five hundred fancy heifers all in one breath, was too much to be expected. He whirled to an exuberant halt, finally, at the wheel of a camp wagon driven by Sweetwater Smith.

"Yip-a-yai-yip-a-yah!" Johnnie yelled.

Sweetwater slapped his whip at the tip of Johnnie's nose.

"Toss a rope on him, Slim," advised Sweetwater. "Since we seen him last he's been feedin' on loco."

"Where 'd yuh git that braunk, kid?" Slim Coxon was a horse lover and his eye beamed approval at Muchacho.

"Is this here the Pecos?" Ogallala demanded. "In that case load up yer guns, cowboys. I hearn they ain't no law t'other side of it."

They were all at the wagon now, letting the heifers drift on. Johnnie tried to ask fifty questions at once and answer as many from his friends. "We sure made a sensation, Johnnie," Rosy grinned. "Seems like the natives out here never seen any cowstuff like this before. We sure had 'em lined up battin' their eyes when we driv these ballies through Las Vegas."

"We driv slow," Ogallala said, "so we wouldn't ga'nt 'em none."

"Let's push 'em on to water and quit gabbin'."

Riding between Slim and Ogallala, Johnnie trailed on after the cattle. It made him proud to look down the straight, broad backs of those heifers. Five hundred of them, all two-coming-three years old. Blocky stock with chunky legs and short horns and low-hanging dewlaps. Glossy red cattle except for white at the face and tip of the tail. Dewlaps were white like satin, too, and sometimes the white carried back along curly manes to the shoulders.

Beef cattle. The vanguard of vast herds destined to displace dogies from the range.

"Look 'em over!" Slim exulted. "Even after bein' driv three hun'erd miles from Granada, you still can't see a rib. Betcha they'll weigh better 'n eight hun'erd pounds a head right now."

"Notice how they walk to water, Johnnie?" grinned Ogallala. "If they was Mexico stuff, they'd 'a' started runnin' soon as they smelled a crik. These here stuff of ourn has sure got dignity, Johnnie."

"You can't hardly push 'em out of a walk," Rosy boasted. "Soon as they stop walkin', they start feedin'. Soon as they stop feedin', they bed down. They ain't nervous like them longhorns we usta drive north from Texas."

Ogallala took a bite of plug cut. "I recollect it allers usta take two hands to count them Texas cattle, Johnnie. One to say 'Here they come,' and another to say 'There they go.'"

The herd had arrived at the Pecos and were watering now. Johnnie rode the bank to admire them. Among the five hundred heifers, he counted ten yearling bulls.

Sweetwater pulled the wagon up beside Johnnie's campfire. By the time Johnnie returned from his inspection, bacon was sizzling in the pan.

The coolish September twilight deepened. "Come and grab it," yelled Sweetwater Smith.

"Them critturs won't graze far," Ogallala opined. "Easiest stuff to handle I ever saw."

"What about these here outlaws you writ about, Johnnie?" Slim questioned.

"The pozo's full of 'em, Slim." Around the supper fire, Johnnie gave a brief sketch of his encounters with Montoya.

"But the rest of these crooks," he finished, "are all gringos. They're squattin' in the pozo right now, waitin' to throw lead."

Ogallala, rolling his tongue into a round, knobby cheek, said nothing. He was older than the others, a blizzard-chiseled little rangeman with the face of a starved owl. Johnnie saw him put aside his coffee cup to begin polishing his Colt's forty-five.

Slim Coxon got up and moved toward the horses. "I'll take a scout upcrik," he said. His lean six feet disappeared in the gloom.

Sweetwater Smith called after him, "If yuh need any help, just holler." He went limping to the wagon for his bedroll. A Comanche bullet had once broken Sweetwater's leg. Less active than the others, he usually drove the wagon.

Rosy Ryan took a comb from his vest and used it on his sleek and reddish hair. The vest was braided and his shirt was the finest silk. Rosy Ryan was a heartbreaker and knew it. He had two hobbies, fancy clothes and guns.

"A tough outfit, huh?" Rosy said. "Then it

looks like a good investment. Take a look in the wagon, Johnnie."

"Rosy blowed himself," Ogallala explained. "He loosened up and brought everybody a present. He figgered we might need 'em."

Johnnie went to the wagon. In the bed of it lay a brand-new rifle. "It ain't never been fired, Johnnie," Rosy said. "And it's all yourn."

"But I already got a rifle," Johnnie said.

"Throw it away. It's outa date, now."

Knowing Rosy to be a crank on firearms, Johnnie picked up the rifle hopefully. It was a model he had never seen before.

"Smack bang outa the factory," Rosy grinned. "I bought one fer each of us and they're the first centerfire Winchesters that ever hit this range."

Centerfire! The significance of it impressed Johnnie. He had never before heard of a centerfire repeating rifle. His old rifle, of course, was the 1866 model rimfire .44.

"This here's what they call the 44-40," Rosy explained. "Shoots twice as far and four times as accurate. So bring on your pozo ladrones."

Johnnie was elated. "If I'd only had this baby back of those rocks, that day they four-timed me!"

"Means we're heeled fer 'em now," Ogallala chuckled. "First time they come moseyin' around our cowstuff, we'll blast daylight through 'em and then feed 'em to the buzzards."

The wagon team had been unhitched and was eating grain from a box on the ground. All the riding horses had been unsaddled except Slim's. Johnnie went to his own saddle and put the new 44-40 in the scabbard there, tossing the old rimfire into the wagon.

Then Slim's beanpole silhouette rode out of the darkness. "Stuff's all right," he announced. "Nobody seems to be hangin' around."

Ogallala cocked an owlish eyebrow. "I figger them outlaws won't bother us none, Slim, till we get to the pozo."

"A feller never can tell," Slim said.

"I'll go out on night herd," Johnnie offered. "You jiggers get some sleep."

"Call me at midnight," said Sweetwater Smith, "and I'll relieve you."

"Sure." Johnnie saddled Muchacho and rode into the cottonwoods.

Fording the stream, he found the heifers scattered along the west bank. Most of them had bedded down for the night. Johnnie rode to the summit of a low hill and dismounted. There, after staking out Muchacho at the end of a long rope, he sat down with his rifle to watch.

Coyotes barked upriver and an owl hooted from the cottonwoods. The glow of a fire on the far bank grew dim. The boys would be pretty tired after the long drive from rails. Johnnie decided to let them sleep.

So at midnight he did not arouse Sweetwater Smith. Johnnie kept a lone vigil all night on the hill. It was a thrill when dawn came to see the heifers grazing in the valley there, like fluffy balls of red and white.

Twenty-five thousand dollars on the hoof. "They'll make prime bait for those ladrones," Johnnie thought. He rode back to camp and aroused his friends.

By sunup they were on the trail to Santa Fe.

"If that pozo grass is so good," Rosy inquired as they rode along, "howcome somebody else ain't already filed on it?"

"Because honest folks are scared of the outlaws there," Johnnie said. "And the outlaws themselves dassent show up at a land office. And if they did file, outlaws never stay long enough in one place to prove up."

Rosy nodded. "I savvy. It takes three years to prove up a claim. A feller's got to build a house on it, ain't he?"

"That's right."

"Look, Johnnie. Why didn't you file claims fer all five of us, just to make sure nobody beats us to 'em?"

"The homestead law," Johnnie explained, "makes each claimant swear he's seen the land he's filin' on. But nobody'll get ahead of us. We'll turn the heifers loose on the Sandoval grant. Then we'll ride into the pozo with our guns limber, and stand on those five waterholes. Then we fill out the blanks and let one man hightail with 'em to the land office."

That same morning, Ramon Montoya rode into the pozo hondo. He was followed by five sleepy-eyed peons. Each peon rode a burro. Montoya guided them to a spring of water which bubbled from the bed of an arroyo, giving a flow about the size of a man's leg. The flow ran about half a mile before disappearing in the gravel.

"This will be your rancho, José," Montoya announced.

One of the burro-mounted Mexicans looked at him with a dumb smile. He did not fully understand this errand. All he knew was that Don Ramon had just given him fifty dollars, which to José Arragon was a fortune. He was a very poor man and his family did not have frijolis for the winter.

"Bueno, Don Ramon."

"Sign this paper, José."

Although painfully illiterate, José Arragon managed to scratch his name on a homestead application blank. He signed it in duplicate. Montoya put one copy in his pocket. He put the other copy in a tin can. Then he drove a stake in the ground by the spring and inverted the can over it.

"Let us move on to the next waterhole, niños," said Montoya.

Riding north across the pozo's basin, he explained that only at five places was water to be found here in the dry season. When snow was melting, water could be found anywhere. But after July fifteenth, stock in the pozo would need to water on one of five quarter sections. "So whoever controls the five waterholes, my niños, will control all of the pozo."

"And what must we do, patron?"

"Nothing. You go home to Santa Fe and spend your fifty dollars. I will build an adobe hut on each of the claims, to comply with law. At the end of three years, the government will give you title to the claims. You will transfer the titles to me. Then I will give each of you another fifty pesos. *Cornprendez*?"

They comprehended only that Don Ramon was a caballero and should be obeyed. And was not this a very easy way for each of them to earn a hundred dollars? They were not ladrones. They had never heard of Fadeaway Fallon. They were just ignorant *pobres* from the back alleys of Sante Fe, and years ago they had been servants in the great house of the Montoyas on Agua Frio Road. Why should they deny their old master such a simple service?

When all five claims were filed, Montoya told them to be on their way. "You will say nothing about this, niños. I myself will mail the duplicate applications to the land office."

The pawns disappeared up a timbered slope toward Santa Fe. A few minutes later Montoya saw Fadeaway Fallon riding toward him.

Fallon reined up truculently. "What's the idea, Ramon? Who you bringin' in here, anyway?"

"They are only ignorant peons, señor." Montoya gave a sly smile. "*Innocentes* who have loaned me their names."

Fallon scowled at a claim stake. "Been usin' 'em to file land, huh?"

"And why not? Now for three years you are sure to have no intrusion in the pozo."

The argument weighed with Fallon. Still, he had planned on letting the pozo be a web in which he could catch twenty-five thousand dollars' worth of cattle. "Things ain't broke right lately, Ramon. We need to cash in on them cows. Did you hear about Billy Clegg?"

"No, señor. What about him?" Billy Clegg's murderer blew cool smoke from his cigarrita.

"He skipped out, blast him, with whatever he grabbed off Martinez."

"Verdad? It is too bad, señor." Montoya hid a smile. It was with cash from the Martinez purse that he had just paid off the five peons.

"So I need to pick off those cows o' Cameron's," Fadeaway insisted. "Why can't you lay off filin' these claims till we get 'em in here?"

155

"They are sure to come anyway," Montoya argued. "At least they will come as far as the Sandoval rancho. You can raid them there. Then you will have the cattle—and I will have the pozo."

"Yeh?" Fallon's lip curled. "You allers figger to git yourn without any fightin', I notice."

Montoya's eyes narrowed and his lips puckered to blow smoke rings. "If you do as I suggest, you will not need to fight, señor."

Fadeaway hooked a leg over his saddle horn. "I'm listenin'." He had a good deal of respect for Montoya's cunning. "Show me how I can run off them cows without a fight, and I'll take off my hat to you, Ramon."

"It is very simple, señor. Five men will bring the cattle to the Sandoval grant. They will camp on the Puerco at this end, so that they will not disturb the sheep. And the next day they will ride over the mountain to file claims here in the pozo. Yes?"

"Yeh, we can count on it that far," agreed Fallon.

"There is a gap they must ride through on top of the divide, before they come down into the pozo. You will hide your best shot in the gap. He is Frenchie Welsh, you have said. With a rifle Frenchie will shoot Cameron. The others will chase Frenchie, who must have a fast horse. While they chase Frenchie for many miles toward Colorado, you are down at the Sandoval rancho driving cattle across the Puerco toward Arizona. So there is no danger for anyone but Frenchie."

"Frenchie's no fool," Fallon protested. "He won't do it. Why should he take all the risk just because you an' me got a grudge agin Cameron?"

"This is a reason." Montoya produced a purse. It was the purse which Billy Clegg had taken from Martinez. From it Montoya boldly drew out one thousand dollars in bills. He handed the sum to Fallon.

"One thousand pesos is a big reason, señor. It is Frenchie's if he takes the risk. He has taken bigger risks for less, no?"

Fallon thumbed through the bills, then looked up with suspicion. "Thought you was busted, Ramon."

"Last night I have won this money," Montoya asserted, "at roulette."

The assertion satisfied Fallon. "Aw right," he agreed. "Frenchie gets a thousand fer knocking over Cameron. And while Cameron's pals chase him north, we drive the cowstuff west. You allers did have a head on you, Ramon."

CHAPTER 14

Mᴀᴋɪɴɢ ᴅᴜsᴛ ᴀɴᴅ history up the Santa Fe trail came a drove of Hereford heifers. At villages along the route, brown faces stared curiously from doorways. In all New Mexico, cattle like these had never been seen before.

"Que bonitos!" What pretty cows! But weren't they being driven the wrong direction? Heretofore, cattle had always been driven from and not toward the ranges of the Rio Grande. The markets lay east, not west. This was taking coals to Newcastle.

"But *mira*, Manuel! These *vacas* are not like our own. Let us follow and learn where they go."

Vaqueros from the ranchos and village boys on fuzzy-eared burros rode out to greet the drovers and to inspect these blocky, deep-dewlapped bovines. Some of them galloped ahead to tell neighbors not to miss the sight.

So by the time Johnnie Cameron and his friends came to a rise from which they could look down upon Santa Fe, an entourage of outriders had joined them. Where did these cows come from? To what rancho were they being taken? Why weren't they branded? Do you need any help, señores?

All of which made Johnnie more and more

proud of an idea. His idea was in the flesh now, a wave of red and white life rolling into Santa Fe.

They turned into the Camino Real and the heifers moved along the same route of parade trod only three weeks ago by Don Diego de Vargas. Now, as then, an applauding crowd lined either edge of the road.

"Get along, little ballies." There was a lilt in Johnnie's voice. He flicked his rope at a straggler.

"Better help Slim ride point," Ogallala said, "and clear the way. Somebody might get run over."

Johnnie spurred down the long red and white line to the front, and joined Slim there. And still curious crowds lined the highway ahead of them. "If these were longhorns," Slim said, "they'd be stampeded by now."

Even these Herefords weren't entirely proof against contagion from excitement. As the chatter on either side arose in volume, the heifers began lowing, looking with half startled eyes to the right and left. "We'll make it through, though," Johnnie said. "Look, Slim; that's the plaza right where you see that picket fence around the alamos."

The point moved into the plaza, swinging west at the Palace of the Governors. Half of Santa Fe was on the plaza. All guests of la Fonda tavern tumbled out. Johnnie saw Stephen Elkins and his customers emerge from the bank.

"How you like 'em?" Johnnie yelled.

Elkins' broad smile proved that he did not regret loaning money on these cattle. Johnnie let Slim point the herd while he himself rode up to the bank steps.

A group of prominent citizens stood with Elkins. One of them owned feeding corrals just west of the city. He invited Johnnie to hold the herd there overnight.

"A good idea," Elkins put in. "Thank you very much, Don Pablo."

He presented Johnnie to Don Pablo Lucero, explaining that Don Pablo was one of the more progressive stockmen of New Mexico.

"It is nothing," Don Pablo murmured. "And perhaps we may do some business, Señor Cameron. Don Stephano has told me that you paid fifty dollars each for these cows."

"That's right, sir," Johnnie said.

"I will give you sixty, señor." Don Pablo brought out a checkbook.

Elkins smiled. He explained to Johnnie: "Don Pablo has a large Spanish grant stocked with longhorns. And now he sees a chance to improve the blood of his cattle."

"No thanks," Johnnie smiled.

"Sixty-five, señor."

"They're not for sale," Johnnie said.

The cows had drifted by now, with Ogallala and Rosy flicking ropes at the stragglers. Last of all Sweetwater Smith came rumbling along in his wagon.

"Pull over, Sweetwater," Johnnie yelled. "Want you to meet some friends."

He presented Sweetwater to Elkins and Don Pablo.

"Some parade, huh?" Sweetwater grinned.

"Reminds me of the one three weeks ago," Johnnie said, "when De Vargas rode in on a white stallion."

"Yes," Stephen Elkins said thoughtfully, "except that this parade is more significant for New Mexico. The other one looked backward, this one looks forward. Forward to the day when millions of these English cattle will feed on the western plains."

Don Pablo hurried to find his horse. He promised to overtake them at his corrals.

"I'll show up there too, Cameron," Elkins said. "Got some papers I want you boys to sign."

Johnnie rode on. Just beyond the Silverado gambling place on lower San Francisco Street, he caught up with the cattle. A score of volunteer outriders were still with them; one and all they offered to show the way to Don Pablo's corrals.

"May we help you brand them, señores?"

Ogallala grinned. "Look like help's cheap out this way, Johnnie."

"These New Mexicans," Johnnie said, " 'll give you the shirt off their back. Fact is they embarrass you. Which reminds me I can't figure out what to do about Don Ygnacio Sandoval."

"He's the gent what give you that chestnut braunk?"

"Yeh, and he's gonna let us use his grass till we get settled in the pozo. Won't take pay. If you offer to pay him, he's insulted."

"Looks like we'd orter make him a present," Ogallala suggested.

"Yeh, but what? We better get some advice from Elkins on that."

Six miles west of town they came to ranch buildings and corrals beside the road. In the corrals were troughs with water piped into them, and feeding racks.

Here Don Pablo Lucero caught up with them. "Enter, señores," he invited.

The heifers were driven into the corrals. Johnnie saw vega hay stacked on the roof of an outshed and offered to buy two loads of it. Lucero agreed and gave orders for it to be put in the corral racks.

In an adjoining paddock Johnnie noticed a handsome white stallion. He recognized it as the one Ramon Montoya had ridden in the fiesta. Then he remembered hearing that Montoya had borrowed the animal for the occasion from a wealthy stockman. Evidently the stockman was Don Pablo Lucero.

Sweetwater pulled up and they made camp by an acequia across the road. It was still only midafternoon, but a few hours extra rest would be good for the stock.

"Here comes your banker friend," Sweetwater said.

Stephen Elkins rode up with a note and a chattel mortgage. Johnnie Cameron had already signed them. Ogallala, Slim, Sweetwater and Rosy now signed.

"The bank," Elkins said, "insists on one condition."

"Anything you say," Johnnie agreed.

"It's that you brand these cattle before you turn 'em out on the range."

"We'd be loco not to," Rosy said.

"We aim to brand 'em in the Sandoval corrals soon as we get there," Johnnie said. "Which reminds me we haven't registered a brand yet."

"Pick a brand," Elkins suggested, "and I'll register it for you myself."

"What about Diamond Cross?" Rosy asked.

"I like Bar Slash better," Sweetwater said. "Only takes two licks with a straight iron."

"Too easy to blot," objected Ogallala.

Johnnie said thoughtfully, "Let's pick a brand that means something."

"What, for instance?"

"We'll figure one out. But first, let's rustle

some land claim filin' blanks so we can file on those pozo claims."

"I brought along a pad of homestead blanks," Elkins said. He handed the blanks to Johnnie.

"Thanks. And now one other thing," Johnnie said. "I don't want to roll up to Don Ygnacio's place empty handed. I mean we got to take him a present."

"A gold watch," Rosy suggested.

"Too much like handin' him money," Johnnie argued. "It ought to be something casual—and something he needs. Just like the horse he gave me when Blazer got shot. There I was without a braunk, so it was the most natural thing in the world for him to gimme one."

"It's a delicate problem," Elkins murmured. "These New Mexico aristocrats don't like to be paid for hospitality. They're very sensitive. Whatever you give him, you must make it look like you're doing yourselves a favor and not him."

"Which hands me an idea," Johnnie said. "We're gonna brand these Herefords in the Sandoval corrals."

"I getcha," Slim said. "We put Sandoval's brand on a few of 'em by mistake."

"Nothin' so crude as that. Listen. Usual way to brand a cow is to rope her, throw her, hogtie her and then brand."

They gaped at him. "What other way is they?" Ogallala wondered.

"I saw it at the Kaycee stockyards," Johnnie said. "You make a brandin' chute in the corral. It's a contraption kinda like a hinged gate, with a squeeze lever. You drive a cow down an aisle that gets narrower until it comes to the squeeze gate. Then you squeeze and pinion the cow, upright on her feet, so she can't move. Then you slap on the brand."

Ogallala didn't like it. Neither did Sweetwater Smith. "Too ladylike," Sweetwater said. "That ain't no he-man way to handle cattle."

"It's an intelligent way," Johnnie argued. "Especially if you're brandin' comin' three-year-old heifers like to have calves in the spring. Look. You throw a cow and drag her and bully her and let her lie there bawlin' while you romp on her with hog-ties and a brandin' iron. And what happens?"

"It don't hurt her none," Sweetwater insisted. "First thing you know you'll have us feedin' these critturs with a spoon, Johnnie."

"What really happens," Johnnie said, "is that the cow loses at least ten pounds in flesh by bein' thrown. Five hundred cows 'd lose five thousand pounds. We just turned down eight cents a pound for these Herefords. We throw 'em to brand—and we lose four hundred dollars' worth of beef. But we can build a stand-up chute for one hundred dollars. We save three hundred. Then we ride off and leave the chute there, casual like. It's our gift to Don Ygnacio Sandoval."

Sweetwater tried to pick a hole in this, but couldn't. Ogallala admitted grudgingly that it wasn't a bad idea.

But Stephen Elkins was tremendously impressed. "Cameron," he said, "it's a fine thing to bring in new cattle. But it's an even better thing to bring in new methods of handling them."

Rosy Ryan brushed back his red hair and grinned. "And what about new guns, Mr. Elkins? We brung them along too. Look." He went to his saddle and took his late model Winchester. "It shoots centerfire ca'tridges," Rosy explained with pride.

"What advantage is that?" Elkins asked.

While Rosy was expounding the superior ballistics of any centerfire weapon over the old rimfire rifles, Johnnie looked west down the trail and saw a rider approaching. The man was on a calico pony. He came nearer and Johnnie could see that he was Ramon Montoya.

Evidently Montoya was on the way from his mine to Santa Fe. His route would take him by the roadside group here, where courtesy would demand that he stop and exchange greetings.

"I just picked out that brand we were puzzlin' over," Johnnie said suddenly. "I thought of one that means something."

"Which is what?" Slim demanded.

Johnnie held his answer, timing it for the

arrival of Ramon Montoya. In the meantime he looked about for a target on which Rosy could demonstrate his new 1873 model Winchester.

Atop of a cottonwood snag about two hundred yards away, Johnnie saw a chicken hawk. He pointed. "Take a pot at that hawk, Rosy," he suggested.

Everyone looked at the hawk. "It's too long a shot," Elkins said, "for any man's rifle."

"You'd never hit it with a rimfire," Rosy admitted. "But look at this." He stepped to the wagon wheel to use it for a rest.

"That's right," Johnnie echoed. "Even Bill Hickok himself couldn't hit that bird with a rimfire. But watch what a centerfire does. My money's on you, Rosy."

At that moment Ramon Montoya drew up beside them. "Buenos dias, Don Stephano," he greeted. "And you, Señor Cameron."

Rosy was drawing a bead on the hawk. Johnnie held his breath. Rosy was the best shot of them all, but even Rosy might miss a test like this.

The rifle cracked. The hawk spread its wings, wobbled on the snag, then fell flapping to the ground.

"Amazing!" exclaimed Elkins.

"Which gives us a brand for these heifers," Johnnie said. "We brand 'em Circle Dot."

"A circle with a dot in the middle, huh?" echoed Ogallala.

"Sure," said Johnnie. "Like the shell cap o' that ca'tridge Rosy just fired. We slap it on these cows of ours. Then every time a rustler starts to steal one, he sees that brand and it reminds him how straight a centerfire rifle can shoot. Don't you think that's a good idea, Montoya?"

Montoya's eyes flickered as they met Johnnie's. His response was a faint shrug. Then, lighting a cigarrita, he rode on toward Santa Fe.

CHAPTER 15

IF FEAR PRICKED AT the spine of Montoya as he loped on up the road, it wasn't fear of bullets. What frightened him was a feeling that Johnnie Cameron would in the end uncover proof and expose him to the Sandovals.

It made Montoya impatient. Impatient for the hour when Frenchie was due to snipe Cameron at the gateway gap of the pozo. When would that be? Not tomorrow, for it would take those gringos at least two days to get those cows over the mesa to the Sandoval rancho. Then they'd be riding to file in the pozo.

A smile straightened Montoya's lips. They'd be too late to file. The claims were already taken. Which reminded him that the duplicate applications were in his pocket now, ready for delivery to the land office. Attending to that was one purpose of this trip to Santa Fe. Another was to put himself far from a scene of ambush, and so have a perfect alibi for Cameron's murder.

Also there were minor errands. With what little remained of the Martinez money, Montoya must in some small degree appease his creditors.

Dismounting in front of la Fonda tavern, he tossed his bridle reins to a boy there. "Take him to the livery, niño." He gave the boy a dollar.

At the tavern desk Montoya insured his welcome by paying half of the several hundred dollars he was in arrears there. "I shall settle the rest soon. Give me the same room."

He was taken to a suite at the rear side of the patio, on the ground floor. There was a bedroom and a small sala, with a private entrance to a street. Upon occasion Montoya received visitors whose approach through the main lobby and patio might be embarrassing. It was in these very rooms that he had arranged for Pancho Archuleta to spy on Cameron from the Sandoval bodega.

Now he groomed himself and went out to the plaza. His first call was at the bank where a vice president looked up hopefully. "We've been expecting you, Don Ramon."

"Here is one-half the due interest, señor." Montoya presented five hundred dollars.

The bank officer's smile faded. "What about the principal? Your notes for—"

"I will tend to them soon, señor," Montoya cut in. He tossed the money on the desk and sauntered out.

At his tailor's he paid a trifle on a long standing account. Proceeding then to various other tradesmen he paid them just enough to keep them quiet for a while. His last call was at a large trading store specializing in general supplies for ranches and mines.

170

He was appeasing the proprietor when a horseman drew up in front. The rider dismounted and came in. With a start, Montoya saw that he was the dudish, red-haired cowboy who had given a demonstration of shooting down by Don Pablo's corrals below town.

The merchant turned politely to the newcomer. "May I serve you, señor?"

"If you ain't too busy," Rosy said. He presented a list of merchandise. "It's some heavy hinges and bolts and chains and a pulley, mister. Also we want eight two-by-ten planks twelve foot long. I reckon we can cut posts and poles to make the rest of it with. This here stuff's to build a brandin' chute with."

"Ah! I remember you rode by this afternoon with those so beautiful cows. You are a customer of Don Stephano Elkins, are you not? Then I am proud to make you my own. Shall I charge this, señor?"

"Much obliged," Rosy said. "And if you don't mind, deliver it to our wagon down the road. We're campin' tonight at Don Pablo's corrals."

"It shall be done, señor."

Rosy Ryan went out. Montoya saw him ride on toward the plaza.

Returning to the hotel Montoya saw him again. The red-haired cowboy was stabling his horse at a livery barn. Having accomplished his errand in town, it was only natural that Rosy should want to spend the evening taking in the bright lights of Santa Fe.

Ramon Montoya resolved to keep well out of his way. A bullet from Frenchie's rifle would take care of Johnnie Cameron. And Cameron's friends didn't greatly matter, since they could have no first hand knowledge of guilt.

Back in his suite at the Fonda, Montoya looked ruefully at his purse. It was quite flat now. He had reserved just enough to pay five filing fees on as many claims in the pozo. He now put the fees in five envelopes, also enclosing in each the proper application. His own name did not appear on them at all. Now he stamped the envelopes and mailed them to the land office.

That done, he went into the patio and dined. Nothing to do now except to keep conspicuously in Santa Fe while Frenchie ambushed Cameron, and while the rest of Fadeaway Fallon's gang made their raid on the cattle.

"Send a bottle of claret to my rooms, mozo," Montoya ordered. He retired to his sala and was sipping wine there when he heard a knock. Someone was at the private entrance giving to a dark side street.

It might be a creditor. So Montoya peered cautiously from a window. Yes, it was a saddler to whom he owed an old bill. Evidently the fellow had heard he was in town paying a few accounts. Now the rest of his creditors would be after him like a wolf pack. Montoya did not open the door. When the man had gone away, he locked it.

Three more glasses of wine made Montoya heady. Then came the sound of carriage wheels on the side street. They stopped at the curb. Again came a knock. Again Montoya peered discreetly from his window. This time he saw a woman. She was plump, middle-aged, and her face was almost hidden by a long, black mantilla.

La Marta Calaveras! Evidently she had heard of his arrival in Santa Fe.

Montoya kept quiet while she knocked three times. Then the carriage wheels creaked away and he gave a sigh of relief.

Marta, he admitted, was a problem. He considered it broodingly over more wine. How does one handle such an affair? She knew nothing of his connection with the pozo gang. She knew him only as a fine caballero. And she was tenaciously in love with him.

Until recently he had kept her on a string, in case anything went wrong in his arrangement with Josefita Sandoval. It was now time to break off. He could do that only by keeping out of her way.

As he was brushing her from his mind, Ramon Montoya heard another step outside. A furtive step, this time. Then a knock at his door.

Peering out, he saw a man dressed in shabby

173

range garb. The man had bowed legs and a bullet head. Montoya recognized him as one of the pozo gang. Frenchie Welsh! Here was the killer who was to deal with Johnnie Cameron. He had been selected because he was the best shot and owned the fastest horse.

A risk for Frenchie to appear in Santa Fe! Only something important could have brought him here.

Montoya opened the door and Frenchie slipped shiftily in.

"It ain't enough," the man said. His narrow, bloodshot eyes fixed sullenly on Montoya.

"What's not enough?" Montoya asked coldly.

"A thousand pesos. Too much risk fer chicken feed like that. You expect me to salivate that Cameron kid and then run a hoss race with four of his pals."

"I thought you had nerve," Montoya jeered.

"I got nerve if the ante's big enough. This time it ain't. You got to hike the ante, Ramon."

Montoya winced. It always stung him to have one of these backwash outlaws address him as an equal.

"How much do you want?"

"I'll take a chance fer five thousand," Frenchie said.

"I haven't that much," Montoya admitted.

"Aw right. Then pick yourself another sniper." Frenchie was edging toward the exit when

Montoya called him back. "Help yourself to wine, Frenchie, and we'll talk it over."

Frenchie poured himself claret and sat down.

"I haven't any more," Montoya said. "But I can tell you how to take some of the risk out of this affair."

Frenchie leered suspiciously. "I notice you ain't takin' none yerself. You're holed up fer an alibi in Santa Fe, leavin' me to run a race with slugs."

"Some bullets go straighter than others," Montoya said. He told about Rosy Ryan shooting a hawk at two hundred yards. "He has a new kind of rifle, Frenchie. It is better than yours, because it shoots centerfire bullets."

"Just like my forty-five?"

"Just like your forty-five. Only it's a rifle. With it you could not miss Cameron. Also you would have an advantage when they chase you."

Frenchie was interested. "Where is this rifle?"

"It is in a saddle scabbard at the Gomez livery barn. The man leaves his horse there while he takes in the sights tonight, here in Santa Fe. You can enter the barn by the rear and find the saddle on a rack there. Then you can exchange his rifle for your own. He will see only the stock sticking out of the scabbard, and so will not suspect the exchange until morning. By then you are back in the pozo."

It was an inducement, Frenchie admitted. "But

175

a thousand pesos ain't enough. You got to jack up the ante, Ramon."

Montoya leaned forward and lowered his voice. "If I tell you where you can get twenty-five thousand, or perhaps even fifty thousand, this very night, will you do it?"

Frenchie stared. His tongue curled out to lick his lip. "Fer twenty-five thousand," he said, "I'd shoot up the plaza."

"*Bueno*. Then listen. You know the gambling sala of Doña Marta Calaveras, on San Francisco Street?"

"I tossed dice there once."

"The doña's office is at the rear of it. Back of that is the apartment where she lives. The apartment has a door to the side street. You will slip in there a little before midnight, and hide."

Frenchie shook his head.

"It's outa my line, Ramon. I ain't no hand to pick locks."

Montoya's smile was sly. "You don't have to. At one time the doña and I were—well, shall we say very good friends? She gave me a key to her house. This is the key."

Montoya gave a key to Frenchie. Still doubtful, Frenchie held it gingerly between his fingers.

"Always at midnight," Montoya explained, "the dealers take their money to la Marta. They leave her alone with it. She counts it, then puts it in her safe. When she does that tonight, you step out of your hiding. You hold her up, not only for what she has in hand but for all there is in the safe."

The prospect brought a flush to Frenchie's face. "Criminy!" he breathed huskily. "It don't sound bad, Ramon. With a haul like that, we don't need to drygulch nobody fer a cowsteal. You an' me could split an' say nothin' about it to Fallon."

A threat hard as flint came into Montoya's eyes. "No. You must deal with Cameron as arranged. We are not safe if Cameron lives. You and I will divide the money, *muy bien*, and we will say nothing about it to Fallon. But this tip and this key are your pay for dealing with Cameron."

"Aw right," Frenchie agreed sullenly.

Montoya warned him: "There's a federal warrant out for you, Frenchie. If you cross me on this, I will see that it is served. Do this exactly as I say. Whatever you take from la Marta tonight, leave half of it in the hollyhocks that grow at this end of Burro Alley. Then ride to the pozo and make ready to receive Cameron."

"I'll scout the lay," Frenchie promised. "If it looks safe, I might take it on."

Montoya's watch said eleven o'clock. "You should make the rifle trade first," he advised. "Then slip into la Marta's house at eleven-thirty."

Frenchie went out without committing himself. Montoya could only hope he'd go through with it.

He himself went into the tavern lobby and took a conspicuous position. Other patrons came by and he spoke to them all. A nervousness grew on him as midnight approached. To cover it, Montoya sat in at a poker game with a group of wool buyers.

The game lasted until one o'clock. It broke up when a late-homing guest rushed in with a sensational report.

"Have you heard?" he cried. "A ladron has held up la Marta!"

The poker players stared. One of them asked, "You mean the woman who runs that gamblin' joint on Frisco Street?"

"Si, señor. He has hit her with a gun and she is dead."

Montoya got shakily to his feet. He didn't need to fake his shock. "Carramba!" he murmured. "Always la Marta has been my good friend. Are you sure it is true, señor?"

"But of course, Don Ramon. Was I not at play there myself? The dealers say she has been robbed of thirty-eight thousand pesos."

Instantly Montoya's mind divided that sum by two. With half of it, he would be rich again. He could even redeem the old Montoya mansion on Agua Frio Road.

For another hour he continued to make himself conspicuous about the tavern. His own alibi was perfect. No one could possibly suspect him. Nor was he greatly afraid that Frenchie would evade a division. Only by dividing with Montoya could Frenchie hold out on the pozo gang. It would be cheaper for Frenchie to give half to Montoya than to give more than half to Fadeaway Fallon. At last Montoya retired to his suite and remained there until daybreak. Then he went out to a café for coffee. Returning toward the tavern, he made a point of passing by an end of Burro Alley. From a corner of his eye he saw a sack half hidden in hollyhocks there.

Montoya made sure that no one was looking. Quickly he slipped the sack under his coat. Arriving at his rooms he counted the money in it. Nineteen thousand dollars! It meant that Frenchie had been afraid to cross him. They need say nothing about this to Fallon. But Frenchie would carry on at the pozo.

CHAPTER 16

"SNAKE ROSY OUTA them blankets," Ogallala demanded. He was boiling coffee over a fire by the road. Beyond piñon hills to the east, dawn was just breaking.

"How late was yuh out last night, Rosy?" Slim jerked the covers from his red-headed friend. When Rosy only rolled over and groaned, Sweetwater Smith threw a bucket of water in his face.

"I hearn him ramble in about four A.M.," Sweetwater insisted. "He was all likkered up and whoopin' like a Piute. Roll him in that irrigation ditch, Johnnie."

Rosy staggered to his feet, rubbing his eyes. "It's early yet," he grumbled. "Why can't you horned toads let a gent sleep?"

"Look at him!" scoffed Ogallala. "We send him to town fer some hardware and he stays out all night!"

"I was in camp before one o'clock," Rosy protested. He sat down to pull on his boots, then turned at the sound of hoofbeats from the direction of Santa Fe. "Who's that comin', Johnnie?"

An enormous Mexican galloped up and reined to a halt by the fire. The man's face was triple-chinned and a cigarette drooped indolently from his lips. He was armed with both a rifle and a revolver. Johnnie saw a sheriff's badge on his shirt.

"*Como estan?*" he greeted softly.

"Howdy, sheriff," Johnnie said. "Not lookin' for anybody this early, are you?"

"Si, señor. There has been a murder in Santa Fe."

"A killin', huh?" echoed Ogallala. "Anything we can do to help? Light and pour yerself some coffee. My name's Murphy. These here other broke-down hairpins is named Coxon, Ryan, Smith and Cameron."

The sheriff got ponderously to the ground and accepted coffee. "I call myself Gonzalez," he said. "Yes, señores, I am told by my friend Don Stephano Elkins that you camp all night by the road here. So I come to inquire if you have heard anyone ride by after midnight."

"Rosy here rid in about that time," Slim offered. "I didn't hear nobody else. Didn't throw down on anybody in town last night, didja, Rosy?"

"I was plumb peaceful," Rosy insisted. "When and where did this killin' come off, sheriff?"

"It was at exactly midnight," Gonzalez said, "at a gambling place called el Silverado. A ladron has held up the proprietress there and has taken away much money. He hit her with his gun and she is dead."

181

Johnnie asked quickly, "You mean Marta Calaveras?"

"Si, señor. It is very sad. Her place is always orderly and has never given me trouble. Thirty-eight thousand pesos the man has taken. If we catch him, he will hang."

"One of the pozo gang, maybe," Johnnie suggested.

Gonzalez shrugged. "The pozo hondo is not in my county, señor. Sometimes I have ridden there with posses from Rio Arriba and Sandoval counties, but it is no use. When we arrive, always no one is there."

"Well, nobody rid by here after midnight," Sweetwater said. "He'd 've woke me up, 'cause my bedroll was within ten feet o' the trail."

Gonzalez turned his lazy eyes upon Rosy. He appraised the redhead for a minute and then said: "It is all I wish to know, señores. Gracias."

Rosy took a cup of coffee and sat down on his saddle. It was one of five saddles by the campfire. Rosy had no more than seated himself there when he exploded: "Hell's fire! Look!" The stock of a carbine showing from the saddle scabbard had caught Rosy's eye. Sight of it agitated him so violently that he spilled his coffee.

He snatched out the rifle. "It ain't mine!" he yelled. "I been robbed. Last night it was dark and I didn't notice. Look! It's an old style rimfire."

"Shoot me if it ain't!" Slim exclaimed.

"Somebody switched saddle guns on me," Rosy raged. "It must 've been at the livery barn." He made a run for the corral to get his horse.

"Where you goin'?" Ogallala demanded.

Rosy came back across the road with his horse. His face flamed redder than his hair. "I'm foggin' to town," he announced, "fer a showdown with that Montoya buzzard. It was him done it. Nobody else knew I had that new '73 model 44-40. He seen me shoot a hawk with it yestiddy, and it's a cinch he wanted it fer hisself."

Sheriff Gonzalez stared in confusion. "What is this, señor? It cannot be Don Ramon Montoya. He is a very fine caballero."

"He's a very fine ladron," Johnnie Cameron cut in. "But I'll admit we can't prove it, sheriff."

Gonzalez stiffened. "I am afraid you are mistake, señor." Evidently he didn't like to hear strange gringos cast aspersions on one of the old Santa Fe families.

"Let it pass," Johnnie said. "Soon as we can corral some proof on Montoya, we'll let you know. And Rosy, calm yourself down."

"You'd only get your carcass in jail, Rosy," Ogallala said.

"Think I'm gonna let him get away with that new rifle o' mine?" Rosy flared. "I'll grab it away from him and then spin him around the plaza on his ear."

"No you won't," Johnnie retorted. "How could we handle these heifers with you in jail? Sit on him, Slim."

"You can catch him out in the pozo sometime," Sweetwater advised, "and work on him there."

"Likely it wasn't Montoya who swiped your saddle gun, Rosy," Johnnie suggested. "He'd have somebody else do the job for him. That's his style. Like the time he had Pancho Archuleta jimmy mine at Sandoval's. Bet it wasn't Montoya who cracked down on the Calaveras woman, either."

This last almost shocked the breath from Gonzalez. "Are you mad, señores? Of course it is not Don Ramon who killed la Marta. He was at the hotel in a poker game when it happened. Besides, he would have no dealing with ladrones. He is a very fine—"

"I know," Johnnie interrupted bitingly. "He is a very fine caballero. That's what they all say. La Marta told me so herself the other day. She even called him the top caballero in all New Mexico."

Gonzalez squinted through smoke from his cigarrita. "You knew la Marta, señor?"

"I had a talk with her," Johnnie admitted. "Never mind about what." He wasn't going to drag Josefita's name into this.

The sheriff sighed. "You have made a very sad mistake, señor. It is not wise to insult our best people. And now, since you cannot help me, I shall ride back to my duty."

The fat man pulled himself to his saddle and rode back toward Santa Fe.

Rosy looked after him with a scowl. "No wonder they never catch any ladrones out here!"

"It's sunup," Ogallala said. "Let's get them heifers started down the trail."

"Wagon's packed," Sweetwater announced. "Includin' that hardware and stuff what was sent out from town." He limped across to the corral for the wagon horses.

The others threw saddles on their mounts. As soon as Sweetwater had the wagon team in traces, Slim opened the corral gate. Five hundred and ten Herefords drifted west down the road.

Sight of them brightened Johnnie a little. With a faint, contented lowing the heifers strung out ahead of him, the morning light slanting on sleek red backs. "Anybody tries to rustle 'em," Johnnie said, "is in for a fight."

"And me with only a rimfire carbine!" Rosy mourned.

"Take mine," Slim offered. He insisted on trading rifles. "You're the best shot in this here outfit, Rosy."

From the wagon seat Sweetwater remarked hopefully: "Whoever grabbed Rosy's rifle won't have any ca'tridges for it. None for sale out here either, on that new model. So he'll have to send plumb back east to the factory."

"Not till he fires fifty rounds," Rosy gloomed. " 'Cause mine had sixteen shells in the magazine. And I had about twice that many in a bullet pocket on the saddle scabbard, and they're gone."

He rode to the head of the herd to point the trail.

By noon they were at the Rio Grande and forded there.

"Do we make Sandoval's by night, Johnnie?" Slim asked.

"No, Slim. It's a two-day drive from Santa Fe."

"This here's a big country," Slim admitted, looking ahead toward a skyline of mesas.

"Plenty o' room to run cows in," Johnnie said.

They pushed the heifers on and at sundown made camp in an aspen park just under the east rimrock of a mesa. High, mountain bluestem was sweet there. "Look at 'em go after it!" Ogallala chuckled as the cattle spread out to graze.

"It cures with a head just like grain," Johnnie said. "Puts plenty o' tallow on a cow's ribs."

"Puts big bones in a calf, too, this mountain grass does," Sweetwater chimed in. "Betcha our calf crop next fall 'll weigh four hun'erd pounds each at weanin'."

The night was divided into five watches, each man taking a two hour turn. "We're not likely to be bothered here, though," Johnnie predicted.

Rolled in blankets under the stars, he breathed in the pine-scented air and wondered just what fate awaited him across these mesas. The warm hospitality of the Sandovals was there, he knew, and beyond that lay the hazards of the pozo. Somewhere a bullet with his name on it was waiting for Johnnie Cameron.

He considered the prospect calmly. The bullet, he felt certain, would be inspired but not fired by Montoya. Montoya the fine caballero! Montoya who was only waiting for a girl's eighteenth birthday.

"I gotta put a kink in that!" Johnnie murmured.

"Put a kink in what?" Slim demanded from the next bedroll.

"In a wedding bell," Johnnie said. He told Slim about a baby girl found wrapped in a buffalo robe on the Santa Fe trail; about her adoption by the Sandovals and her betrothal to Ramon Montoya. "We got less 'n three months to work in. If that jigger gets me first, you start in where I leave off, Slim."

"Is she good lookin'?"

"Makes no difference about that," Johnnie retorted. "I mean we can't let him get away with this just by drygulchin' the only witness he's afraid of."

Slim nudged Sweetwater. "Did you hear that, Sweetwater? Johnnie wants to break up a weddin' and he needs our help."

"Ain't it awful!" Sweetwater jibed. "You wouldn't 've thought it of a nice boy like Johnnie."

"With all the troubles we got," Slim sighed, "he wants us to start botherin' about a woman."

"When you see her," Johnnie retorted, "you'll be the first to begin slickin' back your hair."

"Sure he will," Ogallala put in. "Don't pay any 'tention to them two bowlegged crowbaits, Johnnie. Now shet yer traps and go to sleep."

In the morning they crossed the mesa and drifted the cattle down into the Springs of the Saint's Soul Grant. Grouse whirred through the timber. Rosy, riding point, flushed a flock of wild turkey.

"It's just like this over in the pozo," Johnnie assured them. "Game everywhere."

"That grass is what looks good to me," Slim said. He pointed out toward the Puerco flats where miles of range were dotted with sheep.

Centering it all stood the ancestral hacienda of the Sandovals.

In midafternoon they drew near it. And Johnnie saw the entire Sandoval household riding out to meet them. "Mind your manners, you bunkshack bums," he warned. "These here folks are mighty polite."

A girl came galloping up on a pony. "Hello, Señor Johnnie," she called. Her cheeks were red and her long black hair flew behind her in the wind.

"Hi, Josephine," Johnnie grinned. "Meet the best lookin' herd o' cowstuff in New Mexico."

"They are all so alike!" enthused Josefita. "Such pretty heads! How can they be so fat after such a long trail?"

If Josefita was impressed by the Herefords, Slim and Sweetwater were no less impressed by Josefita. Johnnie saw them edging up with hats off, and sleeking back their hair.

Rosy Ryan, at the head of the herd, was already being greeted by Don Ygnacio and the other Sandovals. Ogallala was driving the wagon this morning. When he rumbled up, Johnnie presented his friends to Josefita.

Ogallala was old enough to say what Slim and Sweetwater couldn't. "Johnnie's been tellin' us about how purty you was, miss," said Ogallala. "We're sure proud to find out he's so truthful, fer once in his life. Is this yer grandpa?"

Don Ygnacio approached them, his small, goateed face beaming. "We are happy you are home again, Señor Cameron." To the others he bowed. "My rancho is yours, caballeros."

Then came Don Santiago with all the nephews and primos, ranging down to seven-year-olds on burros. Back of these came the house servants, as well as numerous sheepherders and vaqueros.

"We are glad you come home, Don Juan," they shouted.

"See what pretty cattle he has brought here!"

Slim whispered behind his hand to Sweetwater: "Hear that? They're calling our Johnnie names."

Vaqueros took proud charge of the heifers and drove them on toward the corrals. Don Ygnacio wanted to take every man, horse and cow right into his household, but Johnnie wouldn't hear of it.

"It wouldn't be right to clutter you up, Don Ygnacio. With your permission we'll just camp on the upper Puerco for a few days, till we get the stuff branded. Naturally we don't want to turn it loose till we get our iron in it."

Ogallala stopped the wagon by the corral gate and began unloading certain hardware and planking from it. "You don't mind if we rig up a brandin' chute, do yuh?" he asked casually. "Don't see any sense in it myself. But Johnnie figgers we ought to pamper these heifers."

They were quite welcome, Don Santiago said, to build anything they wanted.

Looking over the corral fence, Johnnie saw a shabby old man with a flowing white beard. Around him were a dozen little children from the peon quarters. They were holding a milk bottle to the mouth of a baby antelope.

"Hi, Jason," Johnnie yelled.

The old prospector shuffled forward, grinning. "Caught a fawn antelope up near my camp," he explained. "Its mammy got clawed by a panther.

So I fetched the little feller down here fer the kids to play with."

"Any devilment been goin' on over in the pozo?" Johnnie asked.

"Nope. Quiet as a graveyard over there." Old Jason renewed the cud in his cheek and then squinted from man to man of Johnnie's companions. "When you fellers figurin' on goin' over there to file claims?"

"Bright and early tomorrow," Johnnie said. "Soon as we file, we'll come back over here and brand."

"Takin' a chance, ain't yuh?" Jason cautioned. "Leavin' them ballies without a herder while you ride over there to file?"

"We've got to get those claims staked," Johnnie said. "Only take us a day. While we're gone, we get Don Ygnacio to put a few of his vaqueros with 'em."

"Reckon that orta make it safe," Jason said. "Well, I got to fork my mule now and be a-ridin'."

Persuasion from Johnnie and the Sandovals was futile. The old man mounted his mule and rode north toward the pozo hills.

"Queer old codger," Rosy murmured.

"Yeh, there's a mystery back o' that old beard," Johnnie said.

Don Ygnacio readily consented when Johnnie explained his plans. "I regret that you will not

191

stay even for comida, señores. So I myself will show you to good grass on the upper Puerco. And early tomorrow I will send you my three best vaqueros."

Josefita came along too. She rode with Johnnie at the head of the herd as the others trailed it northwest toward an upper corner of the grant.

"I like your friends, Señor Johnnie," she said. "I hope all of them will come to my wedding."

"Montoya passed us on the road," Johnnie said. "He was headin' into Santa Fe."

Some brusque quality in his voice made her look at him curiously. "I do not believe you like Don Ramon, señor."

He forced a laugh. "Of course I don't. I'm jealous."

She refused to take this at face value. "Please, Señor Johnnie, why do you not like Ramon?"

"I gave you one reason. There's another."

"What is it, señor?"

"If I tell you, you'd be offended."

"Perhaps it is because you have been talking with el Viejo."

"Old Jason Holt?"

"Si, señor. He too does not like Ramon. Today he came down to bring a little antelope—but it is only an excuse to see me. He has called me aside and talked to me about Ramon."

"What did he say?"

"El Viejo is a good man, but he has lived alone

in the hills so long I think maybe he is a little crazy. Today he has told me terrible lies about Ramon and has begged me not to marry him. But of course I will. It has been arranged a long time, and Ramon is a—"

"A very fine caballero," Johnnie supplied dryly. "Yeh, everyone says that. Suppose we drop it. I don't want you thinkin' I'm crazy too."

Don Ygnacio spurred to a place beside them. "*Mira*, Señor Cameron. There is ten thousand acres we do not use for the sheep." He pointed to a wide stretch of vega along the upper Puerco. "You must make yourself at home there until your house is built in the pozo."

"A thousand thanks," Johnnie said.

"I think we had better turn back here, Papacito," said Josefita.

"Come along and have supper in camp with us," Johnnie urged.

"I am sorry, señor."

Josefita's voice seemed a bit cool as she turned back with Don Ygnacio toward the hacienda.

CHAPTER 17

THEY MADE CAMP in cottonwoods along the Puerco. And again that night each man stood guard in turn over unbranded cattle.

The first blush of daylight brought three vaqueros from the hacienda. The segundo himself made one of them. The other two struck Johnnie as likely to make a better showing in a fandango than in a gunfight. They moved with languor. Their round brown faces, smiling from beneath the wide brims of beehive sombreros, were honest enough. Heavy spurs, chaparejos, wide striped serapes and brass-studded leather cuffs weighted them down.

You couldn't draw a gun very fast, Johnnie thought, in trappings like that. These fellows wore holstered revolvers but carried no saddle rifles.

"Betcha they're handier with a guitar than anything else," Slim murmured.

"What difference does it make?" argued Sweetwater Smith. "We'll be back by sundown. We can't file them claims till we see 'em, can we? So let's ride."

"We can trust you not to let the cattle scatter too far, señores," Johnnie said.

"But of course, Don Juan," promised the segundo.

"And don't let 'em cross the river," Rosy said. "Looks like dawggone good rustler country over there."

"You may rest easy, señor."

Directly after breakfast Johnnie and his friends took trail for the pozo hondo. The way led them into steep high country heading a fork of the pozo.

"Got them filin' blanks, Johnnie?"

"Yeh, and they're all filled out," Johnnie said. "All we gotta do is to tie one to a stake at each of those waterholes. Then we mail duplicates and filin' fees to the land office."

"Get a jog on," Slim urged. "I'd sure hate to get back and find them cow critturs raided."

Johnnie took the lead and they pushed on another hour up a brushy trail. It led them to a bald plateau with a gap between rocky red shoulders just ahead. "That gap," Johnnie announced, "is our front door."

"Nice place to get drygulched," Slim suggested.

"Keep your guns limber," advised Ogallala.

Johnnie pulled his 44-40 from the scabbard and held it across his saddle. They advanced then, riding abreast, toward the narrow gap which made a gateway for the pozo hondo.

Frenchie Welsh saw them coming. Well concealed, he was perched high in a crevice of the gap's left shoulder. Atop the shoulder was a thicket of wild cherries. In it was hitched Frenchie's horse, the fastest in the pozo.

One shot would do it. That was Frenchie's contract with Montoya. The price had been paid in advance. It was a tip which had netted Frenchie nineteen thousand dollars. The money was in his saddlebags right now.

Those fellows were still a good four hundred yards away. Frenchie knew they couldn't ride up here to get him without going a long way around. The face of the shoulder was sheer. And by the time they could scramble up afoot, he'd be a long way off.

He waited, setting his sight for one hundred yards. The feel of this centerfire Winchester gave him confidence. He had practised a few shots with it, since pilfering it from a scabbard in Santa Fe, and had been impressed with its performance. At a hundred yards, and with a broad-chested target like Cameron, he couldn't miss.

The others would chase him. Frenchie would have to risk that. If he didn't, Montoya would set a federal marshal on his heels. Also Montoya would tell Fadeaway that Frenchie was holding out loot.

Fadeaway and the others would swarm all over him, if they knew. They were tough hombres. Right now they were riding to the Puerco to make off with a herd of Herefords. Nobody watching those heifers except a few lazy, slow-fingered vaqueros. Fallon would get away with 'em, all right. By leading off Cameron's buddies and losing them in hills to the north, Frenchie could guarantee Fallon a long start. By then it would be night time. Fallon could push on through darkness and lose his trail in the San Juan.

Frenchie poked the muzzle of the 44-40 through a crack in the rocks. With a steady rest, he drew a bead on Johnnie Cameron.

Two hundred yards. One hundred and fifty. Frenchie was a shrewd judge of ranges. His angle of fire was downward. Easy to bounce Cameron out of that saddle.

One hundred yards! Frenchie pulled the trigger.

Crack! The hills threw back a hoarse echo. Frenchie saw Cameron pitch to the ground. It was a breast hit, he knew. Frenchie himself scurried up through a notch in the craggy shoulder. They couldn't see him from below. He pressed his way into cherry brush and to the horse there. Jumping to the saddle, he dug in with spurs and was off.

Ogallala swung to the ground and caught Johnnie as he fell. He saw blood spread in a crimson blotch over Johnnie's vest. "We'll get him, kid," Ogallala promised.

His voice was savage but his arms were gentle as he pillowed Johnnie's head there.

Rosy, Slim and Sweetwater were firing at a ball of white smoke which drifted from a crevice of the gap. They hadn't seen the sniper. No way to tell how many men were ambushed there.

"We're wastin' lead," Rosy rasped. "Let's circle and find a way to that brush on top." He galloped up a hillside and Slim followed.

Sweetwater dismounted and came limping to Ogallala. "How bad's he hit, Ogallala?"

"Dead center," Ogallala announced grimly. "He ain't conscious, but he's still breathin'. Let's take him to the shade of them aspens."

They carried Johnnie to the aspens. There they removed his vest and shirt. The bullet had entered just over the right lung and had emerged at the back, below the shoulder blade. "He's tough," Sweetwater muttered. "He might pull through if I can stop this blood."

He stripped off his own shirt and bandaged the wound. Ogallala gave his coat for a pillow and they put Johnnie's head on it.

Sweetwater found a tiny pool of water standing from the last rain. He filled his hat and came back to bathe Johnnie's chest and face. He tried to be hopeful. "The way I figger it, the kid's too tough to let one stinkin' little slug finish him off."

"Sure he is," Ogallala agreed grimly. "You just

stay here and take care of him while I go help Rosy and Slim."

"Better let me go," Sweetwater said.

"Nope. I'm the best tracker. Rosy's handy with a gun all right, but he might lose that buzzard's trail."

Sweetwater's eyes smouldered. "When you ketch him, bring his ears back to me."

Ogallala started toward his horse. Then he saw Johnnie's empty saddle. The big Spanish gelding was easily the best mount of them all. So Ogallala took Johnnie's horse, leaving his own standing there. Carbine out, he galloped up a slope along hoofprints left by Rosy and Slim.

It was a slow, circling climb to wild cherry brush high on the gap's shoulder. Ogallala found Slim and Rosy looking over sign there.

"They was only one sniper done it," Rosy announced. "And look! Here's what he done it with." Rosy picked up an empty shell which had been ejected from Frenchie's rifle.

"Centerfire!" Slim and Ogallala exclaimed in a breath.

"Which means," blazed Rosy, "that he done it with my rifle! The one he snitched in Santa Fe. That model's too new for this country, 'cept the ones we brought out here."

"Let's go," Slim urged, and swung back on his horse. "He's got twenty minutes start of us already."

Ogallala took the lead on a trail easy to follow. The killer's horse had crashed through brush, leaving plenty of sign. "He figgers to outrun us," Slim said.

"You fellers turn back and leave him to me," Ogallala insisted.

They wouldn't do it. "He shot Johnnie with my rifle," Rosy argued bitterly. "That makes him my meat."

"Besides," Slim put in, "it's a cinch he's headin' fer some more of his own kind. They's supposed to be a whole pack of outlaws in this pozo. So three of us ain't too many to shoot it out with 'em."

Ogallala pushed on and his keen range eyes missed no print or broken twig. Soon they emerged from the brush and miles of the open pozo basin spread out below them.

"There he goes!" Slim yelled. All of them saw a fugitive horse at a hard gallop on the far side of the basin.

"Lay yer ears back, Muchacho," Ogallala said. "We gotta ketch that skunk."

They raced off. Ogallala pulling well ahead of the others. He didn't need to watch hoofprints now. Hooves thundered as three men followed one in a race to avenge Johnnie Cameron.

Then timber on the far slope of the pozo swallowed the fugitive. Ogallala pinned his eyes on the spot and kept hard on toward it. Arriving there, he had to begin tracking again. Slim and Rosy caught up as the older man was forcing his way through brush.

"Why the Sam Hill don't you fellers turn back?" Ogallala snapped over his shoulder.

"Why don't *you?*" Rosy retorted. "I'm turnin' back just as soon as I flip a forty-four through that jasper."

"Johnnie said for me to carry on in his place, if anything happened to him," Slim argued. "Out of my way, Ogallala."

"You'd lose the trail in five minutes," Ogallala shot back. "You know dawggone well I'm the best sign finder."

Pushing through glade and canyon on the killer's trail, they continued to wrangle. Each man wanted the other two to turn back. Each wanted to deal retribution himself, with a hail of bullets, to the man ahead.

" 'Tain't right to leave Sweetwater alone with Johnnie back there," Ogallala fretted. "One of you son-of-a-guns orter be helpin' him git Johnnie down to the Sandoval place. T'other of you orter be foggin' fer a doctor."

The tracks turned up a barranca and came out on a bare, limerock bench. The surface of the bench was smooth and hard. It left no more sign than a concrete pavement.

Ogallala swore. "Take us half a day to find where he cut away from this rock. Which means we can't ketch him afore nightfall. Blast you ornery bums, Johnnie'll bleed to death while you're messin' around here."

"Aw right," Slim conceded grudgingly. "We'll match for it. Odd man keeps on after the drygulcher. The other two ride back to Johnnie."

Rosy agreed and produced a coin. The others did likewise and all three flipped at the same time.

"Yours is heads, Rosy," Ogallala crowed. "Yours is too, Slim. Mine's tails. Now git to heck outa here, both of you."

A bargain was a bargain. Rosy and Slim turned back.

And Ogallala quickly found where the sign left the limestone bench. He did it more with his head than with his eyes. The man would keep as much as possible to the screen of timber. Timber grew only on the upper side of the bald. Riding there, Ogallala lost only a few minutes in finding the trail again. From here it angled up toward the rim of the pozo.

Scanning the rimrock shrewdly, the tracker saw but two possible niches of egress. Both of them, he reasoned, would emerge on a bare mesa. So Ogallala deserted the tracks and made speed toward the nearest of the niches. He didn't care whether or not it was the right one. The fugitive could hardly be more than thirty minutes ahead. And a lead that short would expose him on the open mesa.

Ogallala pushed on up the slope, emerging on the mesa with the sun still about two hours high. A wide, open tableland ahead now. And on the far rim of it Ogallala saw a loping dot. He was off at lathering speed after it, having gained at least ten minutes by deserting the trail.

Muchacho was blowing hard. It was a punishing gait. But Ogallala knew the fugitive horse would be no less winded. "It's you agin him, Muchacho. Keep a-lopin'."

At the far edge of the mesa the fugitive stopped, whirled his mount, whipped a rifle to his cheek. Ogallala saw a puff of smoke, then heard the rifle bark. He didn't waste a precious minute to fire back. "We'll have him cornered afore sundown, Muchacho. Leastwise he dassent stop to feed. I figger that braunk's got good legs all right. But he ain't got a chest on him like yourn, old hoss."

The man ahead dipped down over the fair rimrock. When Ogallala arrived there he could hear the man crashing through timber below. Ogallala jumped his horse down a stairstep niche in the cliff and went smashing after him. The sun was setting but there'd still be an hour of light. No rest for that fellow. "Ride him down, Muchacho."

The fugitive broke out upon a barren hogback and raced hard for the nose of it. He twisted in his saddle to shoot and the bullet whistled over

Ogallala's head. The wiry little rangeman took his own rifle from the boot. His thin, blizzard-bit face, as wise as a starved owl's, at the same time revealed the tight-toothed tenacity of a pit bulldog. "He can't shake us off, Muchacho."

With each stride Muchacho was gaining. Sweat lathered his flanks and his breath came like a bellows. Another bullet whirred from the fugitive. "He can't hit nothin'," Ogallala muttered, "ridin' like that."

They raced off the hogback and down into a cottonwood bottom. The fugitive disappeared from sight and Ogallala heard him splash through a creek. Then the hoofbeats stopped. Presumably the man had dismounted to take a post of defence back of trees.

Ogallala drew Muchacho to a quick halt. Dropping reins to the ground, the old trailsman advanced on foot with his rifle. The shadows were long as he stalked in among the cottonwoods. A gun roared beyond the creek; its bullet chipped bark from a tree by Ogallala. He dropped to his stomach and crawled on like an Indian.

He could see the other man's horse beyond the creek. Then he saw a rifle barrel poking through brush. Ogallala rolled to one side just as it flashed. He was behind willows now. He stood up and made his way downstream, screened by the willows. Then he waded the stream and circled to a position back of his man.

In the gloom Ogallala had him covered before the man knew he was there.

"Throw down yer gun and h'ist 'em!" Ogallala plowed sod between Frenchie's legs with a bullet.

Frenchie dropped his gun. He got sullenly to his feet and raised his hands.

Ogallala came up and took a forty-five from his holster. Then he picked up a Winchester rifle.

"Lie flat on yer belly," Ogallala ordered, "while I get a tie rope on yuh."

He kicked the man's shins and Frenchie dropped flat. Ogallala took a rope from the saddle of the horse standing there. With it he tied the man securely.

"Now set up and let's talk," suggested Ogallala. "How much did Montoya pay yuh fer this job o' drygulchin'?"

"What drygulchin'?" Frenchie retorted. "Blast you, you can't pin nothin' on me!" He cursed his captor and then compressed his lips stubbornly.

Ogallala took a look through his saddlebags and found a fat roll of money. Counting it, Ogallala whistled. The money came to exactly nineteen thousand dollars.

"I reckon yuh didn't steal this centerfire Winchester from Rosy Ryan, neither!"

"I found it on the range," Frenchie asserted.

Ogallala did some shrewd figuring. Nineteen thousand dollars happened to be exactly half of the loot taken from the murdered Calaveras woman. It was a murder which had occurred on the same night this 44-40 had been stolen from Rosy in Santa Fe. The answer seemed to be that here was the murderer, and that an equal partner in the crime had the other half of the loot.

When he explained this reasoning to Frenchie, blood drained from the man's face. Ogallala saw beads of sweat on his brow.

"You're too ornery to use up a good slug on," Ogallala said. "So I reckon I got to drag you in to be hanged."

The pallor deepened on Frenchie's face. "Don't take me in," he begged. "If you'll let me go, I'll give yuh every cent of that money."

"Which I already got my hands on," Ogallala said. "Come again, you mangy coyote. What else you got to trade with?"

"I ain't got nothin'. I ain't done nothin'. I found that money in Burro Alley."

"If you'll spill the dirt on Montoya," Ogallala sparred, "I might give yuh an even break."

"I don't know Montoya."

Ogallala tied him hand and foot to a cottonwood. Then he crossed the creek and retrieved Muchacho. After unsaddling both horses, he watered them and staked them out to graze. Then he built a fire and squatted by it, squinting across it at his prisoner.

Dark had fallen. From far down the creek an owl hooted.

"You're plumb skeered o' this Montoya, I reckon. Is that why yuh won't spiel on him?"

"I don't know him," Frenchie insisted.

Ogallala baited him for half an hour but could get no admission about Montoya.

"Aw right. Then it looks like yuh ain't got nothin' to trade. Soon as the braunks is rested, I'll pack you in to the sheriff."

Again the owl hooted down the creek.

"Too bad you won't talk," Ogallala said sadly. "'Cause if yuh was to tell me anything right interestin', and it sounded convincin', I'd give yuh an even break."

"Whatta yuh mean, even break?"

"I'd cut yuh loose, put yer forty-five in yer holster and keep mine in mine. Then next time that owl hoots, we could both go fer our guns."

Frenchie's eyes flickered. He licked his pale lip and said nothing.

"An even break's better 'n no break at all," Ogallala baited. "Know anything interestin'? Time's short." He looked at his watch. "I'll give yuh just five minutes to make a deal."

The minutes ticked by.

The strain of them broke Frenchie. "For an even break," he said hoarsely, "I could tell yuh about a cow steal. I ain't got nothin' to do with it, understand."

"A cow steal, huh? If it's important enough, and sounds convincin', it's a deal," Ogallala agreed. "You got one minute left."

"Aw right. Them heifers o' yourn are bein' run west to Arizona right now."

Ogallala blinked. Instantly he was convinced, because it was all so logical. In a flash he understood that the sniping of Cameron had been to lure them in a long chase across the mountains north, giving time for the rest of the gang to drive cattle west from the Puerco.

"When did this cow steal start?"

"Early this morning," Frenchie said, "just as soon as you got outa sight an' sound. Do I get that even break?"

"I allers keep a promise," Ogallala said, "even to a skunk like you."

He used his knife to cut Frenchie free. Then he stuck a forty-five in the man's holster. Ogallala's was still in his own.

The fire blazed between them. "Wait till the owl hoots," Ogallala said. "Then go fer yer gun."

He knew the man wouldn't wait. He'd be sure to snatch for an advantage by beating the owl's hoot. So Ogallala kept his eyes on a slowly clawing right hand.

When it darted to a holster, Ogallala drew and fired. Frenchie stiffened. Then he pitched forward across the fire, deadcenter between the eyes.

CHAPTER 18

WHAT TO DO NEXT worried Ogallala. He had a dead man and nineteen thousand in loot on his hands. Certainly it was his duty to deliver both the corpse and the money to Sheriff Gonzalez at Santa Fe.

"But if I do that, I'd be ast a peck o' questions I can't answer."

More than that, he'd be delayed in getting back on the job with Slim and Rosy and Sweetwater Smith. Five hundred prime Herefords were being driven west by the pozo gang. At least this outlaw had admitted as much with his last breath. An itch burned Ogallala to be after those heifers.

A faint distant light down the valley suggested a way out. A ranch or Mexican settlement of some kind was no doubt there. Ogallala put out his own fire, then saddled both horses. He lifted the dead man to a horse, jack-knifing it across the saddle.

Ogallala put the money in his own saddlebags and also took possession of Rosy's rifle. Mounting Muchacho, he led the other horse down valley toward the ranch light.

Moonlight was bright, so he kept to the shadows of the creek cottonwoods. An hour's riding brought him to a corral smelling strongly of sheep. A dog barked. There should be no alarm, though. People in the house would merely assume that coyotes were prowling near.

Ogallala fished an old scrap of envelope from his pocket. On this he printed in large letters:

THIS MAN MURDERED MARTA CALAVERAS. HALF THE MONEY HE STOLE FROM HER WAS FOUND ON HIM. IT WILL BE DELIVERED TO SHERIFF GONZALEZ AT SANTA FE.

Ogallala pinned the message to the corpse, which was still balanced across a horse. Then he tied the horse to the corral gate. Inmates of the house would find it there in the morning.

Loping back up the creek on Muchacho, Ogallala decided not to try to make it back to the pozo before daylight. Crossing that mesa in the dark wouldn't be too easy. And Muchacho needed rest.

So at the top of the creek Ogallala made camp for the night. He staked Muchacho in good grass there and waited until the first peep of dawn.

He rode up through aspens, then, and crossed the mesa. From its farther rim he could look down and south into the pozo hondo.

A few spots of brighter green gleamed in its basin, indicating permanent water flows. Two of them lay directly on Ogallala's route back to the Sandoval grant.

So after Ogallala had ridden down into the pozo, he took pains to cross one of the watered quarter sections. A spring there made a tiny rivulet which twisted a short way through a lush meadow before sinking into sand and gravel. This would be one of the claims they would file to control the pozo.

A stake with a tin can inverted over it caught Ogallala's eye. He concluded that Rosy or Slim, en route back to join Sweetwater yesterday, had stopped here for a minute to file.

Yet Ogallala failed to see fresh hoofprints by the stake. The ones he did see had been made before the last rain, and were burro prints. A worry creased Ogallala's brow. He dismounted and took the can from the stake.

Inside he found a land claim blank, properly filled out. The name on it was José Arragon. By the scrawled signature, Arragon might be an illiterate peon.

Ogallala swore softly. "Somebody beat us here, plague take 'em! Wonder if they grabbed off them other waterholes too."

He spurred on a mile to the next bright green spot. Here again he found a can inverted over a stake. This quarter section had been filed on by a Manuel Chavez.

Depression settled over Ogallala. He couldn't doubt that it was all a carefully laid plot to forestall himself and his friends. To keep them out of this pozo. It made a convincing pattern with the sniping of Johnnie in the gap, and with the running off of the cattle by rustlers.

More sure than ever now that the herd had been raided, Ogallala spurred at a savage gallop toward the gap. He didn't expect to find anyone there, though, or even at the cow camp down on the Puerco. While Sweetwater was occupied with Johnnie, and while Slim and Rosy and Ogallala were chasing a decoy sniper, the main force of the outlaws must have swooped down on the Puerco. And the sleepy-eyed vaqueros left on guard there could hardly have put up much resistance.

Muchacho was tiring again by the time Ogallala reached the divide between the pozo and the grant. He found no one at the gap there. Hoofprints revealed that Slim and Rosy had passed on into the grant. Had Johnnie been taken to the hacienda and was he still alive?

With these uncertainties flogging him, Ogallala plunged his mount on down into an upper Puerco canyon. It was past noon when he broke out of this and sighted vega flats, and cottonwoods along the riverbank there.

Then he pulled up short and rubbed his eyes. He saw grazing cattle. White-face heifers! They were spread out like fluffy red and white balls and grazing contentedly on the vega.

Ogallala saw a campfire in the cottonwoods.

He rode to it and found Rosy Ryan frying bacon. At a nearby stump, Slim was slicing a steak from the hindquarter of an antelope.

"Where's Johnnie?" Ogallala demanded.

Slim's grin quickly reassured him. "He's laid up with lead poisonin', Johnnie is."

And Rosy added: "With a good-lookin' nurse feedin' him. Some guys have all the luck."

"Time we got to the Sandovals' yestiddy," Slim explained, "Sweetwater had him in bed there. It was that Josephine girl herself what rid all the way to Bernalillo fer a doctor, an' she broke all the records gettin' back. Better light an' feed yerself, Ogallala; you look tuckered."

"Did you ketch up with that drygulcher?" Rosy demanded.

"Deadcenter," Ogallala reported. "And speakin' of deadcenters, here's yourn, Rosy."

Rosy was elated to get his rifle back: He prodded for details, while Slim flipped flapjacks for the famished Ogallala.

"Ain't nobody raided these heifers?" Ogallala demanded.

"Nope," Slim said. "We found everything plumb peaceful."

Ogallala puzzled over it.

"Reckon that feller just strung me along with the first thing he thought of," he concluded, "so I'd give him an even break."

"Looks that way," Slim agreed. He dumped

another stack of flapjacks in front of Ogallala.

"Still, it sure sounded logical," the older man brooded.

"You can't believe everything you hear, Ogallala."

"And so quick as Johnnie gets well, we won't be any worse off 'n we was before."

"We'll be a heap worse off," Ogallala frowned. "I fergot to tell you them pozo homesteads is already filed."

"The heck you say!" Slim exploded. "Who filed 'em?"

"Names don't matter." Ogallala said. "What counts is who's backin' up them names. Me, I nominate Ramon Montoya."

"You mean he ran in some ringers to grab that land for him?"

Ogallala wolfed another pancake. "Looks like it. Anyways, somebody beat us to them water claims. Means if we file in the pozo now, we gotta file dry."

Gloom settled over the camp.

Ogallala broke the silence to ask, "What became of the vaqueros?"

"They went back to the hacienda," Slim said. "Sweetwater's usin' 'em to get that brandin' chute started. He's honin' to get the Circle Dot on these critturs."

Rosy punched a ramrod through the barrel of his cherished Winchester. "What I'm honin' for," he muttered, "is to get the Circle Dot on Montoya."

"You'll have to smoke him into the open first," Ogallala advised. "A slick hombre, that feller is. Allers works under cover."

"Who's that comin'?" exclaimed Slim.

They saw an old graybeard riding down the mountain on a mule. "Shapes up like that broken-down prospector, Jason Somebody," Rosy said.

"Johnnie claims he's all right," Ogallala reminded them.

The ragged oldster rode up to the fire and squinted at them from rheumy eyes. The plug cut he was chewing caused yellow streaks to trickle down his beard. Balanced across the mule was a double-barreled shotgun.

"Any grief around here yet, gents?" he wheezed.

"Nope, pardner," Ogallala answered. "'Ceptin' that Johnnie Cameron got drygulched and somebody beat us to them claims. I mean we ain't had any rustler trouble yet."

A slyness came into Jason's eyes. "The way I figger it," he cackled, "them rustlers has cleared plumb outa the country. Betcher they won't be back fer a coupla weeks."

"Howcome?" Slim asked.

"'Cause they allers hightail ever time they think a posse's comin'," Jason explained.

"Generally they hide out in the Navajo country for a while, then they come slippin' back to their old ha'nts in the pozo."

"You mean a posse just rode in lookin' fer 'em?"

El Viejo stroked his beard and chuckled. "Nope, gents. But I made 'em think one was comin'. It was like this: when I found out you boys aimed to ride into the pozo and file claims yestiddy mornin', I figgered that gang might try a cow steal while you was gone. Then I got an idear. I remembered seein' a smoke signal half a dozen times in the last few years. Sometimes it was white smoke. Sometimes it was black smoke. Whenever it was white smoke, I allers seen them outlaws a-comin'. Whenever it was black smoke, I'd see a posse show up only to find the outlaws had faded away."

The Circle Dot men stared. "Well, whatta yuh know about that?" Slim exclaimed.

Rosy said:

"Looks like somebody on the east rimrock tips 'em when to come and when to run."

"It sure looks that way," Jason grinned. "So on account of you fellahs ridin' in to file yestiddy, I thought it was a good time to start 'em runnin'. So I made a black smoke fire on the rimrock. Like as not, they thought it meant a posse was comin' and so they hightailed to points west."

Rosy slapped the old man on the back. "You're

a smart hombre, Jason. Looks like that drygulcher gave Ogallala the straight goods after all. Only it didn't pan out."

Ogallala agreed with him. More than likely a raid on the Herefords had been planned, but had been circumvented by Jason's column of black smoke.

"They'll be mad as hornets, Jason," he warned, "soon as they find out it was a false alarm. They'll git together with Montoya one of these days. When Montoya says he didn't throw any smoke signal, they'll figger it was you done it."

"That's right, Jason," Slim agreed soberly. "So they'll put your name on a bullet and lay for you."

Jason spat on his hands. "Let 'em lay!" he challenged. "I got a shotgun with two barrels in it." Shouldering the shotgun with a cocky grimness, he rode back toward the timbered mountain.

CHAPTER 19

THROUGH THE OPEN window Johnnie could smell burning hair. From the corrals came the yelling of men and the bawling of cattle. The chute was finished and five hundred and ten young Herefords were being branded Circle Dot.

Josefita sat beside Johnnie's bed and was reading aloud to him. The book was Prescott's Conquest of Mexico and she read from it in Spanish. Johnnie could not understand every word. But he liked to see her sitting there and hear the soft music of her voice.

She finished a chapter and looked over the book reproachfully. "I think you have paid no attention, Señor Johnnie. You think only of those cattle out there."

"No such thing, Josephine. I heard every word. Great guys, those old caballeros."

"I should not be here, señor. Only Don Eusebio says you must be amused." Don Eusebio was the doctor from Bernalillo.

"I told him you make a top hand at nursing," Johnnie said.

"Your wound does not pain you today, señor?"

"Not when you're around. It burns like the devil, though, every time you leave the room."

A flush mounted her face. "When you are well I shall be angry with you, señor."

The old manservant, Miguel came in with a bowl of broth. Since Johnnie must still lie flat on his back, Josefita fed him with a spoon.

"Tell me about your life here, Josephine. Where did you go to school?"

"When I was very little," she said, "Papacito sent me to a convent in Santa Fe. After that I went for three winters to Mexico City. Have you even been there?"

"Never got below El Paso."

"Where else have you been, señor?"

"I was raised on a Missouri farm," he told her. "Went to a little red schoolhouse on the hill. Lost all my folks when I was fifteen. Been knockin' around ever since, mostly between Texas and Dakota. I had to do most anything for my board and keep. Ogallala found me sweepin' out a Wichita barroom."

"You have been with Señor Ogallala ever since?"

Johnnie nodded. "He taught me how to skin buffalo. Then we threw in with Slim and Rosy and Sweetwater Smith. Summers we been hazin' cattle and winters we been huntin' buffalo. Time we're settling down on a rancho, don't you think?"

An odd smile lighted her face. "I am interested in the buffalo, señor. Did you ever see my robe?

The one I was found in when I was very small?"

Miguel came in for the tray and Josefita said: "You will bring the robe from my cedar chest, Miguel."

Miguel brought in a very old buffalo hide. It was lined with silk and had been well preserved from moths. The hair on the top side was soft and shaggy.

"Don Ygnacio told me about it," Johnnie said.

"Papacito has been so good to me, señor. I love him very much."

Johnnie's hand stroked the smoothness of the robe. "Ogallala and Slim and Rosy and Sweetwater and I shipped thousands of these hides into Kaycee," he murmured. "They weren't fixed up nice and pretty like this 'n, though. Look, Josephine. Would you mind leavin' this robe here till the boys drop in? They'll be wantin' to see me after brandin' hours. This buffalo skin oughta make 'em feel right at home."

"But of course, señor."

She draped the robe over the foot of the bed. "If it is cold tonight, I shall have Miguel put it over you."

Johnnie pretended to shiver.

"I'm practically freezin' right now, nurse. Tuck me in yourself."

"You are such a baby, Señor Johnnie." She laughed as she spread the robe over him. "And now you must go to sleep."

When she was gone he lay snugly under the silk-lined hide and listened to the bawling of fresh-branded cattle. The branders were knocking off, he knew, for the sun had set and the chill of an October twilight breezed crisply through the window.

Johnnie tried to pin his mind on those filings over in the pozo. How could they file on land already taken? What could they do with these heifers now that they were branded? Trading on the Sandoval hospitality couldn't go on forever.

Miguel came quietly in. "Señor Slim is here to see you, Don Juan."

"Tell him to wipe off his boots," Johnnie said. He could see Slim just beyond Miguel. As the tall, thin cowboy came in, Johnnie demanded, "What's the idea bustin' in here smellin' like a corral?"

Slim cocked his eye at a pink cushion, then at a robe which covered Johnnie. "Sure looks like a lady's boudoir," he said.

They exchanged banters until Miguel withdrew. Then Johnnie lowered his voice to inquire, "Where's Ogallala?"

"He just rid off to Santa Fe," Slim said. "He's got to get shed o' that money he took off the drygulcher. Not wantin' to be held there for questions, Ogallala says he'll just wrap it up and toss it through the sheriff's window."

"How's the brandin' comin' along?"

"Take us another day to get done."

"You'll be short-handed without Ogallala, won't you?"

"Nope. Because old man Jason Holt's gonna squeeze on the pinch bar in Ogallala's place tomorrow. He just rid down from that cave in a rimrock he calls home."

"Roll me a cigarette, Slim."

Slim rolled one and put it between Johnnie's lips.

"You know I can't figger that old coot out, Johnnie. I mean Jason. He never does much prospectin', far as I can see. His tools are all rusty. Just lives like an old hermit up there, and keeps nosin' around."

"I noticed that myself, Slim." Johnnie puffed thoughtfully for a minute. "He's takin' a big chance up there, Slim. Wonder to me is those pozo ladrones haven't shot him fulla holes long ago."

"When they come back and find out about that false alarm smoke fire," Slim predicted, "they'll blow him plumb outa the pozo."

"I'd like to talk to him," Johnnie said. "Send him in here, Slim."

Miguel came in and lighted an oil lamp. And shortly after Slim withdrew, old Jason Holt shuffled into the room.

His eyes fastened on the robe which covered

Johnnie. The intensity of his gaze made Johnnie ask, "Ever see it before, Jason?"

"See what?"

"This buffalo hide."

"Sure I seen it before. It's Josefita's. She showed it to me once."

"Sit down, Jason. A bee's been buzzin' in my head, and I want you to listen to it buzz."

The old prospector sat down a bit nervously. "Can't quite savvy what you're gettin' at, young feller."

"Lots o' things I don't savvy either, Jason. For instance, why would a prospector stay six or eight years under the pozo rimrock, without makin' any strike, when there's plenty o' better minin' country further on? Why doesn't anyone ever see him with a muleload o' samples? Why are his picks and drills always rusty, which they wouldn't be if he used 'em regular?"

"Reckon that's my business, ain't it?" Jason retorted.

"The way you figured out that smoke signal business," Johnnie went on, "you've been spyin' on goings on between Montoya and the pozo gang a long time. Why? Ain't it because you want to see Montoya convicted before wedding bells ring in December?"

"Sure I do," Jason admitted. "And so do you. We shook hands on that, didn't we? We sure got

223

to git the deadwood on that hombre afore the fifth o' December."

"You mean December twelfth," Johnnie corrected.

"Sure," the old man amended hurriedly. "I mean the twelfth."

Johnnie smiled wisely. "You gave yourself away, Jason. Might as well come clean, now. I won't tell anybody."

"Whatta yuh mean?"

"How come you know Josefita's real birthday?"

The question confused Jason. His eyes evaded Johnnie's. "I only know what folks around here told me," he mumbled.

Then he arose nervously and shuffled toward the door.

Johnnie called him back. "Lay your cards face up, Jason. Even Don Ygnacio doesn't know the girl's birthday. He had to guess at it and he missed it a week. That slip you made just now about December fifth tipped your hand, Jason. It ties up with other things, too. Why you've lived like a coyote in the hills for six years just to be where you can see Josefita once in a while. Why you're standing pat there in spite of hell, high water and horsethieves. Why you've put in your time tryin' to get the deadwood on Montoya."

Something like panic came into Jason's eyes. "It ain't right fer her to know it," he pled huskily.

"You ain't gonna do no talkin' about it, air yuh?"

"Not unless you say so, Jason. But let's you an' me work together. We both want the same thing, don't we?"

"Reckon we do," the old man admitted. "I'd feel a heap better if it was you she was a-marryin', stead o' Montoya."

He sat down on the edge of the bed and whispered: "Reckon you guessed it, kid. I'm her grandpa."

"Tell me about it," Johnnie begged.

"I made the run to Californy, like I told you," Jason confided. "But I didn't hit pay there. I'd ambled back as fer as Colorado when word come from my married darter in Illinoy. That was in '56. The letter said a baby girl had been born to her on December fifth of the year before."

"Did you go back there?" Johnnie asked.

"Nope. I was busted, and sort o' down and out like I am now. But I'd just shot a prime buffalo, so I had the hide cured and I sent it to the folks in Illinoy. Didn't hear nothin' more from 'em. I kept knockin' around the continental divide, chippin' rock off ledges. Finally word come from old neighbors that my darter and son-in-law and baby girl had gone west to take up land in the fall o' '56, and hadn't been heard of since.

"That skeered me. But I couldn't get no track of 'em. It was in '66 than I hearn a yarn about a girl on a New Mex ranch what had been picked up as a baby on the Santa Fe trail, after Injuns had kilt off her folks. They said this baby was wrapped in a buffalo robe. So I came down this way to check up. Don Ygnacio put me up here, just like he would any other old tramp prospector. Josefita was goin' on twelve then. One look and I knew she was my granddarter."

"You mean she looks like her mother did?"

"Just enough so I could be sure of it," the old man said. "Then I hung around till I got a look at this buffalo robe." A gnarled hand reached out to stroke the robe which covered Johnnie. "I'd had to shoot that bull twice, once in the right shoulder and once in the left rump. If you'll feel around on yer bedcover, young feller, you'll find bullet holes right in them same two places."

"I'll take your word for it, Jason. But why didn't you tell 'em who you are?"

Jason Holt looked down at his shabbiness. "What good would come of it?" he protested. "She was in a fine family that was bringin' her up like a lady. What was the use o' saddlin' her with an old packrat like me? She's eddicated, and I ain't. Nope, young feller, I'd a heap ruther she'd never know."

"I won't tell her," Johnnie promised.

There came a knock at the door and Josefita's voice called:

"Are you awake, Señor Johnnie?"

"Come in."

"You have a visitor," the girl announced. She was followed into the room by Ramon Montoya.

Montoya smiled at Johnnie and ignored old Jason Holt. "I am distressed to hear of your trouble, señor," he murmured.

The nerve of him! Johnnie made himself remember that Josefita was present, and that he was her guest. "Thanks," he said.

"Please call on me, señor, if I may be of service."

He made a handsome figure standing there. Josefita's eyes met Johnnie's and seemed to say, "You see, is he not a fine caballero?"

"Josephine's takin' good care of me," Johnnie said. "In a few days I'll be up and fightin'."

Montoya laughed easily and one of his small slender hands flicked ash from his cigarrita. "Why should there be any fighting, señor?"

"If they's any fightin'," old Jason broke in, "let's hope it'll be in the open. I sure don't like this here drygulchin' style some folks go in fer."

Johnnie saw Montoya stiffen. The man's eyes flickered toward Jason.

Through a silent minute of challenge Josefita glanced in puzzlement from Johnnie to Jason to Don Ramon. These three seemed to hide a secret from her. Johnnie broke the tension by asking, "Did you show Don Ramon that sketch I made, Josephine?"

227

It was a ruse to get her out of the room for a few minutes.

"I want him to see it," Josefita said. "If you will excuse me, I will get it now." She went out.

"What Jason means," Johnnie said levelly to Montoya, "is that these drygulchers don't usually get away with it. Take Frenchie, for instance. He got branded Circle Dot between the eyes."

The announcement jolted Montoya. Johnnie followed up in rapid fire order: "That's what you been wonderin' about, ain't it? You been holin' up in Santa Fe, sittin' tight on an alibi, and waitin' fer Frenchie to show up and report. No use your waitin' any longer. Frenchie's dead. On him was exactly half the money stolen at the Calaveras murder. Know where the other half is, Montoya?"

Montoya had recovered his poise and his eyes defied Johnnie. "If you are trying to insult me, you are very stupid, señor."

Josefita came in with a pencil portrait of herself—a pleasing likeness which Johnnie had sketched while she sat by his bedside.

"*Mira*, Ramon!" Josefita held the sketch before Montoya. "Is it not like me? With only a few quick lines he has drawn this. He has such excellent talent; is it not so, Ramon?"

Montoya agreed graciously. "Señor Elkins has told me you sketch cows and horses, señor. I did not know you draw ladies."

"He can put all things on paper, Ramon," exclaimed Josefita. "He has made one of Papacito, and Miguel, and all the household." She turned impulsively to Johnnie. "Will you not sketch also Don Ramon, Señor Cameron?"

"Sure," Johnnie agreed. He reached for the sketch pad and a pencil.

Deftly he began sketching Montoya. With less than fifty quick lines he made a recognizable likeness.

He exposed it to Josefita and she was delighted.

"It's not quite finished," Johnnie said. He took it back from her and his pencil stroked a few more lines. This time he handed it to Montoya.

Montoya saw a likeness of himself—except that a mask covered the upper half of his face. Also a noose was drawn tightly around the subject's neck, the rope reaching up to some unseen support above.

Only Ramon Montoya saw this. His face flamed. He could not show it to Josefita.

"You are very clever, señor," he said.

CHAPTER 20

MONTOYA'S RETREAT was hurried but not ungraceful. Josefita urged him to stay for comida and so did Don Ygnacio.

"But you have only just arrived!" the hacendado protested.

"Affairs await my attention at the mine," Montoya said. "I stopped by only to pay my compliments to you and to Josefita."

Don Ygnacio drank a parting glass of wine with him. "Your health, Don Ramon. It pleases me that you will soon be one of my family."

"I am counting the hours, Don Ygnacio."

Outside, Montoya swung to the saddle of his calico pony. He loped off into the dark, and only then did he permit himself the luxury of a curse. He tore a sketch into tiny bits and let the pieces fly in the wind. That gringo Cameron! He was more dangerous than ever now. Dangerous because he lay abed wounded in the house of Sandoval, and therefore would draw sympathy from Josefita. Could the fellow win her confidence? Or Don Ygnacio's?

Would they believe when he told what he knew about ladrones? Many times Montoya had assured himself that they'd never take the word of a strange cowboy against his own. But now he wasn't so sure. Josefita was sitting by him as a nurse, and he was drawing pictures of her pretty face.

But what most alarmed Montoya now was the prospect of facing two accusers instead of only one. True, the second one was just an old vagabond prospector. El Viejo, they called him. Sight of the old man seated confidentially at Cameron's bedside had startled Montoya.

Until now, he had never considered Jason worth a worry. Yet after all the man was a human witness. For six years he had been pottering around the pozo rimrocks, living like a packrat there. Sometimes in the rigors of winter the Sandoval hacienda had given him shelter. The fact now for the first time disturbed Montoya. Josefita, he remembered, had always seemed rather fond of the old man.

Evidently Jason had joined forces with Cameron to discredit Ramon Montoya.

So they must *both* be put out of the way. It was a thing he must do himself. Montoya knew he must not risk any more bungling. Three times he had placed faith in agents who had failed. Montoya swore bitterly as he recalled the trap set in a deserted house on Agua Frio Road. Cameron had shot his way out of that trap. Next Montoya had put his faith in Pancho Archuleta. But sabotage on Cameron's rifle had availed nothing. And finally Frenchie Welsh, sniping from ambush, had placed his bullet an inch too high.

"I must attend to it myself," Montoya vowed. He was still barely a mile from the hacienda and loping toward the mountains.

All at once he saw bovine shapes about him. Cattle were grazing there—fat, blocky heifers with white faces and short, down-curved horns. Cameron's cattle, these were. They had just been released from the branding corral and had scattered out over nearby grass.

Riding through them, Montoya saw a big brown circle on the ribs of each cow. In the center of the circle was a dot. Circle Dot. Like the exploded cap of a centerfire cartridge! Johnnie's warning recurred sharply to Montoya: "These drygulchers don't usually get away with it. Take Frenchie. He got branded Circle Dot between the eyes."

The threat echoed through Montoya's brain, burning there like a hot bullet as he rode on to his mesa mine.

It was past midnight when he arrived home. The place was dark and silent, the few miners who still worked the shafts on shares having retired long ago. Montoya put up his horse. He was turning into his house when a figure startled him by stepping out of the shadows.

"Don Ramon?" The voice was nervous and apologetic.

"What are you doing here, Pancho?" It was Pancho Archuleta, one time clerk in a Taos store and now supposed to be a pot-cleaner for Fadeaway Fallon.

"Has the posse gone away, señor?" whispered Pancho. "Señor Fallon has sent me to find out."

Montoya gave a hard stare. "What posse?"

"The one you announced with the signal smoke, señor."

"I didn't make any signal, you fool. And there has not been any posse."

"But we saw the smoke at the place you always make it, Don Ramon! It came just as we were riding to raid cattle on the Puerco."

To Montoya it was all bitterly clear now. "Tell Fallon he has been very stupid. I have been in Santa Fe all this time. If there has been a smoke signal, then that old crow-bait of a prospector must have made it."

"But why, señor?" Pancho was completely confused.

Montoya wasn't telling. He knew that old Jason had tricked the outlaws into flight.

"Ride west and find Fallon," Montoya snapped. "Tell him to bring his men back to the pozo right away."

"I am not sure he will come, señor," Pancho murmured. "He says he is tired of running at every black smoke. He talks now of making raids in Utah where there is much Mormon wool."

Montoya wasn't ready to be deserted by Fallon. He needed the pozo outlaws to match guns with Cameron's crowd. And so he searched his wits for an argument to induce the return of his allies.

"Attend carefully, Pancho," he said finally. "You ask why did el Viejo make a signal fire to send our friends in flight from the pozo. I will tell you why. It is because el Viejo has at last located the lost wagonload of gold coin from Mexico. For six years he has searched the pozo for it, as Señor Fallon has so often suspected."

Pancho's eyes widened. "Si, Don Ramon. I have heard this tale. I did not know if it is true."

"I never put much faith in it myself, Pancho. But now I know it is true. A carreta of gold was buried there one time by men who were being chased by sheriffs. And at last it has been found by el Viejo, who has pretended to be only a prospector with a pick and a mule. He was afraid Fallon's men would see him packing it out, so he frightened them away with smoke."

"Carramba!" Pancho gasped. "Is it much money?"

"A king's ransom, Pancho. I have found a few of the old gold coins at Jason's cave under the rimrock, so I know he has found all of it. But there will be many mule-loads for him to pack out. He knows that I watch him. But I cannot watch all the time. I need the eyes of Fallon and his men."

"I will tell them to come back quick," Pancho promised.

"Remind him that five hundred fat heifers are waiting for him here, too."

"It is better than wool of the Mormons," Pancho agreed.

"One other thing, Pancho. Tell Fallon that five peons who filed homesteads in the pozo will soon begin building cabins on them. Tell him not to interfere. These peons are only names which I use to gain control of the pozo myself."

"Señor Fallon will understand that. It will be as you say, Don Ramon."

Pancho slipped into the shadows and Montoya heard him ride away.

Montoya himself went to bed. His errand here was to keep an appointment at eight in the morning.

The man expected arrived promptly on schedule. Montoya received him at breakfast. "Buenos dias, Señor Lopez. Our business is a small matter which we shall accomplish with dispatch."

"I shall be glad to serve you, Don Ramon," answered Lopez, who knew Montoya only as an honorable caballero.

"You contract for building houses, do you not, Señor Lopez?"

"Si, Señor. In Bernalillo and Albuquerque I have made more than a hundred houses. I have much men and tools."

"Then come with me." Montoya led him outside to a row of adobe cabins which for years had served as workmen's quarters at this mine. They were now vacant and in poor repair.

"Five men have filed homesteads in the pozo hondo," Montoya explained. "To receive a patent from the government, each man must build a cabin on his land. So they have come to me and bought five of these mine cabins. They have also left with me money to have them moved to the claims in the pozo. That will be your work, Señor Lopez."

"But adobe bricks are too heavy, Don Ramon, to be packed far by a mule. It will be easier to make adobes directly at the claims."

"*Seguro*," agreed Montoya. "So you need merely wreck five of these mine cabins. Take the door and window frames, the roof poles, the furniture and everything except the mud bricks. With many men you can make new bricks in the pozo. The money left with me is liberal, Señor Lopez."

Lopez agreed to begin at once and rush the work. After receiving specific instructions and a down payment, he rode away to assemble men and equipment.

Ramon Montoya returned his mind to the hazards of Johnnie Cameron and Jason Holt. Jason, he knew, was at the Sandoval corrals today helping to brand cattle. Therefore the old man's rimrock camp would be deserted. Montoya decided to pay it a visit.

He saddled a horse and rode a few miles along the rimrock to a crevice which descended to Jason's camp. The niche was so steep that he had to lead his horse down. Then he tethered it in aspens and moved along the cliff's face to a cave with an old canvas hanging over it. On the ground outside were rusty tools, sacks of rock samples and battered camp equipment. Looking at it, the sensitive nostrils of Montoya sniffed in contempt. Why should he worry about such a derelict old tramp as el Viejo?

He pulled back the curtain and stepped into the cave. Upended on an empty powder keg stood a half used candle. The intruder lighted it. Light revealed a pile of spruce boughs covered with dry grass. On the grass were spread a pair of worn blankets. The old man's bed! Again Montoya sniffed.

Wires from the cave roof supported a shelf of aspen boughs. On this Jason Holt had stored a few provisions and whatever else of his disreputable estate that needed to be kept out of reach from packrats. Montoya's eye fell upon a small tin box.

He opened it. Inside he found matches, a twist of tobacco and two ancient, yellow envelopes.

Montoya examined the letters curiously. They were addressed in a round, womanish hand to

Jason Holt at Denver. Both of them had been posted at Springfield, Illinois, and had been carried west by Pony Express.

Montoya withdrew the enclosures and took them to better light. The first letter, dated December, 1855, began:

My dear father:
  You will be happy to learn that I have a little girl. She was born on the fifth of this month and we are very proud—

Skimming through it, Montoya could see nothing in the letter which need concern himself. It was signed: "Your Devoted Daughter, Ida."

The second letter was dated July, 1856, and began:

My dear father:
  Thank you for the fine buffalo robe you sent us. Your little granddaughter is lying snugly on it right now, playing with her tiny pink toes and perhaps wondering why Ed and I are so excited. It is because Ed has just decided we will go west and take up land. We do not know where, but will let you know as soon as we are located.

Montoya reread this and it brought to him a conviction of the truth. Josefita Sandoval, he knew, had been born close to the end of the year 1855. Other details came vividly to Montoya.

The buffalo robe; ill-fated homeseekers on the Santa Fe trail.

Unquestionably old Jason Holt was grandfather to Josefita. These letters proved it. Then why hadn't the old man made his identity known to the Sandovals?

Perhaps because for shame of his poverty and social rating, as weighed against refinements at the Sandovals'. At any rate he hadn't told them. Otherwise Josefita would have confided the relation to her fiancé.

Nevertheless, the old man might tell them at any minute or hour. The instant he did so, he would become a force in Josefita's life. His voice would command respect, then, when he used it to denounce Montoya. To that voice could be added Johnnie Cameron's—and the testimony of these long-treasured letters.

The thought made Montoya take up a lighted candle. With it he ignited the letters and burned them to an ash.

Proof was destroyed now. Or was it? Could el Viejo still, if he chose, convince them he was a kinsman of Josefita's?

In any case he was dangerous. Even more dangerous, Montoya decided, than Johnnie Cameron.

Emerging from the cave, Montoya went to his

horse and took a rifle from the saddle. With it he returned to the cold camp of Jason Holt and sat down to wait. This hazard was something to which he must attend personally. He would wait here until el Viejo came home. Today, perhaps. If not today, then tomorrow. Time did not matter, so long as he made sure of silencing el Viejo Jason.

CHAPTER 21

NOT THAT DAY, BUT the next, Jason Holt rode home after helping them brand at the Sandovals'. Usually he rode up the Puerco and through the gap giving into the pozo, and then skirted the timbered slopes of the pozo to his own camp.

But this time a canny caution made the old man choose a more open route. A lifetime in the mountains had given him a sixth sense for danger. He knew that danger can be checkmated only when one sees it from afar.

So el Viejo rode his mule first to the east mesa and followed a rimrock north from there. That way he could see far out over the grant, until he had passed it, and then he could see far out over the basin of the pozo hondo.

By midmorning he sighted the old Montoya silver mine on the tableland ahead. Jason redoubled his caution. He stopped the mule while he made sure his shotgun was loaded. Before advancing, his eyes searched all horizons. For years Jason Holt had scouted through the Indian country with just such caution.

This morning he saw nothing. He heard nothing. And yet some uncanny sense kept forewarning him of danger. He was opposite his own camp now. It was just below the rimrock here. He need only lead his mule down a narrow niche of the cliff and be home.

Instead, the old man dismounted. Soundless in his moccasins, he moved afoot to an overhanging ledge at the rim. Lying flat there, he could look down and at an angle along the cliff's face to his camp. More than once before he had spied from this lookout to make sure that his camp hadn't been preempted.

This time he saw Ramon Montoya. Montoya had a rifle and was seated in a pose of long, patient waiting. A look at his face left no doubt of his errand here. Its purpose was murder. Jason was sure of it instantly, and a smile creased the ruggedness of his cheek.

He drew back and considered what to do. Temptation whispered that he himself could settle everything with the shotgun. Montoya was at his mercy, down there. One squeeze on a trigger and there'd be no wedding in December. And why not? Montoya was a killer and a thief.

But Jason Holt couldn't do it. He wasn't made that way. Potting Montoya in cold blood wasn't the way to save Josefita.

He thought of another plan. A bold and sure plan. The idea chilled old Jason, and he flinched from it. Maybe it could be avoided. He must consult with Johnnie Cameron.

Miguel had just brought broth to Johnnie that evening when Josefita came in.

"El Viejo is back again, señor. He wishes to see you."

Johnnie wondered why Jason should return so soon from the mountains. He had protested vigorously against the old man's going there. Now he felt relief at his quick return. Also there must be some important reason.

"Send him in please, Josephine."

Jason Holt shuffled in. His weathered old face, above the beard, wore a pinched and haggard grimness as Johnnie greeted him. They waited until both Josefita and Miguel withdrew.

Then Jason announced:

"Found a drygulcher waitin' at my camp. He had the hammer all cocked ready to burn one through me."

"One of the pozo gang, huh?" Johnnie questioned.

"Nope. It was Montoya hisself. Looks like he figgers to tend to his own killin' from now on."

"All right. Stay away from that cave, Jason. Stick close to Slim and Rosy and Ogallala. They're campin' over on the Puerco with the cows."

Jason was stubborn. "Nope. Reckon you an' me got to make a showdown on this, young feller. It's us that's the most concerned about Josefita, I figger. Why don't we call Don Ygnacio in here and spill all the dirt we know?"

"He wouldn't believe us," Johnnie protested.

"Won't hurt to try, will it? If it don't work, I got somethin' else up my sleeve, Johnnie."

Johnnie frowned. "Maybe you're right, Jason. But it's daggoned nervy of us, to tell tales on Montoya right in his fiancée's house. It'll sure play whaley with our welcome here."

"It's our duty," Jason persisted.

"All right. Go ask Don Ygnacio please to come in. Let me do the talkin'. You just sit by and back me up."

Jason went out. In a few minutes he returned with Don Ygnacio Sandoval. The hacendado came in cheerily, a cigarrita between his lips, his goatee combed nattily to a spike point.

"I hope you feel better, señor," he murmured.

"I'll be outa here in a few days," Johnnie promised. "Right now I got to get something off my chest."

The grimness of his eyes brought a stare from Don Ygnacio. "If there is any way I can serve you, Señor Cameron, please tell me."

"I should have told you before," Johnnie admitted. Embarrassment made his cheeks red. Then he plunged on doggedly:

"You remember the time we were held up in Cimarron Canyon? One man was masked and he got away. Later I had a run-in with that same fellow at Taos. He outsmarted me there. I didn't report him to either you or the sheriff, because I wanted to round up better proof."

Don Ygnacio looked both surprised and hurt. "But you should confide in me, Señor Cameron, even if you had no proof. You are my good friend, are you not?"

"Wait till you hear the rest of it. In Santa Fe I tangled with this gent again. He's a smooth customer. He knew I was on to him, account of a glove I'd picked up in Cimarron Canyon, so he tried to have me knocked off. He baited me into a trap where he had three killers spotted, but I shot my way out of it."

The hacendado's eyes were getting rounder and rounder. "Who was the man, señor?"

Johnnie ignored the question. "This same fellah kept right after me. He even planted a spy here at your hacienda. First night I was here, the spy jimmied my rifle. Next day I rode into the pozo and who should I meet there but our friend the ladron of Cimarron Canyon! He called in four gunmen to help him blast me down, but I had plenty of luck and got away."

Sandoval leaned forward, his attention breathless, and it was clear he did not yet guess to whom Johnnie referred. "You should have told me all these things, señor."

"I'm telling you now," Johnnie said, "because we can't stand off a showdown any longer. Which brings me to why I'm here with a hole through me. This ladron we're talkin' about hired a gunman named Frenchie to drygulch me in the gap. He and Frenchie had just murdered a gambling house woman in Santa Fe to steal a pot o' money. When Ogallala caught up with Frenchie, exactly half the money was on him. But the number one killer got away, as usual. Do you want to know where he is right now?"

"Where?" Sandoval asked tensely.

"He's squattin' up at Jason Holt's camp, waitin' there to kill Jason when he goes home. Why? Because Jason knows everything I've just told you is true."

"It sure is," Jason chimed in vigorously. "He's a skunk-livered killer, that feller is. And don't you never doubt it."

"But who is this man?" demanded the hacendado. "Do I know him?"

"His name," Johnnie said, "is Ramon Montoya."

Don Ygnacio whipped to his feet. The blood drained from his face. All the warmth left there.

"Have you lost all reason, sir?" he inquired icily.

"I was afraid you wouldn't believe me," Johnnie admitted wearily.

"Of course I do not believe you, señor. It has no sense. Don Ramon will soon be of my own family. His children will be my children. He is a fine—"

"Caballero," Johnnie supplied. "Sure. Well, I figured it was my duty to tell you. There's no proof except my own word and Jason's here."

"Without proof, you should not insult a fine

caballero like Don Ramon." The hacendado was growing stiffer and more incensed every minute. "You are my guest, señor. While you are in my house, you will receive every courtesy. Buenas noches, señor."

He turned on his spurred heels and marched from the room.

Johnnie exchanged forlorn looks with Jason. "We sure wore out our welcome," Johnnie said. "Means as soon as I can sit a saddle, I gotta ride off this rancho for good."

Jason took a thoughtful chew. "In one thing you were wrong, young feller. You told him we ain't got any proof. Well, maybe you ain't got any. But I have. I'm gonna flash it on him right now."

"What is it, Jason?"

"Never you mind." The old man's eyes grew sly and stubborn. "You jest ease up yer blood pressure while I go spread this proof face up in front of Ygnacio."

He went out and found Don Ygnacio in the sala. The hacendado was pacing in front of a fire and biting hard on a cigarrita. He turned coldly as the old prospector appeared by him. "I do not wish to hear more, señor."

"We sure hate to see yuh get riled," Jason said humbly. "On the other hand, yuh got to admit it's a sight better to find out the truth afore it's too late. If Josefita marries that skunk-livered—"

"You will please stop insulting Don Ramon," Sandoval broke in angrily.

"Aw right, I won't mention no names," Jason agreed. "Allasame, I got absolute proof if you feel like takin' a look. It's eye-witness proof, and you'll be the witness. I mean you can just take one look and you'll know everything Johnnie said is true."

Sandoval's chin was still high. His stare was still icily indignant. Yet the word "proof" had impressed him. He inquired stiffly, "Where is this proof, señor?"

"On the mesa," Jason said. "You jest fork a braunk and ride up there. You can take one look and then thank me fer savin' you a mess o' grief."

"What proof is on the mesa?"

"I'll show yuh when yuh git there. I'll amble along ahead now. Two hours after sunup tomorrow mornin', I'll be at that little lake midway of the upper mesa. Meet me there if you're interested in proof."

Jason turned and passed out through the six-foot-long tunnel which made a door for the house. He mounted his mule, riding again toward the mesas. The mule was tired and Jason let him go at a walk.

The hacendado might or might not follow. Jason's guess was that he would follow. However indignant the man might be, he would also be humanly curious. "He'll show up fer proof,"

Jason muttered, "even if it's only proof I'm a locoed liar."

Two hours after sunup he was waiting at a tiny lake on the upper mesa. Below him to the west lay the pozo hondo. Less than half a mile away, and directly under the rimrock, was his own cave camp. Due north at a distance up the mesa loomed the buildings and derricks of Montoya's mine.

Jason's eyes were fixed on a trail leading toward him from the south. He saw a horseman approaching there. Ygnacio Sandoval. The hacendado came up with reproof in his eyes. His thin face was haggard and testified to a sleepless night.

"You have said you will show me proof, señor," he said stiffly.

"It's waitin' fer yuh," Jason said. "Better leave yer braunk here and we'll go on afoot."

Don Ygnacio dismounted. Leaving his horse beside Jason's mule, he followed the old man to the mesa rimrock.

"Keep quiet," Jason cautioned. "If we make any racket, we might skeer this proof away."

A flat overhanging rock lay before them. "My camp's right below it," Jason whispered. "Peek over the edge and get a look."

Advancing, Don Ygnacio peered over the rim. He saw Jason's camp down there. On a stump directly in front of a cave sat Ramon Montoya.

Montoya had a rifle across his knees and wore a holstered forty-five. Because of the man's sombrero, Ygnacio Sandoval could not see his face. But the pose suggested that Montoya had resigned himself to a long, patient vigil. On the ground about him lay the stubs of innumerable cigarritas.

Sandoval drew back and rejoined Jason. "You have a visitor," he admitted. "He is a gentleman of honor. I am humiliated to spy on him, señor."

Jason's smile was grim. "Reckon you don't believe he's waitin' there to kill me?"

"I know that he is not," Sandoval asserted with complete confidence. "He is there only in friendship. Perhaps he has some business with you—"

"Sure he has. His business is murder. Ain't no other way to convince you—'ceptin' to let him go through with it. Pick yourself a gallery seat. And I'm leavin' my shotgun right here." Jason laid it on the ground. "Pick yourself a gallery seat and watch him blast me down."

The idea more than shocked Sandoval. "But it only proves you are crazy, Viejo. Don Ramon will not harm you. He would not—"

"Then I'm perfectly safe," Jason cut in. "You ain't takin' any risk to watch what happens."

"Nothing will happen," Sandoval insisted.

He was so certain of it that he could not with consistency protest against the test. To protest would be to confess a lack of confidence in the integrity of Montoya.

"If nothing happens," Jason said, "then it proves I'm a locoed liar. But if it *does* happen, then you ain't likely to keep on nominatin' him fer an A-one caballero."

Jason turned abruptly and walked to his mule. Unarmed, he mounted and rode toward the crevice which made a trail down under the rimrock. He could see Ygnacio Sandoval at the lookout post a little way back from the rim. However much it might outrage his dignity, the hacendado was sure to observe what transpired below.

Jason spurred his mule into the crevice, causing a clatter from sliding stones. The descent was almost sheer, but the mule was used to it. Man and beast arrived at the foot of the crevice and emerged on a narrow sideslope between the cliff and the aspens. A hundred yards along the face of the cliff was Jason's camp.

Jason was now in plain sight of Montoya. He saw Montoya stand up, rifle in hands. Motive of his presence here darkened the man's face. Jason even saw the thumb of a narrow hand snap back the rifle's hammer.

To advance was suicide. But Jason rode boldly on. "Howdy, mister," he called. "Been waitin' here long?"

He was fifty yards away. Now he was forty,

now thirty. The bullet would come within a split minute now. No help for it! No other way to save Josefita. Only by exposing murder to the naked eyesight, like this, could he read aloud to Sandoval the clear titles of a felon. Sandoval would see and he must then know the truth. He would ride humbly home and apologize to Johnnie Cameron.

It was a hard trail to ride, for Jason. It made his face ashen above the tangle of his beard. For years he had used his wit to cheat death. Now he used it to tempt death. But why should it matter? He was old and his race was run. He was insuring Josefita against marriage to a ladron. And what finer heritage could he leave her?

The midmorning sun, shining aslant, threw shadows of the rimrocked cliff on the aspen slope below. One shadow took a peculiar shape. It was the shape of a small beehived cone with a wide flange.

It was the shape of a caballero's sombrero.

Montoya saw that shadow and it made him alert. It whispered to him of a witness peering over the rimrock. Montoya had no faint idea who that witness could be. He assumed one of the cowboy *compañeros* of Johnnie Cameron.

So Montoya did not raise his rifle. His voice went silkily to Jason: "Buenos dias, Viejo. A long time I have waited for you here."

"What fer?" Jason demanded.

"To warn you, señor. As a neighbor it is my duty."

"To warn me agin what?"

"I have learned," Montoya asserted, "that outlaws in the pozo are hunting for you. Their purpose is to kill, because they believe that sheriffs have put you here to spy on them. They are evil men, señor. I could not rest well until I warned you."

Jason's jaw dropped. He could tell that Montoya had sensed a trap and was slipping out of it. The man's position was perfect now. In the eyes of a rimrock witness, Montoya had made his integrity more secure than ever.

"Much obliged!" Jason mumbled. There was nothing else to say.

"Will you promise not to stay here any more, señor? It is best that you find a safer place."

Jason fixed a meaning eye on Montoya's rifle. The hammer of it was still cocked, but such a detail could hardly be seen by the rimrock witness. "You're sure right," Jason said. "I sure orta find me a safer place."

"Without delay, señor. And now I must leave you. Adios." Montoya turned into a copse of the aspens and mounted the horse he had tied there. With a gracious wave of his hat toward Jason, he disappeared down the timbered slope.

In stinging chagrin old Jason prodded his mule up through the crevice to the mesa level. Don

Ygnacio met him with stern eyes. "Do you not feel shame, Viejo, for telling lies about such a fine caballero?"

"Nope," Jason said. "Skunks are smart, sometimes. It's kinda hard to ketch 'em in a trap. This 'n sure slickered both of us."

Don Ygnacio was in no temper to discuss this. He went to his horse, mounted and rode south down the mesas toward the cross-trail leading into his own grant. Jason followed him for miles, occasionally spurring his mule alongside to renew his indictment of Montoya.

It was no use. Finally Jason gave up. Don Ygnacio rode on to his hacienda, while the old prospector turned off to join Johnnie Cameron's friends encamped on the Puerco.

CHAPTER 22 "WHY," JOHNNIE
demanded of Miguel, "doesn't Josephine come
in to see me any more?" He was still abed at the
hacienda and knew that he must convalesce here
another week at least.

"The señorita is very occupied, Don Juan,"
Miguel explained. "Carramba! All the women of
the house—they sew dresses for her wedding."

But Johnnie sensed another reason for
Josefita's desertion. More than likely she'd been
commanded to stay away from him by the
hacendado. Don Ygnacio himself came in each
day to inquire, with stilted courtesy, about the
welfare of his guest. But Johnnie knew it was
purely formal. Friendship was dead. Don
Ygnacio could never forgive what he considered
an attempt to besmirch Montoya.

Nor would he risk the possibility that Johnnie
might repeat those charges to Josefita. The bride-
to-be must not be shocked by any such wild
accusations. That, Johnnie felt sure, was why the
girl had been excluded from his room.

Ogallala dropped in one evening to report:
"We're sure blowed up on that pozo pasturage,
Johnnie. Took a scout over there today and what
do yuh reckon I found?"

"Outlaws," Johnnie guessed.

255

"Them skunks 've come back all right. They're holed up at the old sheep camp under the west rim, right where they was before. But that ain't what I mean. They's a flock o' workmen in the pozo and they're throwin' up five shacks."

"A cabin to hold each claim, huh?"

"That's right. I talked to the man who's puttin' them up. He ain't a outlaw. He's just a contractor from Bernalillo. He says the hombres that filed the claims also bought five empty shacks at Montoya's mine. They're payin' him to move 'em into the pozo."

"It means Montoya's back of the whole play," Johnnie said.

Ogallala nodded. "I rid into Santa Fe and talked to the land office people. They say them claims are plumb legal and we dassent jump 'em. They say Montoya's name don't appear anywhere on the papers. They say they'll have to issue patents of title if the claimants build homes and otherwise comply with the law."

"Which leaves us out in the cold with five hundred heifers," Johnnie gloomed.

"With winter comin' on, too. We had a flurry of snow today, Johnnie. And some of them heifers is springin'. A few of 'em are likely to be droppin' calves any time."

"Roll me a cigarette, Ogallala."

It took Johnnie three cigarettes of profound meditation before he could summon even the ghost of a plan. Then: "Listen, Ogallala. We know those claimants are ringers who're simply lettin' Montoya use their names. If they were bona fide homesteaders, the pozo outlaws wouldn't stand for 'em. They'd be smokin' that contractor outa their front yard."

"Sure they would, Johnnie."

"The way I savvy this homestead law," Johnnie went on, "the government put it on the books for the benefit of sincere homeseekers. Settlers who're representin' themselves and not somebody else. You and me and Slim and Rosy and Sweetwater are representin' ourselves. So we're more entitled to those claims than five dummies who're just lettin' Montoya use their names."

"Sure we are, kid."

"All right. Let's figure the government 'll see it that way in the end, providin' we show up Montoya. The whole deal depends on us showin' up Montoya."

Ogallala scowled out the window at falling snowflakes. "That buzzard'll sure be hard to ketch up with, Johnnie. He flies high and don't leave any tracks."

"And look, Ogallala. We can't mooch on the Sandoval grass any longer. So let's push the heifers over into the pozo right now."

"What about water? If they was to fence those five waterholes they filed on, our stock couldn't get to water."

257

"That's only in the dry season," Johnnie said. "July to October. Rest of the year there ought to be plenty of pools from snow and rain. This is November, which gives us eight months before we have to worry about water."

"Suits me," agreed Ogallala. "We'll push the stuff into the pozo."

Johnnie brooded through another cigarette. "We might dig a well," he suggested. "Dig it just a little way below where the biggest flow of spring water disappears in the gravel."

"Slim was sayin' the same thing," Ogallala said. "He wants to file a dry claim on the next quarter section below the biggest spring, and then dig a well on it."

"Dig the well first," Johnnie advised. "If you hit shallow water, then Slim can file a homestead."

"Only trouble with that idear," Ogallala protested, "is that a feller can only use his homestead right once. So if Slim files this dry claim, he can't ever take up land again. Then if we can bamboozle Montoya's Mexicans into relinquishin' them five water claims, there'd only be four of us left to file."

It was a sound point. Johnnie solved it by suggesting: "Let old Jason Holt file the dry claim. That'll leave the rest of us free to file water claims later."

Ogallala banged a fist into palm. "You hit it,

Johnnie. Old Jason's thrown in with us, mule and all. I still got those homestead blanks and I'll slip one of 'em to the old man. When we get the well dug and the claim filed, we can throw up a rock shack."

"Oughtn't to take long," Johnnie agreed eagerly. "Plenty of niggerhead boulders over there. Sweetwater can haul roof poles in the wagon—and you can make a sod roof."

Ogallala grinned. "Not much of a ranchhouse. But I've wintered in worse."

"I'll join you soon as I can," Johnnie promised.

Prospect of action revived Ogallala's spirits. He stood up, hitching at his gun belt. "Don't fret none about them heifers gettin' driv off, Johnnie. The outlaws 'd have to round 'em up and drive 'em out through one of seven gaps in the rimrock. Before they could do that, we'd be right there a-shootin'."

"They won't likely want to raid cattle while those Bernalillo workmen are over there buildin' cabins," Johnnie thought. "That ought to give you a few weeks of peace, long enough to throw up our own rock shack."

"So long, Johnnie. And don't strain your luck gettin' outa bed."

When Ogallala was gone, Johnnie tried to resign himself to patience. It was pretty hard to lie there while his friends faced trouble in the pozo.

The lazy life of the hacienda went on about him, and day by day Johnnie could hear its echoes. Servants padding through the hallways. The strumming of guitars. The bleating of sheep coming in each evening from the range.

But Johnnie saw no more of Josefita.

As November dragged by, he realized how short a time remained before her marriage with Montoya. And how slight his own chance to expose the man. Fretting over this brought a relapse, and when the doctor from Bernalillo called again he forbade Johnnie to get out of bed.

"Perhaps not for another month, señor."

"I won't stay cooped up here!" Johnnie protested. "They need me over in the pozo."

"I am the doctor; so you must do as I say. Is it not right, Don Ygnacio?"

The hacendado nodded gravely. "We must not let him exert himself too soon, Don Eusebio."

Alone with the doctor, Johnnie prodded for news about Santa Fe. Don Eusebio was of a gossipy temperament, and often made calls at the capital.

"Did they ever catch the fellah that murdered the gamblin' house woman?" Johnnie questioned.

"You mean la Marta Calaveras? Si, señor. That is, a dead ladron has been delivered to the sheriff with a note pinned on him. The note says the man has guilt of that crime. Also the sheriff has received half of the stolen money."

"And the other half?"

"Quien sabe?" The doctor gestured with spread palms. "The casa Calaveras," he confided, "has always been a place of mystery."

"A mystery? Why?"

Don Eusebio, lighting a cigarrita, crossed his chubby legs and settled back. "Have you heard the story, señor, about a cart of gold coin held up twenty years ago on the Chihuahua trail? The ladrones packed it into the pozo hondo and it was buried there."

"I heard about it," Johnnie admitted. "A posse chased the thieves, killed some of them in the pozo, hung a few of 'em, and the rest scattered."

"And now," resumed the doctor, "about that lost gold we have two theories. One is that it is still buried in the pozo; and that other ladrones watch all who come there, in case someone should return for the gold."

"I heard that 'n. What's the other slant on it?"

"It is that one of the original ladrones was a faro dealer named Manuel Calaveras. He was among those who scattered and escaped. Some believe that he returned a year later and recovered the gold. That he took it to Santa Fe and used it to open a gaming house. And that at his death the gold became the foundation of his widow's fortune."

"You mean his widow was this same Marta Calaveras?"

"The same, señor."

"Why would people think Calaveras dug up the gold?"

"Two reasons, señor. First, when Calaveras came to Santa Fe he put much gold coin in the bank. The coin was from Old Mexico and stained with earth. The bankers think it had been buried at least a year. This was a little more than a year after the fight in the pozo hondo."

"And the other reason?"

"Is Enrico Robles. He is a man with only one eye, and he tended bar at la Marta's."

"I saw him there," Johnnie remembered.

"Enrico Robles knew all the secrets of Manuel Calaveras. He was mozo for Calaveras long ago in El Paso, when Calaveras dealt faro there. After Calaveras was dead, Robles served the widow by tending bar. I am a doctor, and so I know that Robles lost an eye because of a gunshot wound. The posse of the pozo fight say that one of the escaping ladrones was shot in the eye. Perhaps it was Robles."

It was fairly convincing, Johnnie thought. Robles would hardly have been content to tend bar nineteen years if he knew of gold still buried in the pozo.

"But we cannot be sure," Don Eusebio shrugged. "Maybe that money is in the estate of la Marta, and maybe it is buried in the pozo."

"How big is the estate?"

"Bastante, señor. Perhaps more than a hundred thousand dollars."

"Who gets it?"

Again the doctor shrugged. "It is strange about that, señor. Enrico Robles says there is a will. He says la Marta called him in to witness it. He does not know who was named in the will. He only knows that he signed it as a witness a week before the woman's death. But officers of the court cannot find the will."

"She likely tore it up," Johnnie guessed.

"Perhaps, señor. But Robles has a sly look in his eye when he speaks of the will. He says it is only misplaced and will turn up later."

Johnnie had plenty of time to think this over when the doctor was gone. Whom would the gambling woman leave her fortune to? Why not to the man she loved? Ramon Montoya!

A windfall for Montoya. And yet unfortunately timed, since he was soon due to marry a young and sensitive girl. Would not the fact of a huge inheritance from the gambling house widow embarrass Montoya? Would it not betray his old affair?

All of which could be solved simply by suppressing the will until after the wedding. In that way Montoya could gain for himself both the innocence of a new love and the spoils of an old one. Once married to Montoya, it would be too late for Josefita to take offense.

It fit. And there might be dynamite in it for Montoya.

A day later Sweetwater Smith rode over from the pozo.

"First time one of the boys goes to Santa Fe for supplies," Johnnie suggested, "have him get a line on a one-eyed bartender named Robles." He reviewed his talk with the doctor.

"We'll look into it," Sweetwater promised. "Meantime, everything's goin' fine in the pozo. Three inches o' snow don't bother them heifers any. 'Cause in the swales the grass is belly high."

"You dug a well?"

"Sure. Hit water six feet down. Got a rock and sod shack halfway up already. That Bernalillo contractor is a good hombre. He loaned us a mason who's sure an artist with adobe mortar. I hauled a set o' spruce poles for the roof. Brought in poles fer a horse corral, too."

"What about the five cabins on those waterholes?"

"They're about done now." Sweetwater had nothing further to report. Soon he went limping out.

It was a week before Johnnie had another caller. This time it was Slim who came in with news that the Bernalillo crew had finished its work and was gone from the pozo.

"First day after they left," Slim reported, "we had a little run-in with ladrones. Coupla 'm caught old Jason out in the brush and stuck a gun in his ribs. They started to bully him about a cache o' gold coin. If he didn't tell 'em where it is, they'd blast him wide open."

Johnnie sat straight up in bed. "The devil! What did Jason tell 'em?"

"He said he hadn't found no gold, and wasn't lookin' fer any. But seemed like the more Jason denied it, the more sure those buzzards was that he was holdin' out on 'em. 'Bout that time Slim and Rosy rid up and popped a coupla slugs their way. They high-tailed up the timber and we ain't seen any more of 'em."

"It's ten to one," Johnnie said, "that the gold was dug up long ago by a man named Calaveras."

"Yeh, Sweetwater slipped us that angle. So when he driv to Santa Fe for supplies the other day he tried to look up a one-eyed bartender."

"Enrico Robles. Did he find him?"

"Nope. This Robles done a fadeout. Nobody's seen him around Santa Fe for a week."

Digesting this information, Johnnie concluded that it might connect with the Marta Calaveras will. If Montoya were the beneficiary and wanted the will suppressed until after December twelfth, he might consider it wise to hold Robles under cover. Or perhaps Robles was playing some private game of his own.

"While Ogallala was in Santa Fe," Slim

reported, "he went to the land office and got the addresses of the five pozo homesteaders. He dropped in on one of 'em and asked if he was actin' fer himself, or fer Ramon Montoya. Couldn't get him to admit anything, though. Seems funny."

Except that the heifers were doing well, and that the rock cabin on Jason's dry claim was nearly completed, Slim had no more information.

When he was gone Johnnie looked fretfully at a wall calendar. This was the 28th of November. Only two weeks remained before the Montoya-Sandoval wedding. Would it be here at the hacienda?

Johnnie inquired about it when Miguel came in with broth.

"It will be at the iglesia in Santa Fe, señor," Miguel said.

"Church weddin', huh? Night time or day time?"

"It will be at noon, señor."

"I'm pullin' outa here tomorrow," Johnnie said firmly.

Miguel protested. Later, Don Ygnacio also protested. Others of the household insisted that Johnnie was too weak to ride.

But early in the morning he was up and pulling on his boots. His wound had healed. But two months in bed had left him pale and twenty pounds underweight. His gunbelt hung loosely when he strapped it on.

Walking out into the patio made him a little dizzy. Johnnie kept his chin up, though, when he saw the entire Sandoval household lined up to say good-bye.

Miguel was holding the bridle rein of Muchacho. Sight of the horse embarrassed Johnnie. It was a gift from Don Ygnacio. Many other benefits he had received from Don Ygnacio, while Johnnie had given in return only a homemade branding chute. And he had offended the hacendado. Still, Johnnie realized that it wouldn't be good taste to renounce the gift of Muchacho.

He swung to the saddle.

Josefita was standing there beside Don Ygnacio. She could see Johnnie's pallor and that it taxed his strength to mount. "Please do not leave us." There was a tremulous concern in her voice. "You are not well, Señor Johnnie."

"I have tried to persuade him," Don Ygnacio echoed. "Will you not remain with us longer, Señor Cameron?"

"Thanks," Johnnie smiled. "But I've bothered you long enough. Got to be helpin' my compadres over in the pozo. Mille gracias, Don Ygnacio, and Josephine, and all of you. Adios."

"Adios," came in a chorus from the Sandovals.

Johnnie's eyes met Josefita's. It was his first sight of her for many days. Because it was cold here in the patio, the girl wore a mantilla which exposed only her eyes and cheeks. The cheeks were as pink as ever, but the eyes seemed nervous and afraid. Johnnie wondered if she'd heard any echo of his charges against Montoya.

To find out, he rode close to her and asked in a pretense of bantering, "Am I still invited to your wedding, Josephine?"

"But of course, señor."

"I'll be there," Johnnie promised.

CHAPTER 23

HE RODE OUT through the gate at a slow jog. In a moment he turned to wave his hat, and saw Josefita whispering to Miguel.

Ten minutes later Johnnie was riding north toward the pozo, with the hacienda two miles behind. Hoofbeats followed him. Johnnie twisted in his saddle and saw Miguel coming along on a wiry little mustang. The old servant did not try to catch up. He merely followed at a distance, loping when Johnnie loped, pulling to a walk whenever Johnnie slowed down.

Miguel, Johnnie knew, would follow him to within sight of friends in the pozo. And for that he could thank Josefita. The girl wasn't risking any possible dizziness which might sway Johnnie from his saddle far from help on the range.

"She's the right kind of folks, Muchacho," Johnnie confided. "Only trouble is she needs help herself and don't know it."

Snow lay in patches on the vega, and the mountains were steep walls of white. Plenty of feed for stock, though. Johnnie passed a flock of Sandoval sheep under herders on the windswept bare spots. He rode on to the upper Puerco and took a steep canyon trail toward the gap.

Near the top of it he found drifts. This made the going slow and it was nearly noon when he came to the gap. Here Frenchie had ambushed him. He wondered if Josefita had sent Miguel along partly for that reason; so that Miguel could be a witness in case of another sniping here.

This morning only frosty mountain air met Johnnie at the gap. He sat his saddle and looked down into the pozo hondo. In its basin he saw patches of white on the tall, cured vega grass. And red dots grazing there. Hereford heifers were at home in the pozo and the sight of them brought a glow to Johnnie Cameron.

The five pozo waterholes had been taken by outsiders. Josefita was about to marry a ladron. Everything else had gone wrong—except an idea. The idea was now fulfilled; Scotch-English cattle were feeding on New Mexico grass. Whatever else happened, a page of range history had been turned.

Johnnie rode on down to the rim of a broad bench which shouldered out over the basin. From there he could see six cabins scattered at wide intervals over the basin. Five were brown. He knew they were the adobe shacks erected by Montoya in the names of dummies and purely to comply with the land laws. The five adobes were without smoke or sign of life.

But a rock cabin a half mile below the central waterhole gave a wisp of smoke from its chimney. The warmth of life was there. Life which meant sincere and permanent settlers.

Johnnie turned to find Miguel directly back of him.

"Thanks for seein' me home, Miguel. I can make it from here on."

"The señorita was afraid to let you come alone, Don Juan."

"Thank her," Johnnie grinned. "And good-bye, Miguel."

He rode down into the basin with Miguel still watching him from the bench. The old servant wouldn't take an eye off him until he had been received by the boys below.

Riding toward the rock cabin, Johnnie passed close to some of the heifers. They were in fine flesh, with the hair winter shaggy, and a few of them were heavy with calf. The sunshine glittered on snow no whiter than the curly bovine manes and soft milky dewlaps hanging low to the grass. "They sure look contented, Muchacho."

The cabin, Johnnie saw, had a rude pole corral back of it. In the corral were two riding horses. Which meant that the others were in use or had been turned out to graze. The big trail wagon stood empty by the corral and Johnnie saw its team watering at a branch of melted snow. Plenty of stock water everywhere now. It would be a different matter next summer, though, if the five dummy claimants should fence off their quarter sections.

The rock cabin had a door and two windows framed crudely from hand-hewn spruce poles; oiled paper covered the windows in place of panes.

Johnnie swung to the ground and tried the door. It was locked. At his knock the door was pulled suddenly open from the inside. Sweetwater Smith stood there with a forty-five in hand.

"Heck, it's only Johnnie." Sweetwater's glare faded to a grin. Beyond him Johnnie saw Slim broiling venison on a tin stove.

"Fer all I knew," Sweetwater explained, "it might be one of our neighbors up the hill."

Slim came forward anxiously. "You look like a ghost, kid; like you might keel over. Why didn't you stay in bed?"

"I'm all right," Johnnie said. Actually the ride had exhausted him but he was determined not to show it.

A look about informed him that the cabin had two rooms, each with a gravel floor. In the rear room were three sets of double-deck bunks.

In the front room, six kegs made as many seats. The table was a raft of aspen poles bound together by rawhide and supported on axe-hewn legs. Saddles, blankets and sacks of beans made untidy heaps in the corners.

"All you fellas need," Johnnie suggested, "is a

couple o' pink cushions and a home sweet home motto. Wait'll I go unsaddle my braunk."

"I'll tend to him," Sweetwater insisted, and went limping outside.

Johnnie sat down on a saddle and propped his back against the wall. "Where's everybody," he demanded, "including old Jason Holt?"

"Rosy and Ogallala and Jason," Slim said, "are out ridin' herd on them ladrones."

"How many cows 've those jaspers rustled off us by now?"

"Nary a hoof," Slim insisted. "Fact is, them outlaws 've been so quiet lately it makes me suspicious."

"What do you reckon their game is, Slim?"

Slim brought a plate of venison steak to Johnnie. "The way I figger it, kid, they're waitin' fer a chance to smoke us out and then drive off the cowstuff. Mebbe fer a new snowfall so they won't leave no tracks outa the pozo. Tambien, they're keepin' an eye on old Jason. Somehow they seem to think he savvies about a cache o' gold coin."

Sweetwater came in with Johnnie's saddle, bridle, blanket, rifle and slicker roll. He stood the rifle in a corner beside two others. "Ain't had no chance to try out these centerfires yet," he complained, " 'cept on a deer or two."

"Rosy knocked over a wild turkey," Slim put in. "More game in this here pozo than yuh can find bullets fer, Johnnie."

273

"Which is a good thing all 'round," Sweetwater mentioned. "'Cause it means them outlaws won't be killin' a cow fer beef."

They heard hooves in the snow outside. A minute later Rosy, Ogallala and Jason Holt trooped in.

"Hi, Johnnie," Rosy yelled. "How's Josephine? Did you beat Montoya's time yet? The way I heard it, she said it was too bad it wasn't me 'stead of you got shot up; she says she'd sure admire to nurse a good-lookin' gent like me."

Ogallala rumpled Johnnie's hair. Then Jason shuffled up and his eyes met Johnnie's with a silent question. Johnnie shook his head, meaning that he had kept his promise not to tell Jason's secret to the Sandovals. It was evident, too, that the old man had not confided it to the Circle Dot crew here.

Slim and Sweetwater picked up saddles and went out. The cattle were not to be left long unguarded.

"Pick your bunk, kid," Ogallala said, "and turn in."

He overrode Johnnie's protests. With help from Rosy, he picked Johnnie up and carried him to a bunk. "You'll need more tallow on yer ribs, kid, when the big showdown comes."

For two nights and days Johnnie rested. His strength returned rapidly, and yet each hour brought a new line of worry to his face. "We got a deadline comin' up," he complained. "And it's the twelfth of this month."

"Ain't we got enough grief," Ogallala argued, "without frettin' about a weddin'? Ferget that girl and let's go out and tally them heifers."

Of a frosty third of December, Johnnie was permitted to ride out with them. The snow was almost gone, although thick gray clouds rolling over the rimrocks promised more. Johnnie looked to the loading of his forty-four-forty, then swung to the saddle of Muchacho.

He could see the Herefords grazing over the basin within a radius of two or three miles. A few were possibly obscured by brush along the lower slopes.

"Fer all we know," Ogallala said, "them outlaws might 've been shootin' some beef. We ain't made a tally since we hit the pozo."

"Let's round the stuff up," Slim suggested. "We can drift it between them two big rocks over there, and let Johnnie count 'em."

"Sure," Rosy grinned. "Johnnie's good at figgers, even if he ain't much good with women."

They spread out and began bunching the heifers in toward the center of the basin. "Don't push 'em none," Ogallala insisted. "Quit yipayain' and flippin' yer rope, Rosy. These here ain't no high-tailin' longhorns."

The Herefords drifted sluggishly toward a

focus. Sweetwater and Slim rode up the brushy slopes and found a few more. Rosy picked up a few at the top of a scrub oak ravine. Ogallala rode the widest circle of them all, high in timber where snow was still nearly a foot deep. At noon he came back to report that the last stray had been herded down into the pozo.

"Take a tally on 'em, Johnnie."

They drove the herd between two house-size boulders. At this gateway Johnnie posted himself and made a careful count. "Four hundred ninety-nine," he yelled when the last of the stock had passed by, "not countin' those ten yearlin' bulls."

"You musta missed one, Johnnie. Count 'em again."

The cattle were driven back through the same gate of rocks and Johnnie checked his count.

"Four hundred ninety-nine comin' three-year-old heifers," he insisted, "and ten comin' two-year-old bulls. We're one short, cowboys."

"Betch them ladrones had beef fer supper last night," Sweetwater growled. "Let's go smoke 'em out."

"Let's find the butchered carcass first," Johnnie suggested. "Then we'll be in the clear."

"Johnnie's right," Ogallala said. "Nobody ain't elected us sheriff of this county. But if we find a butchered carcass, we'll just be defendin' our own property."

They scattered to search the pozo slopes.

Johnnie headed toward a high bench to the north which was studded with wild cherry brush. Snow lay fairly deep on it, and so it had been skipped in the roundup on the assumption that a cow wouldn't choose to hunt feed there.

In an hour Johnnie had climbed to it. He looked into all the cherry clumps but failed to find the skeleton of a cow. Neither did he see any hoofmarks in the snow.

Then he rode into an oak canyon where deep drifts gave no sign. Muchacho floundered through the drifts and Johnnie turned him downcanyon toward the basin.

At the first windswept area where grass reached above the snow, Johnnie saw a seven point buck. The deer stood at a bend of the ravine, head up and alert. Suddenly the animal turned and raced directly toward Johnnie.

It whirled then to go scampering into brush on the slope. But Johnnie knew that the buck had been first frightened by some life beyond the canyon bend.

He held Muchacho to a walk and rode on cautiously. Sounds came as of hooves crunching snow. Johnnie stopped his horse, waited there, reins in his left hand, right hand free on his thigh. Someone was coming around that bend.

The horseman appeared, stopped abruptly at sight of Johnnie. They were face to face, barely ten paces apart. Johnnie saw that the stranger was a small man with a cast in the right eye. A stubble of beard covered his bullet-chipped chin. Johnnie fixed his attention on the man's right hand. One finger of it, he noticed, was missing. The thumb was hooked in the man's cartridge-weighted belt, near the butt of a forty-five gun.

"Howdy," Johnnie said. "Been eatin' any beef lately?"

"Who wants to know?" the man barked back. By the snap in his voice, and his quick flush, he had a dangerous temper.

"Cameron's the name. Better stick to venison, Fadeaway." Johnnie recalled Jason Holt's mention of a four-fingered gun hand.

In the next split second it went into action. Fallon clawed the gun from his holster. In the same flash Johnnie Cameron drew his own and fired. Fadeaway Fallon's horse reared. Muchacho gave only a nervous twitch of his ears.

"You oughta know better 'n to ride a gunshy braunk," Johnnie said. He saw Fadeaway nursing an empty right hand. The gun had been shot cleanly from it and lay in the snow below the man's stirrup.

An oath escaped Fallon.

Johnnie broke into it smoothly: "I could have circle-dotted that cock-eyed mug of yours, Fadeaway. Better start fadin' before I change my mind."

Fallon stared through gleaming slits of malice. Then he looked down at his gun in the snow.

"Leave it lay there," Johnnie said. "Another thing, no use you hangin' around the pozo for any cache of gold coin. It was taken out years ago by a jasper named Calaveras. He used it to start a gambling joint in Santa Fe. If you don't believe it, ask a one-eyed barkeep named Robles."

It seemed to Johnnie sound strategy to give the Fallon gang one less motive for keeping residence in the pozo. He rode close to the man now and plucked a carbine from his saddle scabbard. Also he noted a pair of range glasses in a case tied to a latigo. Evidently Fallon had been spying from some high vantage upon activities in the basin.

"Fade," Johnnie said.

Fallon faded. He rode on up the ravine where his mount floundered in the drifts. Johnnie watched till he was out of sight, then retrieved the forty-five from the snow. He rode briskly on downcanyon to the basin.

Ten minutes later he crossed a dry wash. Just beyond this he came to a swale between buttes where wind had swept the grass clear of snow. Grazing snugly in this swale was a white-face cow. The fresh brown scar of a Circle Dot brand gleamed on her ribs.

Here was the missing Hereford, not butchered

after all. Johnnie saw that her bag and udders were swollen and instantly he knew why she had withdrawn far from the other cattle. Greasewood bush in this swale offered excellent shelter. A cow will always seek aloof shelter, Johnnie knew, to hide her newborn calf.

So well was the calf concealed that finding it took Johnnie half an hour. At last he spotted a ball of red and white curled in a greasewood bush. The calf was barely a day old. It was a bull calf with hair like moist silk and its pink eyes blinked up at Johnnie. Even when he touched it, it did not move or cry, but the mother came close to bellow complaints.

A glow of pride warmed Johnnie. Here was the first increase to the Circle Dot. More than that, here was the first blood of a new breed to be born in New Mexico.

Johnnie left it there. The cow, he knew, would keep it well concealed and would defend it from coyotes.

CHAPTER 24 "'STEAD OF BEIN'

one short, we're one over," Johnnie reported gleefully at the cabin.

He told them about meeting Fadeaway Fallon.

"Why didn't yuh ventilate that buzzard?" demanded Slim.

"I was savin' him for you, Slim."

"Chances are he'll hightail outa here," Sweetwater predicted, "now that Johnnie gave him the right steer on that gold yarn."

"Main grief we got now," Rosy complained, "is them five dummies of Montoya's that filed all the pozo water."

"How about offerin' 'em a hundred apiece for relinquishments?" Johnnie suggested.

"They wouldn't sell," Ogallala thought.

"Besides," Rosy added, "where'd we get the five hundred dollars? We might as well face facts, gents. We're broke with a hard winter comin' on. And no water in sight for the cowstuff next summer."

"And don't forgit we got interest comin' due at the bank," Sweetwater chimed in. "Semi-annual, ain't it, Johnnie?"

"That's one reason I'm ridin' to Santa Fe tomorrow," Johnnie announced. "If you fellahs

281

'll let me pledge next year's calf crop, I'll guarantee to raise some mazuma."

"Help yerself, kid," agreed Ogallala. The others nodded.

Early the next morning Johnnie was off for Santa Fe. He took a route which would miss both the Sandoval grant and Montoya's silver mine on the mesa. Breaking a trail up to the rimrock wasn't easy. Johnnie's consolation was that these same mountain drifts offered a protection to the cattle. It would be hard for rustlers to get them out of the pozo. In any case, such a raid should leave tracks easy to follow.

Beyond the mesa Johnnie found less snow. The trail was bare by the time he reached the Rio Grande. By sundown he was within six miles of Santa Fe. Corrals by the road there reminded him that here lay the suburban hacienda of Don Pablo Lucero.

Johnnie turned in through a gate and dismounted before a long low ranchhouse with alamos standing nude in the patio.

A barking of dogs brought out Don Pablo, who remembered Johnnie and greeted him warmly. "Bien venida, señor. Have you changed your mind about selling me those heifers?"

"Nope," Johnnie said. "But if you feel right liberal I might contract next year's calf crop."

"Come in to the fire, my friend."

Don Pablo declined to talk further business

until Johnnie's horse was stabled, and the guest himself was seated before a sala fire with a glass of wine in hand.

"The stuff's doin' fine," Johnnie said. "We got a winter calf yesterday. Most of 'em 'll come along, though, in February, March and April. By November first we oughta have about a sixty percent calf crop, ready to wean."

"For how much will you contract them, señor, delivered at weaning age to my corrals?"

"Thirty dollars a head," Johnnie said.

A look of pain crossed Don Pablo's face. "But that is too much, señor. Only last week I bought calves for eight pesos."

"Jackrabbit cattle," Johnnie sniffed. "I'm offerin' you real and fancy calfstuff."

"Fifteen dollars," said Don Pablo hopefully.

"Thirty," insisted Johnnie.

"I am sorry, señor. At such a price I am not interested."

But Johnnie knew he was. The man was avid to become the owner of Herefords.

Comida was announced and the business was dropped, since by the standards of Don Pablo one did not haggle with a guest at supper. He insisted, however, that Johnnie stay all night.

Later, over cigarritas, the host offered seventeen dollars. By bedtime Johnnie had him up to twenty-one.

"It's no deal, Don Pablo. If you want any

calves, looks like you'll have to trail clear back to Missouri. Mine 'll cost you thirty a round."

It was after breakfast the next morning that Johnnie dropped to twenty-eight dollars a head and the deal was closed. Don Pablo drew up a contract and signed it. All the Circle Dot increase of weaning age by next November was to be delivered to him at these same corrals.

With the contract Johnnie rode on into Santa Fe and stabled his horse. He called at the bank where Stephen Elkins received him cordially.

"On the strength of this," Johnnie said, tossing the contract on the desk, "we want some more backing."

Elkins read the paper and smiled. "How much, Cameron?"

"First, we want to be grub-staked until next November."

Again the banker smiled. "That won't break the bank. A wagonload of frijolis ought to suffice, considering the wild game in the pozo. What else?"

"We want five hundred dollars to buy relinquishments with." Johnnie explained about the five watered claims. "They're dummy claims," he insisted. "We figure these hombres staked 'em out for somebody higher up."

"Which is contrary to the spirit of the homestead law," Elkins agreed shrewdly. "If sincere homeseekers were to contest these claims, and prove that the filers were merely dummies for someone else, the land office would revoke the original filings."

He provided Johnnie with a pad of relinquishment forms and offered advice as to the manner in which Johnnie should approach the five claimants.

Johnnie thanked him and went out. When his horse had been fed, he rode into a suburban quarter of the city. Here the houses were small and poor, the district being inhabited only by lower class peons. Johnnie consulted names on a list. The first name was Carlos Ortiz.

He found Carlos Ortiz in a squalid mud hut. The man had a flat, unintelligent face and was sitting on his door stoop, cracking piñon nuts as Johnnie accosted him.

"Carlos, I'm not out to do wrong by you. You're a poor man, and no one deserves a little rancho of his own better than you. But do you really want one, or are you just letting some *rico* play dice with your name?"

Carlos stared vacantly. "I do not understand, señor."

"How much did Montoya pay you for the use of your name?"

Carlos continued to stare. "My English is slight, señor."

Johnnie produced a relinquishment blank and

filled it out ready for signing. He dropped it on the sill beside Carlos and then said in Spanish: "If you really want that rancho for a home, tear this paper up. But if you don't, and are just letting another man use your name, then you better go hire yourself a lawyer."

The word startled Carlos. "I have no money for lawyers, señor."

"You'll need one if I contest your homestead. The court will put you on oath and ask you to swear that no under-cover party is in on it. If you perjure yourself, they'll put you in jail."

Again a word frightened Carlos. "I have done nothing to go to jail, señor."

"Not yet. And you don't want to either. I can see you're an honest hombre, Carlos. So am I. If what is on this paper is true, which is that you do not want the land for a personal home, I offer you one hundred pesos to sign it. Think it over, Carlos. If you decide to sign, take the paper to Don Stephano's bank and exchange it for one hundred pesos."

Leaving Carlos to think it over, Johnnie proceeded to four other addresses. In each case he left a relinquishment blank and an offer of one hundred dollars. Each call convinced him more and more that these men were mere pawns of Montoya's. In no case, however, did they admit this. Johnnie couldn't be sure whether his offers would be accepted or rejected.

But it was all he could do. Now in late afternoon he proceeded to a sixth address. This proved to be a shabby cantina on the road leading west out of town.

Only a slovenly Mexican woman was on duty there. Johnnie asked her, "Does Enrico Robles have a room here?"

"Si, señor. But he has not been home for a long time."

"Know where he is?"

"Quien sabe, señor. But I have heard that he has found employment with Don Ramon Montoya."

"As a mozo?" Johnnie asked.

The woman shrugged. "Perhaps. Once he was mozo for the Señor Calaveras. After that he has tended bar for la Marta. How he will serve Don Ramon I do not know."

Johnnie thanked her and rode west to the Pablo Lucero roadside hacienda, where he was again made welcome for the night.

Morning brought a flurry of snow. "Got to get goin'," Johnnie said to Don Pablo, "before those mesa drifts get too deep."

He was off early down a whitened trail. He crossed the Rio Grande and found it slow going to the mesa beyond. From there, fearful of the rimrock drifts further north, he rode down into the Sandoval grant. The spruce boughs wore silver coats as he brushed through them.

Below in the grant basin he saw no sign of life. Sheep had all been corraled for this storm.

Johnnie cut directly toward the upper Puerco, avoiding the Sandoval buildings by five miles. With snow beating against his face he climbed to the pozo gap. There was still an hour of daylight when he rode down into the home basin.

Falling flakes kept him from seeing far. Riding through them he heard no lowing of cattle. It disturbed Johnnie a little. He knew that in a snowstorm the cows would huddle in the more sheltered swales, and that isolated stragglers would low in seeking the others.

But now the entire pozo had the stillness of a morgue. Just as light failed, Johnnie came to the rock cabin. It's chimney showed no smoke, and again he felt worry. He saw no horse in the corral. In the gloom he saw Jason's mule, though. The mule, hobbled to keep it from straying, was trying to paw feed out of an eight-inch blanket of snow.

Dismounting, Johnnie kicked open the door. Darkness. He groped forward and lighted an oil lamp. Then he heard a groan from the bunkroom. He took the lamp in there and saw Ogallala. Ogallala was swaying drunkenly, and holding both hands to his head.

Rosy, Jason and Sweetwater Smith were in collapse on the bunks, and Slim lay in a face-down sprawl on the floor.

A thick mutter came from Ogallala. "Get him, Johnnie. Throw down on that hombre—" Ogallala's voice trailed off in a moan.

"What hombre?" demanded Johnnie.

"That one-eyed skunk named—" Ogallala doubled up in a fit of coughing. His eyes were inflamed and his face was a blotchy yellow.

"You mean Enrico Robles, the ex-barkeep?" Johnnie gasped.

"Blast his hide!" exploded Ogallala. "Grab him quick, Johnnie, before he gets away."

"He already got away," Johnnie said. He took a bucket and went out to the well. Returning, he dashed cold water over Sweetwater. Sweetwater opened his eyes, groaned, stared groggily about the room, then rolled from bunk to floor. He tried to get up, but collapsed. His muscles seemed to be paralyzed.

"He knocked us out cold," Ogallala mumbled.

Johnnie tossed water over Slim, Rosy and Jason. They came to half consciousness with Johnnie firing questions all the while at Ogallala.

The first coherent story came from Rosy. The redhead was able to sit up with nothing worse than a headache. "He rid up and ast fer you, Johnnie."

"When?"

"We was eatin' breakfast. Mebbe it was this mornin'. Mebbe it was yestiddy mornin'. I wouldn't know."

"What did he want to see me for?"

It came out bit by bit. Enrico Robles, it seemed, had declined to state his business to anyone but Johnnie Cameron.

"We figgered he wanted to sell us some dirt on Montoya," Slim explained when his head cleared. "So we set him down to breakfast and told him to make hisself at home till you showed up."

"And him bein' a ex-barkeep," Rosy put in, "he knew all about knockout drops. Don't know what he slipped into the coffee pot. But it could outkick Jason's mule."

CHAPTER **25** "**I**T PUT US TO SLEEP pronto," Slim admitted.

"I come to with a bellyache," Ogallala groaned.

"Round up the braunks, Johnnie," Rosy said, "and we'll track that jasper down."

Johnnie shook his head. "You won't find any tracks. It's been snowin' all day."

He went to the door, looked out, saw nothing but a flake-dappled darkness and his own tired horse. The range was silent.

And now Johnnie knew why he had failed to hear the lowing of storm-punished cattle.

He turned savagely to his five groggy companions. "A fine bunch of cowhands you are! I take a ride to Santa Fe and you let the whole Circle Dot brand get rustled plumb out of the pozo. That's what they were waitin' for—the first big fall of snow."

"So we can't track 'em!" Sweetwater echoed.

"That's it, all right," Slim admitted bitterly. "When we look out in the mornin', we won't even know which way they went."

"They got a twenty-four-hour start toward Arizona!" Rosy guessed.

"More likely they headed north toward Colorado."

"They'll have a longer start than that, time we pick up their trail."

"There won't be no trail, in this snow."

After a chorus of chagrin, Johnnie broke in: "Might as well turn Muchacho loose. He'll find high grass in some swale tonight, or paw his supper outa the snow. In the mornin' I'll use Jason's mule to round up mounts."

"If they ain't all been rustled," Slim gloomed, "along with the cowstuff."

But Johnnie had no choice. He couldn't let his horse stand saddled all night. So he went out and turned Muchacho loose.

Sweetwater tried to be hopeful. "Them rustlers can't push the stuff very fast. We could ketch 'em on burros—if we only knew which way to head."

"Montoya figured this play out," Johnnie said with conviction. "He waited for a snowfall and then sent Robles down here to knock you fellahs out."

"But why," Sweetwater puzzled, "did he have Robles ask for you?"

"Because he knew I wasn't here. He got wind that I'd ridden to Santa Fe. So Robles asked for me on a stall—and you took him in just like one of the family."

"He only stayed long enough to slip them headache powders in the coffee pot," Ogallala said. "I reckon he hightailed to Fadeaway

Fallon's gang, then, and told 'em to help themselves to the heifers."

A moan came from one of the bunks. Rosy said: "Reckon I better go tend to old Jason. This here's hit him pretty hard, and he ain't as young as we are."

While Rosy went into the bunkroom, Slim made a fire in the tin stove. "We got half a sack o' grain left," Slim said. "Means we can give the braunks one good feed in the mornin'."

"They'll sure need it," Ogallala said sadly, "seein' as how we gotta ride half a dozen trails at once."

Slim boiled coffee and warmed a pot of beans. But only Johnnie had an appetite. Ogallala waved his plate away. "I've hearn about folks bein' seasick. And that's just the way I feel now."

"Me too," Sweetwater echoed.

It was a doleful night. Johnnie made the best of it by mapping a campaign for tomorrow. "There are only seven gaps where they could drive a cowherd out o' the pozo," he said. "One goes south into the Sandoval grant, so we can skip that 'n."

They agreed that Fadeaway wouldn't drive stolen cattle south into the grant.

"Which leaves six other outlets. One for each of us. Maybe we can find sign on the brush where the cows pushed through."

He made them go to bed. "You look like a pack

o' sick coyotes. Get some rest and I'll roust you at daylight."

Johnnie himself went to a bunk but couldn't sleep. All through the night his mind grappled nervously with two issues: the Herefords must be trailed and brought back; Montoya must be exposed before December twelfth, exactly one week from today.

Dawn came and Johnnie saw that it was still snowing. The tarp-covered wagon out there made a lump of white against an unbroken expanse beyond. In another direction Johnnie saw Jason's hobbled mule in the lee of a grease-wood bush. No other equine animal was in sight.

But why should there be? Wouldn't the rustlers cheat pursuit by taking the horses too?

The thought desolated Johnnie as he went out with a bridle to catch the mule. He led the mule back to the wagon and gave it a quart of grain there. Then he brought out Jason's battered old saddle and threw it on. The boys could rest while he scouted for the horses.

Half an hour later Johnnie rode the mule to the top of a butte which overlooked most of the basin. Through a curtain of flakes he made out the dim shape of a horse. One only. He rode down to it and found Muchacho feeding on high swale grass.

Tossing a rope on Muchacho, Johnnie led the horse as he rode the mule in a wide circle. He saw neither horse, cow nor hoofprint. The worst was certain, now.

Four riding horses and the wagon team had been driven off with the cattle. Otherwise one or more of them would be in sight. The wagon stock, especially, would be edging in hungrily toward the cabin, hoping to be grained.

"We're afoot in a blizzard and no place to go," Johnnie reported at the cabin.

They were all up except old Jason Holt. Jason lay with closed eyes on a bunk, his face paler than his beard.

"Them knockout drops didn't do him no good." Slim worried. "He's a sick hombre."

"Poor old fellah!" Sweetwater murmured. "His stomach can't do a comeback like ourn can. Looks like this here's his last roundup."

"I got to ride to Sandoval's and borrow some braunks," Johnnie said. "And I'll bring back someone to take care of Jason."

After wolfing a breakfast he saddled Muchacho. "I sure hate to ask any more favors over there."

"While you're gone," Ogallala promised, "I'll use the mule to hunt sign with." He mounted the mule and rode toward the west rim of the pozo.

Johnnie rode south toward the grant. Snow was still fluttering when he reached the gap. And on the high land, drifts made the going slow.

Johnnie pushed doggedly through them and broke a trail down to the Puerco.

It was past noon when he spurred a jaded Muchacho through the barnlot gate. The mayor-domo was lounging just inside the barn, smoking a cigarrita. Johnnie hailed him. "Rustlers cleaned us out, hide and hoof, Arturo. What about borrowin' five fresh cayuses?"

Assent came readily from Arturo. "But of course, señor. Don Ygnacio is not at home, but always he is glad to help a neighbor."

"Where did he go?"

"To Santa Fe, señor. All the family has gone to the casa there, to make ready for the wedding."

"Did they take Miguel along?"

"Miguel? No, señor. The servants will go in later."

"Look, Arturo. Old Jason Holt's in a bad way. He'll cash in if I don't take back someone to look after him while we chase cow thieves. May I borrow Miguel?"

The mayor-domo was not so sure of this. His conclusion was to let Miguel decide for himself. "But I will have horses ready for you right away, señor."

Johnnie stabled Muchacho, then went to the house to see Miguel.

The old servant was sympathetic. "But I must obey orders from the patron, Don Juan. When the snow is over, he is expecting me at Santa Fe.

They will need me for many things. So I cannot go to the pozo."

Johnnie was reluctant to trust anyone else. "It means I gotta tell you somethin', Miguel, that el Viejo made me promise to keep secret. It's a matter of pride with him. I'm tellin' you because it's the only way I can persuade you to go along."

"What is it, señor?"

"You know that Josefita was found wrapped in a buffalo robe?"

"Si, señor."

"Jason Holt shot that buffalo. He's her real grandfather."

Miguel stared. "That is a strange story, señor."

"It's true. That's why the old man's been hangin' around here all these years. It was to see as much as he could of Josefita."

"I have seen him look at her with love," Miguel admitted.

"Will you come then?"

"I do not know if it is true," Miguel said. "But if it is true and I do not go, then Josefita would never forgive me. So I will go with you, and I will take along medicines, señor."

Miguel went to make a pack of comforts and remedies. Johnnie returned to the corrals and found that five skittish mustangs had been assembled by the mayor-domo. "They are small," he admitted. "But they have tough

Mexico legs, señor. They will carry you well on the trail of ladrones."

"Only trouble is we haven't got any trail," Johnnie grimaced.

Arturo helped him saddle two of the mustangs. Then Miguel came out with a pack, and all bundled up in a serape. He and Johnnie swung to saddles. Arturo opened the gate and they drove the other three mounts out before them.

"Head 'em for the pozo, Miguel."

Miguel proved to be a competent drover. "When I was young I have been a vaquero, señor."

North across the white-mantled grant they pushed, driving three free mustangs ahead of them. Light was fading when they made the pass. But snow had stopped falling and the skies were clearing. "The rustlers get another day's start on us," Johnnie said. "But I reckon it's worth it to have fresh braunks."

They rode on down into the pozo and soon after nightfall came to the rock cabin. A hail brought Slim out to open the corral gate. The horses were driven in and the riders dismounted. "Do these mustangs know how to eat grain, Miguel?" Johnnie asked. He knew that many range horses never learn to eat anything but forage.

"These have fed on grain," Miguel said. "We grow oats on the grant."

"We got about two short rations apiece fer 'em," Slim said.

Johnnie took Miguel inside where they found Ogallala, Rosy and Sweetwater grouped gravely about Jason's bunk. The old prospector was barely conscious. Miguel immediately took charge of him, herding the others into the front room.

"What luck lookin' for sign?" Johnnie asked.

"I got a zero score," Ogallala growled. "First, I rid that mule brute up to the west outlet, 'cause it seemed the most likely. The shacks at that old sheep camp up there was deserted. Nothin' but snowdrifts up that way. The mule an' me floundered around half a day but couldn't pick up no sign."

"What about the north gap?"

"Tried that 'n in the afternoon. It's the one I chased Frenchie through. A blank haul this time, kid. Mebbe they went out that way, and mebbe they didn't. They musta brushed snow off the spruce boughs passin' through, but plenty o' more snow came to cover up."

"It snowed thirty hours straight since them rustlers left here," Sweetwater muttered.

They turned in early to be fresh for the next day.

Johnnie awoke to find Miguel warming gruel for Jason. "He is asleep, señor," Miguel reported. "I think he is better."

Johnnie went out and found Slim feeding the last of the grain.

An hour later the horses were saddled. In each saddle scabbard was a Winchester 44-40 centerfire carbine. In each hip holster was a .45 Colt's. "We start throwin' lead," Rosy said, "the minute we sight them jaspers."

"But which way do we look fer 'em?" Sweetwater wondered.

"No use rakin' snow fer sign at the gaps," Ogallala said. "I tried that yestiddy. So we might as well flip a coin to see whether we head west or north."

"Or maybe northeast toward Questa," Rosy offered. "I hear there's some rough country up that way."

"I say straight west to Arizony," Slim contended.

"We'll flip fer it." Ogallala fished out a coin. "Heads we ride north, tails we ride west." He tossed the coin, catching it in his hat.

But no one looked to see how the coin fell. For a sound came to them from the distant northwest. Johnnie knew instantly what it was. Then he saw a red and white lump floundering through the snow.

The plaintive cry of a cow came nearer. The cow ran at a trot, often stumbling in the snow, but keeping persistently on from timber to the open basin.

"Yeow!" Johnnie yelled. "If we'd had any sense, we might 've known she'd come back. We might 've known they couldn't take that four-day-old calf along."

"Sure," Ogallala grinned. "A cow crittur 'll allers come foggin' back to a young calf. So we don't need to flip no coin, fellers."

Johnnie spurred toward the north end of the basin, remembering a swale there where he had seen the newborn calf hidden in a bush.

The others loped after him. "Yeh," agreed Sweetwater. "They always come back. 'Specially if it's a first calf. I've known a wet cow to run all the way from Kansas back to Texas, lookin' fer a calf she was driv away from."

"Gee!" worried Rosy. "Bet this 'n 'll find hers starved or froze. Don't reckon the poor little feller could live forty-eight hour without its mammy."

"More likely a coyote got it," Slim guessed. "If she finds it gone, I reckon that cow 'll bawl her head off."

They rode as hard as a foot of soft snow would permit. The pace put them in the greasewood swale about two minutes ahead of the cow.

Johnnie rode close to a bush and looked into it. He saw red and white life there, as still as a sleeping kitten.

"He's still here, fellahs. Just like Moses in the bullrushes."

301

The cow came up with frantic mooings, braving the horses, and charged to the bush. Her bawling seemed to burst from a broken heart. Then came a feeble cry from the bush. They saw a tiny calf try to stand; but it collapsed on its thin, unnourished legs.

The cow stopped bawling and began licking the calf. Five men drew back out of the way. "She'll lick strength back into it," Ogallala chuckled. "Purty soon it'll stand up and feed."

Johnnie looked northwest. There he saw plain tracks in the snow made by the homeward journey of the cow.

"Chances are she busted away at the first night camp outa here," he said. "Likely she tried to break away from the drive half a dozen times, but they always headed her off. But come night time, she got away."

"Which gives us a trail right to 'em, Johnnie."

"Sure does. Load your guns, you Circle Dots."

CHAPTER 26

OGALLALA TOOK the lead and they rode single file northwest, backtracking a cow whose mother love and swollen udders had forced her home to the pozo. The trail led up through timber and into interlocking hills which the Circle Dot men had never before explored.

Drifts slowed them to a walk. The lead horse broke trail for the others. "Still and all," Ogallala called back cheerfully, "we can make a lot better time 'n they could with them cows. If we could lope, we'd ketch up with 'em by sundown."

The tracks led in a beeline. They followed up to and across a brushless bench and struck timber again. Here the tracks veered slightly to miss the shoulder of a mesa. The shoulder of another mesa interlocked, so that the two seemed from a distance to be one.

"They's a pass out between 'em, though," Ogallala was sure. "An easy way to get out with the cowstuff." The snow was shallower here and he spurred to a trot.

The pass between the mesas was winding and brought them finally to a new watershed. Here the cowtracks straightened out again due northwest.

"Looks like they're headin' for Utah," Slim said.

"Utah or Hades," said Sweetwater Smith, "we'll feed 'em lead and brimstone when we get a bead on them buzzards."

The grade was down now. The pursuers made better time. On the white expanse ahead lay only a single set of tracks, the hoofprints of a homing cow. To follow them in reverse was simple, in or out of timber. On the plain below them a line of naked cottonwoods led off northwest.

"From what I know of this country," Ogallala said, "we're on the headwaters of the San Juan."

"I recollect lookin' at a gov'ment map once," Sweetwater said. "Seems like this here San Juan crik, if yuh foller it fur enough, takes you exactly to where four territories corner. Colorado, Utah, Arizony and New Mex."

They struck cottonwoods at an upper fork of the San Juan by midafternoon. A small stream ran under thin ice there. Directly down the left bank, the tracks of a cow led through eight inches of snow.

A few miles on the tracks stopped.

"The cow was right here when it quit snowin'," Slim said.

"Makes no difference," Ogallala said. "Because we can bet they kept on follerin' the lee side of this crik. Them cottonwoods make a good windbreak. And the crik bottom gives 'em an easy water grade. If they turned away from it they'd have to fight hills and deep snow."

A few miles further on Johnnie saw a charred circle in the snow. Undoubtedly a night camp had been made at this spot. "Right here's where the cow broke away and headed back toward the pozo," Sweetwater guessed.

They pushed on and in a little while a wide swath of hoof tracks appeared in the snow ahead. Rosy cheered. "Here's where the main bunch got to when it quit snowin'. Reckon the fall o' snow stopped here a little before it did in the pozo."

With the trail well broken now, the pursuers advanced at a lope. "We're makin' four miles to one on 'em," Ogallala calculated. "Might sight 'em any minute."

At sundown the swath of trodden snow turned across the stream. On the other bank, Johnnie saw that the cattle had been driven off at right angles toward a saddle of hills.

He spurred to a lope and in ten minutes reached the saddle. Peering over it, he saw the quarry. Nine men were in a pocket down there. They were making camp for the night. Scattered about the pocket stood a drove of tired Herefords. Two horses were picketed near the campfire. Johnnie counted thirteen other horses grazing, or pawing at the snow to find grass.

Johnnie backed his own mount out of sight. "Nine of 'em," he reported as the others caught up. "Seven gringos and two Mexicans."

"Montoya with 'em?" Sweetwater grunted. He

pumped a shell into the chamber of his Winchester.

"He's not there," Johnnie said. "Him bein' a fine caballero, he's likely in Santa Fe gettin' his hair slicked back for a weddin'. But I spotted Fadeaway Fallon, all right."

"For the two Mexicans," Ogallala guessed, "I nominate Pancho Archuleta and that one-eyed ex-barkeep, Robles."

"Let's spread out," Sweetwater said impatiently, "an' take 'em."

They deployed in a front with about ten yards between adjacent horses. Then Ogallala dismounted. "No sense gettin' our braunks shot up," he advised.

"Besides," Slim agreed, "a feller can allers shoot straighter on his feet."

When they were all dismounted, they advanced in an even line over the saddle's brow.

In the snow they made no sound.

They were thirty yards beyond the crest when campers in the pocket saw them. And even then this winter-white land was silent. Nine outlaws, petrified by surprise, stood staring. While five grim cowboys, each with a level rifle, came stalking on across the snow like ghosts of wrath.

Then Johnnie saw the rustlers jump to a heap of saddles and snatch rifles.

Ogallala yelled, "Throw them guns down and

reach up!" He sent a bullet whirring over Fadeaway Fallon.

Two men dropped rifles and threw themselves flat in the snow. The other seven began firing. The range was less than a hundred yards. Johnnie dropped to his knees and drew a bead on the right-most outlaw. A bullet burned his sleeve as he pulled the trigger. He saw his target pitch forward.

Slim and Sweetwater were shooting straight and fast, raking the camp with lead. Two more of the pozo gang doubled up by the fire there. Rosy stood erect, pumping shot after shot. A slug had tipped his hat back and his red hair flamed against a ground of snow. "It's brandin' day," he yelled, "fer the Circle Dot."

Three of the pozo gang were still upright and firing. A bullet plowed snow by Johnnie's boot. He heard a cry to his left and saw Ogallala stumble. Johnnie swung his aim through a short arc and squeezed with his trigger finger. Through white smoke he saw Fadeaway Fallon stagger, then collapse in the snow. "Deadcenter 'em!" yelled Sweetwater Smith. He had been advancing with gunstock at his cheek all the while. His next shot echoed one from Rosy and another outlaw crumpled by the fire.

The last man threw up his hands.

"And just as I had a bead on him!" Slim complained.

Rosy gave a yelp of victory. "Who says the Circle Dot can't brand!"

"Teach 'em not to fool with our cowstuff," Sweetwater muttered. "How bad did they hit you, Ogallala?"

Johnnie was already bending over Ogallala, discovering a bullet through the leg. "Patch me up, kid," Ogallala said hoarsely. "Did we stampede them heifers?"

"If they was Mexico stuff," Sweetwater said as he came up, "they'd be a mile away by now, tails high. But look at these Herefords! Still chewin' their cuds, by jiminy!"

"Shucks!" Slim grumbled as he joined them. "This here wasn't no fight. This centerfire saddle gun o' mine didn't hardly get warmed up."

Rosy and Johnnie used their bandanas to stop the blood at Ogallala's leg wound. "He's tougher 'n a buffalo bull, Johnnie," Rosy grinned. "You can't hurt him."

"I just tallied the casualties," Slim reported. "Four dead and three down, not countin' two Mexicans that quit before it started."

A couch of saddle blankets was made by the fire and they carried Ogallala to it. Sweetwater limped back over the hill for the horses.

Dark came on, and Johnnie fed piñon chunks to the fire until its heat melted a wide circle of snow. At the rim of that circle, covered with their own blankets, lay four dead men. Near them huddled five prisoners of whom three were wounded. "They've rid their last raid," said Sweetwater Smith. "Next time you meet a ladron in some dark drygulch, his name won't be Fadeaway Fallon."

Toes up beside Fallon lay Pete Adler, wanted for the killing of Deputy Billy Biglow at E-Town.

The only unscathed outlaws were Enrico Robles and Pancho Archuleta. These two, with wrists bound securely, were yanked to their feet by Johnnie Cameron. Pancho was close to a panic, while the one-eyed Enrico remained tight-lipped and sullen.

"Gosh!" Slim complained. "Heck of a job we'll have hazin' this outfit back to the pozo! Four hundred ninety-nine cows, ten bulls, twenty head o' horse stock and nine ladrones!"

"And with me all crippled up!" sighed Ogallala.

"Take your time with 'em, fellahs," Johnnie said. "Me, I'm ridin' to Santa Fe with two witnesses."

"What witnesses?"

"Archuleta and Robles."

Archuleta began whimpering. "I know nothing, señor. I was only the cook for them."

"Better start cookin' up a story, then," Sweetwater gibed.

Rosy winked ominously. "He'll look cute kickin' on a rope, won't he?"

"He won't need to do that," Johnnie argued. "If he uses his head, he oughta get off with only about thirty days in jail. You'd settle for that, wouldn't you, Pancho?"

A surprised hope came to Pancho's sallow face. "Only thirty days? What do you mean, señor?"

"Just this. You don't have to admit stealin' cows and horses. You don't have to admit helpin' Fadeaway hold up wagon trains. In your case we'll let all that pass. Just own up to takin' the hammer off my rifle in Sandoval's barn, and say who paid you to do it, and we'll forget the rest."

It was a bargain from Pancho's standpoint. "Do you promise I will be accused only of that, señor?" he asked eagerly.

"Seguro. It oughtn't to get you more than thirty days in the carcel. Beats bein' hanged for a drygulchin' cowthief, don't it?"

"I will do it, señor."

Johnnie turned to Enrico Robles. "And you, Robles, get even a better deal than that. If we laid your crimes end to end, they'd reach plumb to Kaycee. But we'll wash the slate clean except for the dinkiest little chunk of orneriness you ever pulled. How about it, Robles?"

Enrico's one eye narrowed cagily. "You cannot make me talk."

Johnnie shrugged. "Suit yourself. If you'd rather kick on a rope than do thirty days in jail—" Johnnie rolled a cigarette and let Robles think it over.

"What do you want me to say?" Robles sparred finally.

"You don't need to say anything about helpin' your first boss, Manuel Calaveras, hold up a gold shipment and bury it in the pozo. You don't have to admit he came back later to dig it up and start a gamblin' joint with it. You don't have to own up that Ramon Montoya found that out and has been makin' you eat out of his hand."

"Montoya? I do not know him," denied Robles.

"You don't need to confess," Johnnie resumed, "that all the time you were tendin' bar at the gamblin' joint you tipped Montoya to the big winners so that Fadeaway's gunmen could hold 'em up on the way home. You don't even have to admit that Montoya made you dope the Circle Dot coffee, or that you helped Fadeaway steal the Circle Dot stock."

"I did not—"

"Makes no difference," Johnnie broke in. "Because we'll pass up all that if you'll just come clean about the Marta Calaveras will. Why are you hiding it until after the twelfth of December?"

"I did not hide it," Enrico maintained. His eye grew sly as he added, "But if you will make no

311

charge of anything else, I will tell you about the will."

"It's a deal."

"I burned the will," Enrico admitted.

"Come again," Johnnie argued. "Montoya wouldn't have you burn a will that leaves him a pot of money."

"You are mistake," Enrico countered. "The will say she leaves all her estate to *los pobres* of Santa Fe, except one peso."

"Left it all to the poor, did she, except one peso? Who gets the peso?"

"It say the one peso is for Ramon Montoya, and she leaves him also her forgiveness for a broken promise."

Johnnie whistled. Instantly he was convinced, because this solution was more logical than his own. "Gee! No wonder Ramon made you touch a match to that will! That's all you have to admit, Enrico."

CHAPTER 27

WEDDING BELLS were ringing in Santa Fe. Don Ramon heard them from his newly refurbished house on Auga Frio Road. It lacked only half an hour, now, of high noon.

He stood before a mirror brushing back his wavy black hair. His elegance made a smile play on his lips. Fortune was at a zenith, and this ancient mansion of the Montoyas was now redeemed and ready to receive a new mistress. In only an hour he would bring her here, Josefita, the most lovely bride in all New Mexico.

The distant chiming of the bells reminded him that it would not be polite to permit a bride to arrive first at the church. So Don Ramon hurried down to the patio where a friend was waiting with two horses. One of the horses was the same handsome white stallion which had served Diego de Vargas at the fiesta. Once more, for a grand occasion, Montoya had borrowed it from Don Pablo Lucero.

"*Listo?*" inquired Don Pablo.

"Ready," said Don Ramon.

They mounted and rode stirrup to stirrup down the Auga Frio Road. Soon they passed the Sandoval house and saw a carriage drawn up in front. In a few minutes Josefita would emerge on the arm of Don Ygnacio, and ride in the carriage to the church. It was not proper for Ramon to greet her, though, until she met him at the altar.

The sun shone brightly and the snow was almost gone now.

With Don Pablo flanking him, Don Ramon rode on to the plaza. Church bells were still chiming. Avenues merged into the plaza like spokes to a hub and along these came horsemen and carriages. *Ricos* in all their finery were parading to the wedding. And the *pobres* lined the walks as Don Ramon rode proudly by. He tossed pesos here and there.

"We will drink your health, patron," they shouted back.

With Don Pablo he rode on past la Fonda tavern and the palace. Beyond them loomed a tall cathedral tower with ringing bells.

Guests were already alighting from carriages. The elite of Santa Fe were filing into the church. Don Ramon smiled, waved at them, dismounted and tossed the reins to a boy.

Don Pablo did the same. "This way, Ramon," he said, and led the way to one of two anterooms winging from the chancel. This one was for the groom and his caballero. The other one was for the bride and her maids.

Once inside, Don Pablo produced, cigarritas. "To calm your nerves, Ramon." Don Ramon took one and stood puffing in a glow of contentment at a forward window. From it he could watch the guests still arriving.

Don Pablo stood at the door, peering into the chancel. "It is full to overflowing," he whispered.

Don Ramon remained at the front window looking out, to observe the arrival of the bride. In a little while her carriage rolled up with a flourish. The coachman halted it directly in front of the church. Don Ygnacio got out and reached up a hand to Josefita.

A cloak and mantilla covered all but her face and the fringes of her veil. She looked pale, Ramon thought. But she was beautiful. A crowd of *pobres* cheered as she alighted, and then—

Ramon Montoya, observing from his window, was startled by the intrusion of three men. They pushed through the crowd to the elbow of Don Ygnacio. One of them was Sheriff Gonzalez. The other two were Pancho Archuleta and Enrico Robles. Gonzalez held each man of this pair by a wrist, and it was clear that they were here under pressure.

Then Montoya saw Johnnie Cameron. Cameron sat a horse in the background, not intruding, but with his gaze fixed militantly upon the others.

Gonzalez appeared to make some apology to Don Ygnacio. It annoyed Don Ygnacio. Then he turned in arrogant impatience to a cringing

Pancho Archuleta. Pancho made some statement which reached no farther than the group by the carriage. Evidently it shocked both Don Ygnacio and Josefita.

Then Enrico Robles made a statement. Montoya couldn't hear it, but his ears burned. Blood flushed to his cheekbones. Fear and anger thumped at his heart.

He saw Don Ygnacio question Pancho and Enrico. As they answered with vigorous nods, Josefita swayed and Don Ygnacio had to catch her in his arms.

The plaza crowd stood by, gaping and confused.

Montoya saw Johnnie Cameron turn away and ride to a hitchrack on the plaza. He saw Johnnie dismount and sit down on a bench there, and roll a cigarette with the air of one whose work is done.

By this time Don Ygnacio had handed Josefita back into the carriage. She was hiding her face in her mantilla. Montoya saw an usher rush out from the church to inquire, "Is there anything wrong, Don Ygnacio?"

Faintly the response carried to Montoya: "The señorita is ill. I must take her home. You will inform our friends, señor?"

The whole world seemed to crash about Montoya's head as he watched the bridal carriage drive away.

Don Pablo had also sensed something amiss. "I will find out what it is, Ramon." He stepped out into the chancel.

Montoya waited alone there. He saw confused guests emerging from the church. None were more confused than Don Pablo when he returned. "Word has been brought," he reported, "that Josefita is ill. I am sorry, Ramon."

Ramon was too bitterly confounded to answer. He stood at the window staring out toward a distant plaza bench where sat Johnnie Cameron. Sheriff Gonzalez and his two prisoners were no longer in sight.

"You will go to her at once?" suggested Don Pablo.

"Of course," Montoya murmured. But he knew he wouldn't. He could never again go to the house of Sandoval.

He went out now to his horse and Don Pablo followed to inquire, "Is there anything I can do for you, Ramon?"

Montoya managed to mask his bitterness. "Yes, Pablo," he said. "A gringo named Cameron is on a bench in the plaza. I have a slight unfinished business with him. Will you tell him that if he will wait there one hour, I will see him?"

"But of course, amigo."

Pablo crossed toward the plaza. Ramon Montoya mounted and rode up the Agua Frio Road, as though to the house of the Sandovals.

Actually he passed there without turning his head and rode on to his own residence.

Under the shelter of it, his anger broke leash. He poured rum and drank damnation to Johnnie Cameron. Then Montoya removed his wedding coat and buckled on a forty-five gun.

Johnnie waited in the plaza. The sun shone warmly on his face but his heart was heavy and cold. He had hurt Josefita. The shock had been too sudden and brusque, he knew, exposing to her at such an hour the unworthiness of Montoya.

And now had come a message from Montoya. Montoya would meet him here in one hour.

A step back of him made Johnnie whirl about. He relaxed to see that it was only Stephen Elkins, the banker.

"Been to the wedding, Cameron?" Elkins asked cheerily.

"No," Johnnie said.

"It seems to be over," Elkins said. "Crowd's coming out. I meant to go myself but affairs at the bank delayed me. By the way, here's a note for you to sign, Cameron."

He presented a note for five hundred dollars and smiled. "Yes, those five pozo homesteaders dropped in and signed relinquishments. According to our arrangement, I paid each of them a hundred dollars."

"Thanks." Johnnie signed the note.

It meant complete control of the pozo for the Circle Dot.

Elkins hurried away to his affairs. And Johnnie Cameron fixed his gaze on that corner of the plaza which gave to the Agua Frio Road, expecting to see Montoya appear there. Instead he saw an elderly Mexican ride into view on a mule.

The mule was Jason Holt's. The rider was Miguel.

Miguel came directly to Johnnie's bench. "I have brought sad news, Don Juan," he reported.

"About old Jason?" Johnnie asked anxiously.

"El Viejo," announced Miguel, "is dead."

"I was afraid of it, Miguel. He was a bit too old for a jolt like that."

"Before he died, señor, he gave me permission to tell Josefita."

"Don't tell her today," Johnnie warned. "She's got more than she can stand. But I can see how the old man felt, at the last. Living, he didn't want to be a drag on her. But now he wants her to remember that he stood by."

"That is it, señor. And he has asked one other thing."

"What, Miguel?"

"When he is laid away, he wished to be wrapped in the same buffalo robe, señor."

The cigarette quivered between Johnnie's lips. "I think it can be arranged, Miguel."

Miguel rode away on the mule.

Then Johnnie saw a white stallion. Its rider appeared from the Agua Frio Road. Ramon Montoya sat stiffly in the saddle, his face flushed, his eyes rimmed with redness and fixed in malignant challenge upon Johnnie Cameron.

The man rode to a hitchrack and dismounted there. Then he walked at an impatient pace toward Johnnie's bench.

Johnnie stood up. His holster flap was open. He fixed his eyes on Montoya's slender right hand. The hand was gloveless, now, while the left hand was gloved. That in itself forewarned of the man's errand here.

Stopping at ten paces, Montoya made it clear. "I have come to kill you, señor."

"Help yourself," Johnnie said.

Montoya drew and fired. The draw was a flash but Johnnie caused a miss by stepping to the right at the first crook of the man's arm. Then he stepped back to the left as Montoya's gun boomed again.

Johnnie's own gun was out now. Wrist braced against his hip, he squeezed the trigger and saw Montoya fall. The man's knees hit first, then his outstretched hands, then the drifting white smoke curtained him a moment. When it cleared, Johnnie saw Montoya sprawled face down on the plaza grass.

Men came running from the plaza shops. They

formed a circle about Montoya. One of them said to Johnnie, "We saw him shoot first and twice, señor."

Johnnie went to his horse and rode up the Agua Frio Road. The street was quiet. It was the hour of siesta in Santa Fe.

The gate in the Sandoval wall was closed. Tall, brown stalks of hollyhocks grew there, and alamos in the patio reached leafless arms across the wall. Drawn shutters warned of a forbidding privacy.

Nevertheless Johnnie Cameron squared his shoulders and advanced to the door. He knocked, far from sure of his welcome. He wouldn't blame them if they turned him away. But he knew that within the hour Don Ygnacio would be informed of the plaza shooting; and Johnnie much preferred to bring the news of it himself.

The door opened. Don Ygnacio Sandoval's thin figure was framed there, his face still pale from shock, his shoulders drooped, his goatee grayer than ever, his eyes weary and disillusioned.

"Enter, Señor Cameron," he said.

"Maybe you won't want me to. I just killed Montoya."

The hacendado stared for a moment. Then he opened the door a bit wider. "Enter, my friend."

Johnnie stepped into the sala. "He wrangled me into a showdown and so—"

Don Ygnacio raised a hand in protest. "Will

you do me the favor not to speak of it, Señor
Cameron?"

He rang a bell and Miguel appeared.

"Bring the choke-cherry wine, Miguel."

Miguel brought a decanter and glasses. He
served his master and Johnnie Cameron.

"Your health," said Don Ygnacio. He raised his
glass. His face was still pallid and strained.

"And yours," said Johnnie.

"May the winter be kind to your cattle, Señor
Cameron."

"They'll pull through all right."

"I have heard that your calf crop will go to Don
Pablo next year, señor."

"Yeh, he contracted for 'em."

"The year after next, I shall bid for your calves
myself. We must spread the blood of this new
stock through all New Mexico."

"Sure." Johnnie took his hat and stood up. "I
gotta get started for the pozo," he said.

"But you must stay for comida!"

"Not this time. Thanks."

Leaving the house, Johnnie crossed the patio
and passed out through the high adobe wall. He
found Muchacho hitched at the rack there. And
waiting by the horse stood a girl in a long, black
shawl.

"Josephine!"

"I saw your horse from my window, señor," she
said. "And there is something I must say to you."

"I reckon you feel pretty much broke up," Johnnie said.

"I feel like one who has escaped, señor."

Her hands came impulsively from the shawl and Johnnie took them.

"Remember the last thing I said to you?" he asked her.

"What was it?"

"I said I'd be at your wedding. And I still aim to be there, Josephine."

Allan Vaughan Elston was a prolific author of traditional Western novels and many more short stories and novelettes, memorable for the complexity of their plots and the flamboyance of the villains who are often more interesting than either the heroes or heroines. He was born in Kansas City and spent his summers on a Colorado cattle ranch owned by his father. He was educated as a civil engineer at the University of Missouri and worked in various engineering companies in South America as well as his own in the United States before, in 1920, turning to ranching. Times were hard financially at the ranch so in late 1924 Elston tried writing his first fiction. His first story was "The Eyes of Teconce" in *The Frontier* (2/25), an adventure tale set in the rugged Andes, but his second was "Peepsight Shoots High" in *The Frontier* (6/25), marking his debut as an author of Western fiction, in which henceforth he specialized. His second Western story was "Triggers in Leash" in *The Frontier* (7/25), subsequently adapted for the third episode of "Alfred Hitchcock Presents" in 1955. His first Western novel was *Come Out and Fight!* (1941) followed by *Guns On The Cimarron* (1943) prior to his re-entering the U.S. Army during the Second World War. Following the war, he found his stride with *Hit The Saddle* (1947) and *The Sheriff Of San Miguel* (1949). In the 1950s he would average two books a year, an impressive accomplishment for any writer and Elston was already into his sixties. His novels tend to be precisely situated as to year and place and often contain an intriguing mystery. *The Landseekers* (1964) was Elston's final novel to appear in a hard cover edition. Henceforth, he confined himself to writing paperback originals. At his best, Elston was a fine craftsman who could unite novelty of setting and events with a plot-driven complexity to produce a generally entertaining narrative.

Center Point Publishing

600 Brooks Road ● PO Box 1
Thorndike ME 04986-0001 USA

(207) 568-3717

US & Canada:
1 800 929-9108
www.centerpointlargeprint.com